THE DUKE WHO DIDN'T

WEDGEFORD TRIALS, BOOK 1

COURTNEY MILAN

For 岑玉如
who I've never met
but have always known
(even when I didn't know it)

Wedgeford Down, Kent
England, 1891

CHLOE FONG RETRIEVED HER BOARD CLIP FROM beneath her arm on a fateful spring dawn, not realizing that calamity was about to befall her carefully ordered list.

The morning air was still cold enough to sink into her lungs. The low golden glow of the sun, tipping over the horizon, threatened to burn the fog away. But in this luminous hour when day broke, with the earth poised between grey and color, the mists still danced like happy ghosts across the meadow.

It was early enough that her list of tasks was new; she put on her spectacles and examined it. Her board clip was her most prized possession: a thin metal, light enough to be carried everywhere and yet stiff enough to be used as a makeshift writing desk. It had been a gift from her father, handed over gruffly after he returned from business one day. A newfangled clip, a metal holder that snapped into place by means of a spring mechanism, trapped sheets of paper against the writing surface, with room for a pencil as well. It was the perfect invention if one made a daily list and consulted it regularly.

Chloe, of course, did.

Her tongue pressed between her lips as she examined the list, item by item, looking for—there. *Fetch the sauces for tasting.* The basket with the sauce bottles dangled precariously from two fingers beneath her board. Done. One completed…thirty-four remaining.

Was there anything in life more pleasurable than the sensation of striking a dark line through an item on one's list with a pencil? Yes. There was the visceral sensation of taking out one's pencil and striking a dark line through the *last* item on one's daily list. Finishing a list had an almost talismanic quality, as if the act of turning intentions into words, then words into deeds, carried a subtle magic.

Completing today's list, however… She'd need more than magic to get through it all. Chloe had the tasting with Naomi, the visit to the butcher and then Mr. Tanner to oversee the use of his ovens for her pork shoulder. There was the naming of Unnamed Sauce (and how many times *that* had appeared on her list, Chloe could not guess), the making of labels, the pasting of labels…

It was a good thing Chloe was busy this time of year. She needed a distraction.

In a few days, the village would be overrun with visitors to Wedgeford's annual festival. And when it came to visitors…

Every year for nine years, he had come. Every year for the two years after that, he had not.

That first year he had not come to the Trials, she had waited eagerly—anxiously even. She'd put him on her list, and the item had remained stubbornly undone, unable to be completed in his absence. Rationality had set in after that first disappointment. *Think about him only once today* had been on her list for months before she accomplished it even once, and she found herself consistently, illogically, backsliding.

At this point, he'd skipped two years of Trials; this would make year three. He wasn't coming back.

It was time to remove him from her life the way he had removed himself: completely. He had no right to her list. His *absence* had no right to her list. And if maybe now, with the Trials on top of them, a hint of nostalgia reared its head? She would stomp it into the ground. She was far too busy to waste time on moldering melancholy.

Chloe squared her shoulders and put her pencil behind the clip. The sun was now halfway over the horizon, oranges and pinks and golds tinting the sky with a riot of color. The valley was ringed by blue rolling hills; little golden buttercups had popped up all around the meadow.

Sometimes people thought she was cold, with her spectacles and her lists and her plans and her board clip and her hair always in a strict bun. *Miss Fong,* she had been told too many times, *you're intimidating.*

Everyone thought she was cold until they needed her to be efficient. Today Chloe needed to be colder and more efficient than she had ever been. She shut her eyes, inhaled cool air, and—

"Chloe," someone said, interrupting her preparations.

She jumped, startled, and whirled about.

It turned out that jumping and whirling when one was barely holding on to a basket full of little glass-stoppered bottles, was a bad idea. She accidentally let go of both the basket and her board clip; three of the little sauce bottles fell. One broke, splattering glass and reddish-brown liquid on her list.

Her *list*. It felt ominous.

Chloe looked up in agony, and then—when she saw who had spoken—shut her eyes in redoubled agony. She had seen him for scarcely half a second, but she hadn't needed even that to identify the shape of him leaning against the wall of the barn. He looked the way laughter sounded; he was tapping his lips with one finger and smiling down at her with unholy glee. He had *always* looked like he was laughing at her.

He was here. Why in God's name was *he* here?

"You." She reached almost without thought to touch the bracelet on her wrist. *"You."* She took in a deep breath.

She'd been small in comparison with him ever since he'd shot up in height when he was fourteen. But being small had never stopped people from calling her intimidating, so she straightened as high as she could manage and glared at him.

"What are you *doing* here?" she demanded.

He just smiled more broadly. "Miss Fong. What shocking informality after our three years apart. I appreciate it."

He was tall and dark and handsome. The perfect storybook hero, if storybook heroes had ever been half-Chinese. She could see the similarities she shared with him in the planes of his face, the width of his nose, the fold of his eyelids. And he was giving her that infernal smile that had haunted her lists for far too long.

He wasn't like the heroes in any of the English story-books Chloe had read as a child, but he hadn't matched the stories her Ba told her either. There had been a time, back when he'd focused on her so intently, seeking her out year after year, when she'd thought he was a story written just for her.

Stupidity, that. He'd been written only for himself. He had nothing to do with her.

She glared at him. "Answer the question or go away." As always, she regretted the words the instant they came out of her mouth. Why had she given him a choice when she only wanted him to leave? She changed tactics. She was going to have to be horribly inhospitable. "What are you *doing* here?"

There was a lazy humor to the slouch of him. She gritted her teeth as he turned to her.

"We haven't seen each other in three years, but I agree with your assessment—it feels as if no time has passed at all. Of course I grant you permission to call me by just my surname. 'Mr. Yu' sounds all too stuffy between childhood friends, does it not? But 'Jeremy' would do just as well, if not better. You used to call me that."

"*You.*" Chloe took a deep breath. "I was addressing you by a common, indeed, a *generic* pronoun. Not your surname."

Yu wasn't even his real surname; she knew *that*. It was just the one he'd given. Nothing about him was real. Not that easy familiarity nor his laughing eyes. He was a specter, the sort that cropped up every year until finally it didn't. He was the kind of man who made her want to light firecrackers.

Alas. Whatever demons might be expelled by the cracking sound of gunpowder, Jeremy Yu was not one of them.

"Well then," Jeremy said, "let's try a more specific name, then. *Jeremy.*" He leaned toward her again, his eyes sparkling. "You can say that, yes? It's my name. You've used it before."

"I'm busy." She glanced down at the mess at her feet— the broken bottle and her board clip. "I—" She stopped. There was still glass and brown sauce all over her list, blotting out her daily tasks. "Fiddlesticks!"

He glanced down, his eyes falling on the debris. "Oh, no. Chloe, I'm sorry. I didn't think you'd start like that." His mouth twitched. "Or that you'd be carrying glass, for that matter."

"Not that you'd know what I'm doing now—" Chloe started to say, but before she could properly upbraid him, he knelt in front of her, pulling out a handkerchief, picking up the broken shards of glass.

The sight of him on his knees before her... It brought to mind wicked things, things she'd only allowed herself to imagine years before. Even then, she'd known it was foolish.

She'd always known that what they had was flirtation, nothing but flirtation. She'd liked him anyway, knowing the whole time that holding him in any degree of affection was a bad idea. She'd liked his jokes. She'd liked the way he teased her—relentless and yet gentle the entire time.

She'd liked him so much, and knowing that she was being a fool hadn't helped her stop.

She had always known that one day he would go away and never come back. She had accepted that. But here he was, against all expectations: back and looking at her the way he always had, as if she were the center of his considerable attention.

"Oh, give that to me," she said crossly.

She leaned down, reaching out a hand and snatching her board clip from his grip before straightening. The paper was definitely stained; three items weren't even visible, and half the right side of her list had been spattered with sauce. She could smell it now, salt and sweet and sour and savory all at once, the taste of her childhood in liquid form.

"There's nothing you can do. It's ruined." She had to get him to go away. She had feelings, and they were going to come out, and she didn't want him to see them. "Stop pretending to be considerate; I know you too well for that. Just pretend I don't exist. You did it for years; you ought to be good at it by now."

"I beg your pardon." He was still squatting on the ground, looking up at her with a faint smile. "I will accept all of that except the last. I have never had any particular talent at ignoring you, and I definitely did not develop it."

She glared at him straight on. It was the first time she'd allowed herself to look at him in more than glances since he arrived, and it was a mistake. He rose to stand as she watched, and she felt her throat contract involuntarily.

He had always been handsome, but his effortless good looks used to have a boyish quality to them, enough that she'd always been able to remind herself that he was two years her junior.

He had grown up. His shoulders were just a little broader, his jaw just a little more square. His expression seemed so sincere, but like everything about him, his looks were always deceiving. He was dressed in a dark navy suit that highlighted the brightness of his smile, wearing a shirt that seemed impossibly snow white. There was more than a hint of muscle in the thickness of his thighs...and her perusal of his person had officially become ridiculous. She was not thinking about his damnable thighs. She was not supposed to be thinking of any part of him at all.

She turned to look at her spoiled list, face burning.

"I'm truly sorry," he said, "for the untimely demise of your list. But there is one small bright side."

Her entire plan for the afternoon had been blotted out by the spill. "There isn't. Not one. You have no idea how deathly busy I am today."

"No, there is this," he told her with a lazy smile. "When you rewrite it, you can put me on it."

―――――――――

IT HAD BEEN THREE YEARS SINCE JEREMY Wentworth, the Duke of Lansing, had last come to Wedgeford, and in that time he'd thought about Chloe Fong and her lists. He'd thought about her a lot.

He'd imagined telling her to put him on her list about four hundred times and had constructed a dozen separate responses from her, ranging from welcoming (not likely) (incredibly not likely) to downright devastating. Now he was here and she was glaring at him.

It had been a long time, and yet he recognized her plain gown of ecru muslin from a prior visit. He'd thought about her in this gown—or, to be honest, out of it—often enough, thought about untying the big brown bow of her sash or undoing the buttons down her front.

She looked at him with angry, sparking eyes through her spectacles. He had thought his memory of her was crystal clear, but faced with her in the flesh, he could see every point where his recollection had failed. He had forgotten about the silk tassel earrings she wore. Today little golden fringes dangled from her lobes halfway to her shoulders. He had forgotten about the dimple in her left cheek, the precise black of her hair—so much richer in the first rays of sunlight than his memory could reconstruct—the brown beauty spot three-quarters of the way down her neck. God, how had he forgotten that spot? It had once figured so heavily in his imagination.

He'd missed her. He'd missed everything about her.

She straightened her spine and glared up at him. "You are *not* going on my list. It is *my* list; I get to make it."

Ah, that was good. Just a *little* minor repudiation. There was hope. He couldn't help the smile that spread across his face.

"I genuflect to the sovereignty of your list, of course," Jeremy said. "Your list is sacred."

She turned away from him in one sharp movement and strode back to her house.

Chloe had fascinated him from the moment he'd met her. She was a bit more than two years his elder and had sported such a continual air of perfect competence that he'd wondered how it was possible for her to exist.

If he had any talent for plain speech, he might have confessed the depths of his feelings by now and obtained her understanding in return. Unfortunately, Jeremy had none. He'd told her how he felt; but somehow whenever he looked at her, his thoughts never came out as something sober and intellectual like *I respect the things that matter to you.* No. Instead, everything he felt got tied up and turned around into *I genuflect to the sovereignty of your list.*

His words were honestly meant, yes, but the delivery was far less believable. He wished he had a plan for his stupid mouth, but plans were *her* talent. His? Not so much. For now, he followed behind her.

After three steps, she turned back to him, waving a hand in the air. "It's like you've forgotten everything I have ever said to you. Have you made any progress at all? Or are you still—you?"

It was as if she'd heard his thoughts. "No progress at all," he admitted. "I regret to inform you that I will always be me."

She exhaled loudly. "Have you considered a steady course of continual self-improvement?"

"Tried it." He shrugged. "It went about as you'd expect. Don't worry; there's no need to remind me of the charges you laid on me. My memory is, like the rest of me, extraordinary."

She glared at him. "I told you to *be serious.* And yet here you are."

It had been a moonlit night three years ago, after the

Trials had ended. They had both spent the day unsuccessfully attempting to keep another team from crossing a bridge, and then unsuccessfully trying to foil the subsequent victory. Jeremy and Chloe had both been exhausted and frustrated in their team's defeat. Perhaps it had been a mistake, what happened in that particular moment.

He'd convinced her to go on a walk with him and she'd agreed, which had made him feel optimistic. He'd been twenty—he had thought himself so very mature—and young and full of humor; she had walked beside him, letting him twine his hand with hers. He'd gathered up all his courage. He'd made sure they were hidden from prying eyes, and he'd stopped and leaned in, because he'd known her for almost a decade and he'd adored her for approximately the same length of time.

Perhaps it had been a mistake, but the moonlight had lit the light brown of her skin with silver, and nobody had ever accused Jeremy of engaging in lengthy deliberations prior to action. He had tried to kiss her.

She'd set a hand on his chest and said exactly this: "Jeremy, don't do this unless you can be serious."

Be serious. He had known precisely what she meant. It hadn't been a plea for him to stop joking for good; such a thing would have been impossible, and besides, she liked his jokes. She had wanted him to be serious about her. About *them.* For three minutes, not all of eternity.

If Jeremy had been a farmer in Wedgeford, on the strength of such encouragement, he would have bought a ring and proposed the next day.

But Jeremy was not a farmer. At the time, it had seemed like a fair price to pay for a prize like Chloe—

figuring out how to fit her in his life without destroying what he loved best about her. Too bad he'd never succeeded.

So here they were, together again. Jeremy had never been one for plans; he just seized the moments that he found. So he did what he did best: he smiled at her. "That is *precisely* what you told me. I remember it well. It turns out, that is *your* list for *me,* and we have already established that we don't usually get to make each other's lists."

She rolled her eyes and started to turn away. "I wish I *could.* If I could make your list, I would—"

"I said *usually* for a reason." He spread his arms wide, grinning at her. "Congratulations! Here I am to grant your wish!"

The look she gave him would have proven fatal at a slightly lesser distance than the three paces between them.

"Miss Fong," Jeremy said, thinking as swiftly as he could, "as you know, I am a gentleman of some small amount of property."

"Yes," she said with a roll of her eyes. "You're very wealthy. We all know that; it's why everyone calls you 'Posh Jim' around here." Her nose wrinkled. "Congratulations. All your riches must be very nice for you."

Jeremy tried not to grimace. He had actually never said that he was *very wealthy.* He had tried to avoid the topic altogether. But *very wealthy* was a horrific understatement, and the misunderstanding on the topic was entirely Jeremy's fault.

Not that he had ever precisely *lied;* he had just misled. A little. The first year, he had come to the village unaccompanied at the age of twelve. At the time, it had not seemed prudent to announce to a group of complete strangers that the child who had appeared with no guardian in sight was in fact the very wealthy Duke of Lansing. He'd read books, after all. *That* was how wealthy dukes who were also children got abducted and held for ransom.

So he had introduced himself as Jeremy Yu. It was not exactly a lie. Yu had been his mother's name, after all, and it *was* one of his six names…just not his father's family name. Selectively editing out all his other names? A slip of the tongue. Neglecting to mention his title? It *wasn't* a lie; he left off all his titles but the one during most of his introductions anyway. Deleting that one was just…being selective in his speech. Or something.

The *or something* had grown. The second year he'd visited, he had been having too much fun to ruin it by forcing everyone to become stuffy and bow to him and call him "Your Grace." It had been impossible to hide the fact that he had means. His clothing, his accent, his manners, his ability to patronize businesses in Wedgeford… these were all too indicative of his class. But it was easy enough to misdirect. Nobody saw a half-Chinese boy of thirteen and thought, "By George, that child must be a duke."

By the time the ninth year had rolled around, the information he was withholding had become an increasingly awkward weight. He had friends who knew nothing about him. He was in love with a woman who had no idea who he actually was.

She had told him to be serious; he had realized he was in love with her and wanted to marry her. Then he had recollected that he was the Duke of Lansing and she had absolutely no idea. Finally, he'd remembered that his mother had so hated her life as duchess that she had fled the country with Jeremy in tow the week his father had been put in his grave.

Was *that* what he was going to offer Chloe? A life she hated? How could he be *serious* about her under those circumstances?

"I am twenty-three," he told the woman he was in love with. "Do you know what gentlemen of my age and means are expected to do around the age of twenty-three?"

Her nose wrinkled. "Get in drunken brawls?"

"No, that's nineteen. At twenty-three, I'm expected to start thinking of marriage. My aunt will not stop bothering me."

In point of fact, Jeremy was going to have to figure out what, precisely, he would tell his aunt Grace. His aunt always wanted the best for him…but her conception of what was best for her half-Chinese nephew lacked both imagination and experience.

"She insists that I will have to do almost no work in the matter; she'll find me a few good girls—her words, not mine—and all I must do is give her a list of my criteria."

Chloe audibly scoffed at this. "My felicitations on your pending nuptials. How lovely for you. You get to pick among the ladies as if you were shopping for apples."

Jeremy had never actually shopped for apples; he was nonetheless fairly certain that the analogy was inapt on several points, the most prominent being that he had his eye on only one apple, and it was her. "As I said. I have some means available to me."

Chloe's eyes narrowed. "You see? This is how you

always worm your way in. You're setting up an interesting story, not telling me all the relevant information, and tricking me so that I end up listening to you when I have no intention of doing so. None of this has anything to do with me, and I am *excessively* busy. So if you don't mind, I will—"

"It has four things to do with you."

"It has *zero* things to do with me."

"Three, as a compromise." Jeremy beamed at her.

She let out a pained breath. "You may recite two. But *only* two, and then we are finished. Utterly finished."

"Thank you," Jeremy said solemnly. "Here is what it has to do with you: I am bad at making lists, and you are exceptionally good at them."

She tilted her head. "True. I do not, however, see the relevance. We are done. Farewell forever."

"Second—"

"Absolutely not." Chloe shook her head. "That was already two things: your ineptitude at list-making and my competence. You don't get a third. We agreed."

"That was a single thing: our relative capacity at list making."

She let out a huff. "You are such a cheat. You have not changed one iota."

"I do like winning," Jeremy said. "It is, as you have noted, an ongoing talent of mine. Stop interrupting. *Second,* if you were to ask me what qualities I wanted on my list for an ideal spouse—if I wanted a list that best reflected my desires—that list would be a list of your qualities."

As soon as he said it, he realized that it was brilliant.

Jeremy had two problems, as he saw it. First, there was the as-yet-unsolved problem of being a duke—he'd figure that one out somehow. Maybe. But second, and more immediately relevant, there was the problem of Chloe herself.

If he had said, *Chloe, I want to marry you,* she would have thought it a joke and thrown her board at his head— well, maybe not her board, not with her list attached to it —but she'd have found something else. Something like... He glanced at the bottles in her basket. Yes. Rather more like that. Those would shatter.

As it was, she froze in place. She glanced at him through downcast eyelashes. Her voice came out low. "My...qualities?"

The problem had never been how serious Jeremy was about her; it had been how serious *she* thought he was. She had to convince herself first. How better to have her do that, than to make a list? He wasn't precisely sure how that would work itself out, but Chloe had always been better at details.

"Yes," he said. "Your qualities. If I have to marry someone, it needs to be someone like you."

She swallowed. "Like *me?*"

Yes, Jeremy thought. *Someone exactly like you, in exactly every way.* No other woman would do. He nodded.

She inhaled and turned away. When she spoke, her voice was very small. "I don't think you could pay me to make that list."

He hadn't considered that, but actually, now that she mentioned it, it seemed like a good idea.

"On the contrary." Jeremy grinned at her. "I *could* pay you to do it. Do you wish me to do so?"

She shook her head. "I wouldn't do it for *two pounds.*"

She looked so earnest, saying *two pounds* as if it were an immense and insurmountable sum. Of course she had never thought him serious. The difference in scale between them was massive. For her, two pounds was a vast sum—the amount her father might make after working for a few weeks as a chef for hire, and that much only because of his exceptional skill. For Jeremy, two pounds was basically nothing.

"Not for two. What about three?"

She shook her head again, but this shake came more slowly. He should feel bad about bribing her into convincing herself that he was in love with her, but then, he'd already spent years trying to figure out how to convince her every other way, and the bribery had mostly been *her* idea anyway.

"Four?" he offered.

"Not even for five." She truly didn't sound convinced. She was as bad at misdirection as Jeremy was good at it.

For a moment, he thought about offering her a truly remarkable sum—something that would mean something even to *him*. Six thousand, perhaps. But she'd just roll her eyes and tell him to be serious. The amount would be outside her comprehension.

"Seven, then."

"Not for—" She bit her lip, perhaps realizing how many pounds seven was. She swallowed and looked down. "Well, *maybe* for seven." She glared at him. "But you don't really mean to give me *seven entire pounds* just to make one fiddly list. That would be obscene."

He'd been right to keep the numbers low. "If it's a maybe for seven," he said, "it's a yes for ten, isn't it?"

Her lips trembled a moment.

"I will swear a solemn oath on my father's grave. I'll give you ten pounds, and I'll throw in an entire box of the thickest, creamiest, most perfect list-making paper that you have ever seen."

She shut her eyes. "You're not fair. You're never fair."

It was only right that he should warn her. "I didn't come here to play fair."

"What did you come here for?"

There was a simple answer to that. A terrible answer, he knew, but simple. *I came here to convince you to marry me. Then to tell you who I am. And finally to convince you that you should still marry me anyway, after you realize what a bad bargain I would be.*

In the end, he misled her with the truth. "I came here because I intend to get married."

Still, she hesitated. She looked away, her shoulders rising and falling with every breath. "You'll pay me ten pounds? You'll sign a contract to that effect?"

"Of course," he said. "Make that the first item on our list: whoever it is I marry must insist I sign contracts. I like that in a woman."

She looked up to the heavens as if searching the light clouds overhead for patience. "I'm not sure ten pounds is enough. I'm not sure any amount would suffice, but…" She swallowed. "But very well. It's agreed. I'll take your ten pounds in exchange for a list."

THE AIR IN CHLOE'S SMALL HOME WAS SO PERFECTLY aromatic that she could almost taste the dish her father was making. Ginger, garlic, the scent of fermented broad beans, as well as a hint of lingering incense... She shut her eyes and inhaled. This. *This.* This was the smell of home, the smell of comfort, and the smell of her ambition, all wrapped into one. It was the smell of steamed yeasted buns and pork and the Unnamed Sauce her father had spent a decade perfecting.

With ten pounds—*ten pounds,* what a ridiculous amount!—they would be able to start producing Unnamed Sauce in larger quantities. Chloe could hire Tim to assist with the production on a daily basis, maybe come to an agreement with the Wedgeford Collective on the empty space near the river—jars, manufacturing, *everything.* Her father could get the treatments he needed; he might rest more and maybe give the stiffening joints in his hands time to recuperate. He could avoid the flaring headaches that came if he pushed too hard.

She could not have said no to Jeremy.

Still, the idea of making Jeremy, of all people, a list to help him find a woman to marry… That made something in her want to lash out like an angry, cornered ferret. But that *something* was nostalgia and old, small dreams. All of those needed to die anyway, and this would be the best way to murder them.

"Ah Lin," Chloe heard her father say as she kicked off her outdoor shoes and exchanged them for indoor slippers. "You're back. Go and pai to Ah Me."

Praying to her mother was as much a part of her morning routine as making a list. Chloe's first memory was lighting hiong with unsteady hands and looking to her father for guidance.

She set the three unbroken bottles on the table where her father was laying out breakfast things. Then she took a steamed yeasted bun, a mug of tea, and a dollop of brown sauce from the bowl on the counter, before going to kneel before the low table on the far side of the wall.

She poured tea into two little cups, broke two pieces off the bun, and set these in a tiny dish. She then picked up a match and lit two fat, brown joss sticks. Flame sparked, caught, flared, and then subsided until only the tips of the incense glowed with red. The ritual had been like this her entire life. Nobody else in Wedgeford lit incense for their ancestors in twos, but it was how her father had taught her.

"Good morning, Ah Me." She bowed. Two delicate curls of sandalwood smoke rose from the hiong. "I hope you are well."

Chloe's mother had died when Chloe was a baby. Her

memories of Ah Me were only this—her father's stories and an ancestral tablet of carved rosewood with her mother's name engraved in Chinese characters. Those had been some of the first characters that Chloe had been taught. NyukMin—"bright jade"—that was her mother's name. Her father had taught her to read that first, drilling her on stroke order until she could manage to duplicate the characters properly. Only after she knew her mother's name had he gone on to her own. "YiLin," he'd taught her, hand over hers on the pen. "Lin—see? It has the character for jade inside, the way your mother is inside you as well. That's your mother's family tradition."

Her mother's tablet sat among four generations of Chloe's ancestors. She'd learned about all of them a little, but most of all, her mother.

Her father had told her story after story about her mother's childhood; it was all she knew of the woman. In return, Chloe told her mother about herself.

"Here." Chloe spooned a bit of the sauce she'd taken from her father on top of the pieces of bun. "You'll like this one, Ah Me. The broad beans have been fermenting nine months; I think it's the right aroma, don't you?"

As if in answer, a charred end of an incense stick fell off in a cylindrical clump of ash.

"Ah Me." Chloe lowered her voice. "You know Ah Ba and how he is about me and Unnamed Sauce."

For as long as Chloe could remember—ever since they'd landed in the tiny community of Wedgeford, with its population hailing from around the globe—her father had been working on a sauce. *The* sauce, the sauce to end all sauces. The base of the sauce was broad beans fermented with white qu over the course of months. To that, her father added soy sauce, honey, a hint of ground spice, red yeast rice, and some potato vinegar that he also brewed. It was an alchemical triumph, turning bland crops into delicious magic.

What her *mother* would think of her involvement in Unnamed Sauce… That was another question entirely.

"Your mother," her father had told her, "when Taiping Tianguo opened the imperial examinations to women— she was determined to take part. She was much older than her younger brother and had half the education. But she set to studying—pushing him, teaching him when she was herself learning."

Chloe had always listened to these stories with rapt attention.

"She passed the examinations too," her father had told her with a smile. "Better than her little brother managed in any event. They made her a Deputy Chancelloress of the Winter Department. Your mother could do anything; she usually did."

Her father always spoke of her with love in every word, as if the loss of her were still recent and searing.

"But what was she *like?*" Chloe had asked as a child.

"Kind," he had said. "Quick to think, but shy around new people. Always looking out for her little brother, who hadn't half her wits. Taiping Tianguo brought change, good at first, but what followed…"

That was one of the things he rarely talked about— what happened as the Heavenly Kingdom of Great Peace had gone to war.

He just said this: "It was not good." For him, that was tantamount to ranting about death and destruction.

The only thing he had ever told her about the time that came after was that he had made her mother promises on her deathbed: that Chloe would never starve, that he would protect her, that she would get an education, and that she would grow into her name.

Chloe had never quite understood that last one. Her Chinese name of YiLin meant...the tinkling of feathers, maybe? Or perhaps just the sound of feathers. "Your mother picked the name out for you before you were conceived," he had finally said. "And Baba approved. She wanted you to have what she did not."

Feathers made no sound, and she had not been able to square the demure, dainty image that brought to mind with the vibrant, determined woman her father described. Maybe that was what he'd meant—that she had wanted Chloe to avoid the fate she'd courted. Perhaps without that rise to fortune, there would have been no devastating fall at the end. Perhaps the name had been meant as a warning, something like the Western legend of Icarus.

It was faintly unsettling to know that her mother would have found fault with her had she lived. But Chloe had come to know her through these morning interludes. If she objected to Chloe's path, there had been no sign that Chloe could see.

Maybe her mother had resigned herself in death to a daughter who took after her too much. That much she could tell from the tales her father told—story after story from her mother's childhood and none from his own. He'd told her more stories about her mother's youngest brother and what she did for him and how silly he had been. He said barely a word about himself or how he'd grown up. And when he did, he always referred to himself as "Baba," third person—as if he could distance himself from the memory and reduce himself to just a relationship. He rarely said more, no matter how she begged.

Chloe had not really understood how much he'd sacrificed to keep his promises to her mother until she was fifteen and she'd pried the story of Unnamed Sauce from him.

His desire to make the best sauces in all of Britain was the one thing he was doing for himself, not Chloe. He had allowed her to help, but only grudgingly. It was *his* sauce, *his* legacy, *his* revenge, he had said. No reason for Chloe to be involved.

When Chloe had found out the truth, she had cried and she'd promised her mother then that she would never let her father stand alone. So here she was.

"Ah Me," she said. "All I have to do for the next three days…" It was daunting, so daunting. "All I have to do," she said, "is not make a single misstep. I can do that, right?"

Except. There was…also the small matter of Jeremy. For a moment, Chloe thought about mentioning him. But… No. She'd handle him on her own.

"I hope you like the sauce." She bowed one final time, then stood.

"Done, Ah Lin?" her father asked.

He spoke to her in Hakka. Her father could speak many languages. English, of course, and French and Mandarin and Cantonese. But when it was just the two of them, he used the language that his parents had spoken at home. Chloe understood it well enough to follow, but she rarely spoke Hakka with anyone but him, and complex concepts came to her first in English.

She was going to have to handle these next moments with all the delicacy her Hakka skills allowed. She had only barely convinced him to allow her to assist in the matter of Unnamed Sauce. Additional complications would not put him more at ease. If she mentioned Jeremy straightaway, he'd know something was odd. On the other hand, if she mentioned Jeremy not at all during the conversation, he'd become suspicious if he heard the gossip.

She walked to the table. Breakfast was laid out before her.

The upcoming Wedgeford Trials were an opportunity. The daylong game their village hosted had attracted people from all over Britain for centuries. Rich and poor, young and old, from south of London to the highlands of Scotland. Wedgeford was a village of mere hundreds, but for three days—the Trials themselves, and the days before and after—its population would swell to almost a thousand. Those from outside who wanted to take part would be assigned to one of the three teams. They'd spend the day searching and running and shouting.

By the time a team was crowned the winner in the early evening, they would all be starving. And Chloe and her father would be at the booth they'd constructed on the green with steamed pork bao made with Unnamed Sauce and little printed paper squares advertising where to inquire for more.

He sighed. "You're taking on too much. It's not too late to call it off; if we wait until next year, I'll be able to take on more of the burden. And it will give me a chance to make sure the nine-month fermentation is the right one to use..." He trailed off.

"Ah Ba." They had spent the last handful of weeks filling four hundred jars of the sauce. She was going to scream. "I know you want everything to be perfect, but it is *already* perfect. There's no need to wait."

He looked at her from the corner of his eye. It was just a look—nothing that necessarily meant anything. But Chloe knew him, knew the way his eyes narrowed when he was thinking, knew the way his lips thinned when he decided not to speak his doubts. She knew what this meant: he was still uncertain that she should be involved.

He pushed a bowl forward. "Have breakfast."

Idly, Chloe wondered if Jeremy had eaten yet. If she should have—for the sake of his ten pounds, if not old times—invited him in. Instead, she'd told him to meet her on the village green in an hour and a half.

No. Better to maintain a fence between them. He'd offered her money; she'd accepted. That made this a matter of business. Business acquaintances didn't dine together in the early hours of the morning.

She ripped the bun in half and inhaled the scent of yeast, then dipped it in the sauce. The depth of flavor—the roundness on the back of her tongue—that hint of heat right at the end... She let out a noise.

"Perfection." Her eyes slid shut. "You see? It's absolute perfection."

Her father held up a hand. "There is no such thing as perfection."

Chloe held up her bun. "What do you call this then?"

Even the taste of Unnamed Sauce was not enough to distract her. Chloe was lying to herself. And she was bad at lying even if she was the only target.

Really. Trying to fool herself into thinking Jeremy was a business acquaintance? Ha. She'd seen the way he looked at her. She knew how she had once looked at him. If she told herself falsehoods, the truth would take her by surprise, and there was no room for unwelcome surprises at the moment.

Her father frowned. "Something will go wrong if you keep boasting. It's bad luck."

Bad luck. That's what she was courting with these lies. Over these next few days, no matter what she told herself, one thing mattered and one thing alone. She had to successfully launch Unnamed Sauce.

"Boo." Chloe folded her arms and took another bite. "Ah Ba, I'm telling the truth. This is your moment of triumph. People from all over England will take home jars of your sauce. They'll share them with friends and family and—" She paused, not knowing how to say *telegraph* in Hakka, and rearranged her sentence. "They'll write to order more. Just imagine: White and Whistler visit their warehouses one day and realize—"

"That wouldn't happen," her father interjected. "Visiting warehouses is work. White and Whistler visit inns for ale, not warehouses for information."

Chloe waved a hand and altered the trajectory of her imagination. "A man from their warehouses visits them with bad news. Their stock of White and Whistler's Pure English Sauce is only taking space and gathering dust. Orders are down. They start looking for a reason and discover that newspapers are saying that White and Whistler's Pure English Sauce is boring in comparison to…" Well. Her dream would work better if she'd hit upon a name for their sauce yet. She hadn't, and matters were getting rather dire. "Um."

"None of that." Her father frowned, straightening from where he leaned against the table. "And don't insult Pure English Sauce. I made that for them, you know."

Mere details. She waved a hand. "Then they'll say it's unrefined." He hadn't had time to improve it, after all, and they'd tossed him out before he had a chance to apply years of meticulous testing to achieve perfection. "Instead, everyone is buying—"

"Stop," her father said. But the corner of his mouth curled up. "Stop dreaming. Start eating. You're too skinny."

She had never been anything of the kind. But this was what love looked like between them—him cooking her food so perfect that she could cry, while he frowned at her and told her she was too skinny. When she'd been teased as a child for her lists, he'd been there for her, perfecting his sauce as best as he could, serving up plate after plate of food so good that it almost defeated her loneliness.

This—seeing his dream come to fruition—was the only thing she could allow herself to care about right now.

He set a clay pot and a bowl on the table in front of her with a thump. "Eat."

"Ah Ba, I am eating already. I can't eat all that."

He had taken his promise that she wouldn't starve very seriously. That was another one of her early memories— sitting at a different table, feeling a cold chill, and being told to eat.

She had been born in Trinidad, but she had no memory of that country. Her parents had traveled there as laborers. It was there, at the end of her father's indenture, that he had encountered Mr. White and Mr. Whistler, travelers who had quickly become enamored of his cookery. They'd marveled over his dishes and his sauces. Her Ba hadn't had the money to return to China; he'd been considering a second indenture. They'd offered him an exorbitant amount of money to come to England instead.

Spend a few years with them, they had whispered. Develop a method for making sauces that could be produced commercially for the English market. He would end up rich, they had promised, with wealth enough to return to China and set up a household where he could live in comfort and see his daughter respectably married.

He and tiny Chloe had been brought over the ocean in something like luxury. He hadn't signed a contract because they were friends, and friends didn't need such things.

They'd tasted his sauce after the first month and pronounced him a fraud who had fooled them. It didn't matter that he'd earnestly explained that the mix needed time to ferment. They'd tossed him out with no money, no means of returning to China—with nothing but Chloe and his skills as a cook. And when he'd tried to argue, they'd told him he should thank them for the opportunity of being abandoned in a country where he knew nobody.

Some time later, he'd discovered that White and

Whistler had taken the sauce he'd left behind in the barrel, used the instructions that they had written out as he worked, and sold the resulting sauce as "White and Whistler's Pure English Sauce." They'd made a fortune.

Ever since then, he'd started to develop his own sauce. Something better, tastier, richer, more balanced. His cooking had always been excellent, but the addition of spite to every recipe had brought an extra level of brilliance.

Chloe took a pair of chopsticks. The food her father cooked at home was like nothing she had found anywhere else—not in England, not even in Wedgeford, where they were not the only Chinese family, not even the only Hakka family.

The rice in the clay pot was perfect, little holes made by rising steam separating fluffy, individual grains. In the other bowl, fried into soft golden wedges, was a swirl of long strings of salted, preserved radish bound together with beaten egg, dotted with green scallions. Once those scallions would have been sliced into paper-thin circles. Now that it was harder for him to hold the cleaver, the little green flecks were somewhat larger. She took a wedge.

"Mmm." Her first mouthful of egg was soft and fluffy in perfect counterpoint to the salty, chewy radish. The scallions lent a pungency to the dish, no matter their size. "So good, Ah Ba."

"You would be able to eat more if you spent less time praising the food." His words were stern, but the corners of his eyes crinkled in pleasure.

If she was praising the food, she wouldn't have to think about her other problem. Jeremy. Her... Business acquaintance? Had she just told herself she would treat him as a business acquaintance?

Ha. She had been very silly over him three years back, and she could feel those emotions inside her, preparing to be silly once more. She could remember how he'd almost kissed her and she'd said no. In the years that followed, she'd praised herself for that strength of mind, the decency of her principles, her moral and upright stance.

She had also bitterly regretted her stupid principles. She regretted pushing him away *before* the kiss. She should have pushed him away *after.* Then she could have prided herself on the uprightness of her morals, and *also* been kissed.

She could feel warmth rising to her face; her father looked at her, where she'd paused mid-bite, chopsticks poised. Swiftly, she finished her food and nodded at him. "It's delicious."

"Humph." He folded his arms and frowned to hide his pleasure. "We still need a name for the sauce. I like the name 'Lucky Sauce.'" Those two words, spoken in English amidst the flurry of Hakka, sounded almost harsh. "What do you think?"

They'd had this discussion before. She wrinkled her nose. "That's not very British."

His eyes met hers briefly before he looked away, shaking his head. "You may have noticed this, but my sauce is not very British."

"Yes, well." Chloe couldn't figure out how to articulate her thoughts, so she switched to English. "White and Whistler's Pure English Sauce is also zero percent English. British people *love* their non-British sauces, as long as they don't *know* they're not British. It needs a name like…" She trailed off, thinking. "Two Hundred Percent English Sauce: Now Twice as Much English as Pure English Sauce."

Her father still didn't smile at this jest. "That sounds like it's made of English people."

They stared at each other in silence for a moment, before her father let out a snicker.

"Sauce of Britannia," Chloe supplied.

"England in a Bottle."

"Definitely Not Foreign Sauce."

Her father laughed. "The name still needs work. Too bad we don't have any stuffy British people around to use as a test." Not in Wedgeford, they wouldn't; half the village was white, but the last half-century had altered the character of the place.

No, they needed…

Chloe's mind went right back to the person she had been trying not to think about all breakfast. Jeremy. He was *back,* and… And she couldn't have any hopes of him. She never had. She had known precisely what it meant when they'd spent time together: She was a bit of fun to liven his days. He came for the festival; he stayed a handful of days. He was going to leave. He was always going to leave.

But did that mean she should have nothing? Would she always have all regrets and no kisses?

She swallowed.

"What is it?" her father asked, and, well. She had known she would have to mention Jeremy to allay his suspicions. He had enough to worry about. No need for him to harbor further suspicions.

She sighed. "Do you remember...um... The person who would once come at Trials...?"

Apparently, this was not the way to make her father less suspicious. His eyes narrowed immediately. "No," he said, but the firm way he said it sounded more as if he was denying the existence of Jeremy altogether rather than his own memory. "*He's* returned?"

She thought of the wide curve of Jeremy's nose. The planes of his face, so much like hers. His eyes, dark and laughing. "He's returned. And technically, he isn't...*British* British. But I could ask him."

Her father's jaw twitched. "He is *British* British. In most of the ways that matter."

"He's just here for the Trials."

If I have to marry someone, he had said, *it needs to be someone like you.* Her stomach flipped at the memory. *Someone like you. Someone like you.* It was going to be someone *like* her—but it was not going to be her, and she had to remember that. He was *Posh Jim.*

He'd never boasted of his wealth, but the things he took for granted—fancy schools and ice in summer and once he'd mentioned that he had a personal valet who dressed him when he was not in Wedgeford. For God's sake. She couldn't comprehend tossing around money on such frivolities.

Ten pounds was apparently only a minor setback for him. He wanted to marry someone a *little* bit like her. Not a village girl who dreamed of challenging a sauce empire with her father. She *had* to remember that.

But lying to herself about her own complicated feel-ings left Jeremy with all the control. He could seduce her far too easily if she didn't take charge. And she was very afraid she could be seduced.

Her father's eyes went to the place where her hand had wrapped around the jade bracelet at her wrist. "If he's here for the Trials, he doesn't need to see you at all."

He wasn't much for giving advice; he never had been. But he remembered the year Jeremy hadn't come. He remembered the way she'd moped about, waiting. Wanting. He'd hand-pulled thick wheat noodles for her and fried them with pork and scallions, muttering under his breath.

"He doesn't matter to me," Chloe lied. "So it doesn't matter if I see him or if I don't. But if we have a chance to get his opinion…"

"No." He shook his head. "No need to expose yourself to any of this. None of this would be necessary if you—"

She held up a hand, forestalling the conversation they'd had dozens of times already. "*Please* don't tell me not to help you."

"It's not necessary," he groused. "You're young. A girl your age should be spending the Trials having fun, not laboring with an aging man and his bao, selling sauce."

She sighed. How hard was it for him to let her care for him as much as he cared for her?

"Ah Ba," she said gently. "I'm twenty-five. I'm not a girl. I'm not a child. I *should* be pulling my weight."

"All the more reason to stop worrying about my sauce. Especially if it means you have to talk to *him.*"

There was no point rehashing old arguments. He never

argued anyway, which made it terribly hard to win. He just stubbornly insisted that she didn't need to be helping him. He'd made the sauce; it had taken him years to perfect. She couldn't blame him for wanting to be in control of the process; she could only point out that it wasn't possible for him to do everything.

"I need to meet Andrew and Naomi at the inn." She stood. No need to mention that she'd already planned to meet Jeremy first. Chloe had been supposed to bring Andrew the final, definite, absolute name for Unnamed Sauce. She'd been supposed to decide on it in that unfortunate block of time that she now had to give to Jeremy's list. She shook her head, annoyed. She would just have to figure it out on her way there.

"You still don't mind if I choose one?" It was the one thing he had ceded to her, and that made her all the more determined to do this properly.

He waved a hand. "I'm even less British than you. On this, I don't think my input is needed any longer. Name it what you want. It's only right."

She wasn't sure what that meant—*it's only right*—but it was something. All she had to do was find a perfect name between here and the inn, then do everything else without a flaw. She owed him no less.

"Thank you, Ah Ba."

He just looked at her in confusion. "For what? For letting you talk to that man?"

"For breakfast," she said diplomatically. "I don't care about him at all."

He raised an eyebrow, and she tried not to flush. He

probably saw through her even faster than she saw through herself.

There. She'd seen Jeremy this morning; she'd floundered in confusion. Now that she'd had the chance to consider what he was offering in cold, hard daylight, she could recognize the facts.

For all he talked about marrying someone else, the truth of his list was obvious. He was going to heap her with compliments. He always did. And she was—no matter how she steeled herself for this eventuality—going to like it when he did so. She always did.

She didn't think Jeremy had thought hard enough to have formed a deliberate *plan* to seduce her. He was many things, but she could not think him so calculating. But he was definitely charismatic enough to *succeed* at it without trying too hard. And he would certainly do nothing to prevent its fruition.

This realization should have been unnerving. But her horror at the thought was sadly lacking. Even though she knew it would make his inevitable departure all the more painful…some part of her wanted him to succeed.

"Have it your way," he said. "Bring him by. I won't even hurt him."

"Ah Ba."

"Or threaten him."

"Ah Ba."

Her father cracked his knuckles and looked up at the ceiling. "Much."

Perhaps that was exactly what she needed to hear in the moment. Jeremy was going to seduce her…but he needn't seduce her *much*. Accepting that inevitability left her in full control.

Everyone thought her so intimidating, but Chloe knew better. She'd always had feelings, too many of them to let any of them come out. She was vulnerable. She had regrets. She had wants. She was fallible, no matter how often she put on her list that she should not be so. But if she ran from the truth of herself, from the depths of her wants, he would win. She couldn't let that happen.

No. Chloe was going to do what she did best: She was going to take charge.

3

THE VILLAGE OF WEDGEFORD DOWN WAS NOT QUIET, especially not an hour and a half after daybreak two days before the Trials. Roosters crowed. Sheep, somewhere on a nearby hill, bleated. Birds sang. Smoke rose from chimneys; laughter and voices drifted out of windows opened to the late spring sunshine.

Jeremy had returned to the center of Wedgeford after a long ramble around the perimeter. He'd taken his unfortunately named mare out for a bit of exercise, made sure she had the best of care in the stables. After she was settled in and groomed, he walked slowly across the village green, where tricolored bunting was being hung. Near him were the trees that lined the banks of the Wedge. On the far side of the green, where he could make out the silhouette of the inn across the distance, three men were unloading kegs from a wagon. A pair of geese crossed the road near them.

Likely, he knew those men. He had probably made jokes with them over a pint of ale in the past. He no doubt knew their families, their friends—and they didn't know him at all. Just his lies of omission.

He exhaled in frustration.

"Jim? Jim!"

Jeremy turned around and was hit by the rays of the blinding morning sun, beaming directly through a gap in the trees.

"Posh Jim," said a man standing ten feet from him, nothing more than a dark outline. "It *is* you! My mother said you'd arrived late last night, and I could scarcely believe it."

Jeremy blinked, then squinted, then—"Andrew?" He asked. "It's been years; I suppose I should call you Mr. Uchida now."

"Mr. Uchida? You big flat bean; it's Andy, as always. Where have you been?" The man reached out and took him by the arms, giving him a firm shake. "Daft, that's what you are. Utterly daft. You disappeared for three years. I thought you'd forgot about us."

"Forgot?" Jeremy blinked. He'd held all of Wedgeford in his heart these past years, Chloe most of all. Andy, having grown up here, could not possibly imagine what it was like to come to this place at the age of twelve. But Jeremy had been living...not in Wedgeford. Where people looked at him askance and whispered about his eyes and his nose when he was present, and asked ridiculous questions—such as whether his blood was red or yellow—when they became comfortable.

He could feel eyes watching him everywhere he went. *Not from here,* the watchers all seemed to think, although Jeremy had been born in England. *Doesn't belong,* people said, and those suspicions had chafed until he'd come to Wedgeford for the first time and discovered that there was somewhere he *did* belong. Somewhere people looked like him—not just one or two, but an entire community. Wedgeford spanned the spectrum from pale to dark brown in skin color, and Andrew—with his light brown skin and wide nose and dark eyes—fit right in the middle.

He looked around the green. "How could I forget Wedgeford?"

"*You* need to explain that to *me*. Where have you *been?*"

The answer to that question was awkward, and the question sounded mostly rhetorical in any event. It was considered bad manners here to pry too much into affairs, and he could put off even a friend he'd known as long as Andy with little effort.

"Oh, I've been getting a little exercise this morning," he said, purposefully misunderstanding the question. "Wedgeford has altered a bit. The inn... The roof's been changed, hasn't it? And the old well is gone. And—that building, there? What's that? It's new."

"That's the seed exchange," Andrew said. "One of my projects, which I run in my spare time." He gave Jeremy a little glance, and then smirked. "If you've the time while you're here, I'll tell you about it."

"What used to be there, then?"

"An old stable, unused and dilapidated. We performed a little liberation."

"Liberation?"

"It's the fucking duke's land," Andrew said nonchalantly, as if it were no small matter to tear down a building belonging to the Duke of Lansing in order to make space for his own enterprise. "But since he doesn't seem to care what we do around here, it was either let the ruins molder in the middle of the village for no reason, or…liberation."

Liberation. This was the other reason Jeremy had never told anyone who he was.

Wedgeford was largely built on property that belonged to one man: The Duke of Lansing. Unfortunately, this happened to be Jeremy. The dukes of Lansing had collectively practiced benign neglect for over half a century. They hadn't made any of the necessary modernizations, but they also hadn't collected any rents. If anyone in Jeremy's family had remembered that they owned this land, once on a minor stage route, with its only present claim to popularity being an ancient yearly festival, they hadn't bothered to care.

Jeremy had been twelve when he first arrived, scarcely old enough to begin to comprehend his duties—just old enough to want to avoid them, in fact. He'd been absconding from a painful visit with a not-distant-enough relative who scarcely tolerated him. He had wanted to have fun and enjoy the Trials. It had seemed boorish to start conversations with, *Nice to meet you, and by the by, I own your house and you owe me fifty-three years of rents.*

So he hadn't started conversations that way. It had been equally easy to fail to include this fact anywhere in the late-night discussions with his new friends. Years of neglecting this extremely unfortunate piece of information had not made disclosure easier. So here he was, more than a decade later. He was Posh Jim, or Jeremy Yu, and that was all they knew of him.

Alas that his more public persona was not so anonymous. The Dukes of Lansing had forgotten Wedgeford; Wedgeford had not returned the favor. Not that anyone ever referred to Jeremy by anything so civil as his actual title. Here he was known by more flavorful appellations, such as *His Grace Good Riddance* or *The Duke Who Didn't* or—for those like Andrew, who leaned toward saltier language—simply *the fucking duke.*

There had been no point in Jeremy's history with Wedgeford where he had wanted to confess that he was, in fact, the fucking duke.

"Hold up." Andrew frowned at the structure. "I haven't seen you in years. You haven't gone all stodgy on me, have you?"

"Stodgy? About seeds? What sort of seed-hating fiend do you take me for?"

"It's probably not legal, I don't think?" Andrew waggled a teasing eyebrow at Jeremy. "Demolishing a duke's building. Establishing an entire society that abides rent-free on land that belongs to His Grace Good Riddance. You're posh, Jim. Posh people tend to be tetchy about things like 'ownership' and 'deeds' and 'proper permission' and such. They tend to respect conventions. That sort of thing."

Jeremy suspected that if he were to consult his family solicitor, he would, in fact, be advised to be tetchy about things like "ownership" and "permission." Which was precisely why he'd never mentioned the matter at all. Instead, Jeremy did what he had always done when confronted with questions like this. He played along. "Ah, what an insult. You imagine I've changed into some kind of a monster? Fuck the fucking duke and his fucking conventions."

An enormous smile spread across Andrew's face—so large and so accepting that Jeremy could not help but smile alongside him. Dear God. Why would he want *rent* on a minor property when he could have companionship instead?

"Ah, Posh Jim." Andrew bumped his shoulder. "You're a traitor to your own class. I like that in a wealthy man. You've got time for a round?"

By the way, Jeremy did not say, as he had not said for over a decade, *I am the fucking duke you speak of. I am not betraying my class; I am only betraying myself. And it is a great deal of fun.* He should have told them who he was years ago. Instead, he was precisely as they'd named him. He was the duke who didn't.

"I've got—" Jeremy paused, and then frowned. "I'm sure I *do* have time for a round, but not at seven thirty in the bloody morning. Later today. What I have now is an appointment."

"An appointment?" Andrew asked. "Appointments sound tetchy. That's awfully posh of you, Jim."

"It's not that sort of an appointment. It's an appointment with…" He trailed off. Would she want people talking about them? It must be all right. She'd asked to meet him on the green; she was hardly hiding.

"An appointment with whom?"

Jeremy folded his arms. "An appointment with Miss Fong."

Andrew looked at him knowingly. "Ah *ha.*"

"This will come as a complete surprise, I am sure."

From the moment Jeremy had come to Wedgeford—the moment Chloe had been assigned to explain the Trials to him and to shepherd him through the event—it had always been Chloe.

Andrew just looked upward. "Very much so. My mother and aunt see her as something like a second daughter, you know. Don't make me have to pound you into the dust."

"You've nothing to worry about there. I vastly prefer my unpounded state."

Andrew just nodded at him. He said nothing else about Chloe, and it was just as well. The other boys, when they found out that she'd been tasked with his education that first year, had winced and said she was cold and harsh and demanding and intense. And, well, yes. She *was*.

But that had only sparked Jeremy's interest. There was something about a woman who knew what she wanted. It had captivated him even at the tender age of twelve when he hadn't quite understood his own fascination.

Chloe knew what she wanted. Wouldn't it be something if she wanted *him?*

"One moment." Andrew raised an eyebrow. "*Miss Fong,* is it? That seems terribly formal. What *are* you planning with our Chloe?"

"Only what I should have done years ago."

"And that is?"

"I should probably discuss it with her first. She'll have to put it on her list if it's going to happen, and she'd hate to hear it from someone else."

From behind him, he heard a snort. A snort that he

recognized. A snort that he knew from long experience. He pretended not to notice Chloe's arrival.

"But if you must have just a hint," he said, posturing a bit, and speaking a little more loudly, "I'm going to be seeing rather a lot of her, this round of the Trials."

"Are you?" Andrew was openly looking over Jeremy's shoulder at someone who was most certainly Chloe, come to meet him as planned. "What *are* your plans, then?"

"What do you expect?" Jeremy threw his arms out. "I plan to bask in the magnificence of her presence, to whatever degree I am allowed."

Behind him, Chloe choked on something that might have been a laugh. "Be *serious,*" she said.

He just shook his head and winked at Andrew before turning to her. "I *am* serious, my dear. Basking is serious business. You'll see."

4

EFFICIENCY. CHLOE WAS GOING TO EMBODY efficiency in every single part of her plan. She was going to take control. She was going to demand precisely what she wanted, and accept neither one ounce more nor less. Afterward, she'd be free of Jeremy, and it would be *he* who thought of *her* with regret for years.

Surely it would happen that way.

She pretended not to see the arm that Jeremy offered her as they left the green. Instead, she marched ahead of him to a handful of rocks in the shade of some willows along the banks of the Wedge. She settled back on the single tall boulder, arranging her skirts and board clip on the rock around her. She left him to array himself on the flat stones at her feet. This way, she could tower above him.

Petty, she knew, but he'd been gone for three years before turning up like a stray cat, expecting to be fed.

He slouched indolently against the low granite rock a foot away, tilting his head so that she could see an inch of his neck above the points of his collar. "Right," he said, as if this were his usual mode of sitting. "So. How do you want to go about this?"

"I had some time to think over breakfast." Something warm bloomed on her cheeks. "Before we proceed, I would like to make some alterations to our agreement."

"Ahhh." His smile broadened; he took off his hat and leaned all the way back. Sun tilted across the flat planes of his face. "You've realized you can milk me for everything I have, haven't you? Clever girl."

"I don't need you to tell me I'm clever. I've always been able to outsmart you."

His eyes, so mocking, took a leisurely course down her body, from her neck, past her chest, past her waist. Chloe drew her knees in and brushed her skirts down around her ankles.

"Yes," he said in a deep, tempting voice. "You most certainly have. You're doing it right now."

She swallowed back heat. *Control.* She was taking control.

"But it is all to the good that you have raised the point of our relative intelligences; it is a perfect conversational bridge between your depraved conduct and my wishes for our arrangement."

The corner of his mouth kicked up in a grin. "A bridge between my depravity and you? I like that. Please go on."

"I am not stupid," Chloe said. "Nor am I naive nor foolish nor even innocent."

"You aren't?" he breathed, his gaze fixing on her as if this made her all the more fascinating.

"I know quite a bit of the world. I have read extensively."

That smile broadened. "You've read! Extensively, at that! I cannot *wait* to discuss your reading material, Miss Fong. The possibilities are positively delightful."

"This is by way of saying that I know what you are doing." She glared at him.

He put one hand on his chest in something like apparent innocence. "Perfect! That saves me a great deal of time, I should think. Bravo for efficiency." He clapped once, then turned to her. "By the by, just so I know—what *am* I doing?"

Chloe's hand went to the bracelet at her wrist. It was made of curved, polished sections of milky white jade held together by ornate gold filigree. Her father had given it to her when she had turned sixteen.

"This is from Baba," he had said. "It comes from his family."

It was the first time he had mentioned his family.

She'd taken the bracelet and turned it over. Jade and gold were a lot more valuable than the silk tasseled earrings her mother had left for her, more valuable even than the single pair of heavy, curving silver earrings from her mother's family, reserved for special occasions. It said something about where her father's family had come from, this kind of wealth. She'd looked up at him with questioning eyes.

"You're finally old enough that this won't fall off if you wear it," he had said. "Baba wants you to have this. It will protect you."

Maybe it was foolish, but when her fingers touched

that skin-warm jade on her wrist, Chloe always found her courage. And she needed courage now—a generous helping of it.

She looked Jeremy in the eyes. "You are trying to seduce me."

He blinked. He didn't deny it immediately; instead, his brow furrowed, as if he were contemplating the matter. "I suppose," he said after a long moment, "I actually *am,* in a manner of speaking? I had not quite put it that way to myself, but yes, I will accept this formulation, inadequate as it may be. I am trying to seduce you. Are you going to tell me that I will fail?"

Her cheeks flamed. "That depends on your precise aim."

His eyes widened in astonishment. He sat up, leaning toward her. "Really? Does it? That's delightful."

"I am neither naive nor innocent," she said, "but while I am *theoretically* knowledgeable, I am, as a practical matter, inexperienced. I have occasionally thought to myself that I wished it were not so."

It would be easier if he took the moment to offer his expertise, in the detail she suspected he was capable of providing. Then she would not have to say the words aloud; she could simply cut him off when he crossed the line. But perhaps he could sense her want. Instead of speaking—a thing she knew from experience that he was extremely good at—he simply set his chin on his hands and watched her. "Mmm. Do go on."

He was going to make her say it. He was going to make her say what she wanted. It would have to come out of her own lips. She'd wanted control, but…

She shut her eyes so she didn't have to watch him enjoying himself at her expense. "I don't want to be completely despoiled," she said, "but I am going to be very busy for the next decade or so, and I should like to be kissed at least once. You are ideal for this endeavor. You will disappear in a few days. You know what you are doing. You are unlikely to develop unseemly emotions that will entangle me into a relationship that will ruin my business, as you've failed to do so thus far. You also have every motive to avoid detection."

"You made a list!" He sounded delighted. "Look at that—you've already made a list about me. I'm thrilled!"

"I am not attempting to thrill you. I do not care about you; you do not have to share your inner thoughts."

"Well, thrilling me is a perfectly lovely side effect of whatever it is you *are* attempting. Your list lacks accuracy on most major points, but I am honored by your consideration nonetheless."

She ignored this. "I would like to propose a secondary bargain with you. If you will refrain from…despoiling me, I will allow you to kiss me. You will not need to make any effort to secure this result." There. That would put her firmly in control. He could hardly say no.

But he did not say yes, not for a long time. She put a hand over her eyes, to prevent herself from peeking.

Finally, he sighed. "Chloe, sweetheart. Look at me."

She opened her fingers to peer out. For once, despite his words, he didn't look like he was mocking her. He had turned toward her on his rock, and…

Oh, no. She was still fooling herself. She was fooling herself dreadfully. Her hands fell to her sides. She should never have told him she wanted him to be serious, because the way he was looking at her... It felt as if she were the center of his universe. As if nothing and nobody else mattered to him. Her whole body seemed to reverberate with the echo of her heartbeat.

"Chloe," he said. Nothing more for a while.

She wanted to look away. She could not.

"Chloe," he said again. "It's your decision. But please. Please never kiss a man who doesn't think you deserve his effort."

She could hardly stand it—him looking at her and saying things like that when he'd been gone so long. "As you said," she snapped. "It's *my* decision. If *I* want to kiss someone as unworthy as you, it should be allowed."

"Of course." He frowned. "But I'm to be involved in this kissing as well, so I should get *some* say. And *I* think that it's the effort that makes a kiss worthwhile. If you want me for my extensive body of practical knowledge, you should accept my unrivaled expertise on this point. If I simply tow you into the hills and maul you in a transactional fashion, you'll be disappointed, and then *I'll* be disappointed. Neither of us wants to be disappointed, do we?"

"On the contrary. I should very much like to be disappointed. Why else would I choose you?" If he disappointed her, it would be for the best. She'd stew in that disappointment for a week or two, then get angry, and finally, *finally*, she'd forget about him.

He shook his head gravely. "I shall have to disappoint you with your lack of disappointment in me. But I think we have traveled far afield. You weren't bargaining about the kiss; you cared about what comes after. I offer this as compromise: I won't despoil you unless you make a numbered plan leading up to the event."

He actually looked serious when he said that. In point of fact, despite his many witticisms, he'd taken the entire conversation seriously. That felt dangerous too, in a different way.

But it was a good offer. He was saying that he wouldn't fog her reason up with want, the way he was so clearly able. As long as she could hold on to her logic and take her time to think things through, she could talk herself out of anything he talked her into. She'd wanted control; he'd offered it to her.

"So you'll…do it?" She couldn't quite bring herself to meet his gaze as she asked. But she could hear him, hear the delighted intake of his breath, hear the rustle of fabric as he leaned toward her rock.

"What, precisely, is the 'it' that you are referring to? Describe it with particularity so that we are sure to be talking of the same thing."

Damn him. He knew. He *knew* it embarrassed her to say it. "You'll…" Her voice dropped to almost nothing. "You'll kiss me?"

"There's a sixty percent chance I'll say yes."

Oh. Her heart plummeted. She had assumed, based on his teasing words and his seductive looks and the way he nudged her arm and…so many things…that he actually had a cursory interest in her. She had imagined that he wanted her, at least a little, that he'd thought about her when he wasn't here. Obviously, that had been too proud by half on her part. By sixty percent, perhaps.

"And there's a forty percent chance," he said, interrupting this depressing spiral of thought, "that I'll say yes, but loudly."

Chloe shut her eyes and let her forehead fall into the palms of her hands. Had she thought him serious? No. He was *such* a jackass. How had she forgotten that about him? She was going to get her first kiss from an absolute jackass, and she didn't even regret it. She took a deep breath in. Yes, he was who he was. Long exhalation out. But—and this was a very relevant *but*—she was ultimately in charge here. He had hired her. She was getting money. As a completely independent matter, she was also getting a kiss. And then he was leaving and she could forget him and concentrate on the things that mattered: proving her worth to her father and selling Unnamed Sauce to the entirety of the United Kingdom.

She was going to end the Wedgeford Trials this year with all of her dreams fulfilled. All she had to do was set up the terms and manage Jeremy.

She straightened her spine, smoothed back her hair, and picked up her board clip from where it sat next to her feet. "Right. Now that we have all that squared away, it's time to get to business."

"Already? I love how eager you are. But kissing right *here?* I know there's nobody in the immediate vicinity, but we're still visible to others. How very courageous you are."

"Our *other* business." Time to remember that he was marrying someone not herself. "I have come up with a framework for the inquiry into your requirements in a wife, so that we might manage this matter as efficiently as possible. We must make sure that what I have done is adequate for your needs."

"Oh. *That.*" He leaned back on his rock and waved an insouciant hand in the air. "I had quite forgot about that. Please. Proceed."

She dipped her hand in the little pocket at her waist and removed her spectacles, then placed them on her nose before putting her board clip on her knee. "The first step is to identify the key characteristics of a wife. By my count, those characteristics fall into one of four categories: physical properties, intellectual capabilities, emotional character, and ambitions for the future." There. She'd make it a rational exercise. She could do rational.

"You've left off wants," he said lazily. "Desires. Fantasies. We should definitely discuss those, particularly as they pertain to you."

Chloe found her cheeks heating. *Wants. Desires. Fantasies.* She'd already admitted that she wanted him to kiss her; did he honestly want her to tell him everything *else?* To talk about the things she thought about late at night?

She glared at him through her spectacles. "Discussing those would be redundant. The things you list are nothing more than ambitions for the future."

"You are referring to ordinary concerns for day-to-day existence—things like how one chooses to make a living?"

"Precisely."

He turned his head to look at her. "You tell me, Miss Fong. Are the fantasies that keep you up at night composed of nothing but dry ambitions for your future?"

How did he even *know* about her nighttime fantasies?

A flash of memory came to her—thoughts of the last year he'd been here and the way he'd twined their fingers in the dark. How many times had she imagined *not* putting a hand on his chest when he leaned in, *not* begging him to be serious? How many times had she envisioned him pushing into her space with his arrogant confidence, until his body was pressed against hers? Her entire being was singed with heat.

"My ambitions are lofty," she said with a frown. "They are not *dry.*"

"Hmm. *Not* dry. Do you, by any chance, at the moment, find yourself becoming the opposite of dry? Because that would be very interesting."

"*Stop*," she squawked, shutting her eyes. Her cheeks felt hot; how annoying that he had managed to break through her reserve despite her best efforts. "I take it all back. Let's just call them dry. Dry as dust. Dry as a desert."

"Parched," he said with a grin that she could feel clear to her toes, "and in need of a long, cool drink."

"Oh, stick your head in the river and swallow," she snapped.

He let out a delighted laugh. "Right. Put that on the list for me. I want a wife who says *exactly* that to me. With those exact words. If she doesn't say it at *least* once, I won't marry her."

God. She was going to lose her mind. She cleared her throat. "Please recall that efficiency is paramount. Moving along from this pointless diversion and back to the framework that I am proposing for our inquiry. For our second point of discussion, we should identify differences between me and your potential spouse."

He straightened and frowned at her. "No. That's not necessary."

She blinked. "Of *course* it's necessary. I can see that you might want someone who has my steadiness of mind, as you are so severely lacking on that front, but you don't actually want *me*. You want someone who brings her own financial…whatever…to the marriage. Property and family connections and that sort of thing. Which I lack."

"Not necessary," he repeated tersely. "I don't require a list of differences."

Well. He had said that he was going to give the list to his aunt. His aunt would likely trouble herself with the practical matters. It probably *wasn't* necessary.

She let out a sigh. "If you insist. It's less work for me this way, and as I have mentioned, I am excessively busy these next few days."

"Are you participating in the Trials this year?"

"My father and I will be selling buns. It will take all our time."

He turned, swiveling his entire torso toward her. "Will it? So you're not at all involved in…"

Frauds, he didn't say. Chloe was *not* involved this year. She was *not*. It had taken enormous effort to remain uninvolved, but she had done it.

"I'm busy," Chloe told him. "I'm horrifically busy. I haven't time for anything! Not even you! And have you learned nothing? You don't *talk* about that in public like this. You're lucky I'm not actually involved or I'd have to stuff you headfirst into a barrel."

His smile tilted. "I can't believe you'll talk about kissing aloud, but you won't mention…" He trailed off, twirling a finger, not mentioning the thing she wasn't mentioning.

The Trials were, on their face, quite simple. The village of Wedgeford was divided into three where the Wedge met the Wyton. If you lived in Wedgeford, your allegiance was set by the place where you lived. If you came to Wedgeford from outside for the Trials, you were assigned a team on your arrival.

The teams spent a week furtively hiding their tokens, followed by a day frantically searching for tokens from the other teams. Why this was called the Trials—why they even did it—nobody knew. But it had been happening in Wedgeford for as long as history in Wedgeford had been recorded.

"I won't say it then," Jeremy said. And he winked at her.

Jeremy had been assigned to be a Reeler—Chloe's team—when he first arrived. Chloe, at the age of fourteen, had been told to teach him the rules, to make sure he didn't cause any problems. It was how they had become acquainted.

Chloe did not say that participating in the Trials reminded her of him, that it had been easier to say no this year and thus avoid the memories that came with it.

"I'm busy," Chloe told him. "I'm far too busy. I have so much to do." She glared down at the board on her knee.

Jeremy licked his lips. "I can help."

"You will hinder."

"No, think it through. Do you need things carried to and fro? I can carry to. I can even carry fro."

"You?" She gave him a suspicious look. "Do manual labor? Do you even know how?"

He ignored this practical inquiry. "I can save you an hour, maybe three."

"If you spend all your time around me instead of just a handful of minutes while we hash out your list, everyone will talk." Everyone had already been talking about them before.

"I don't mind."

"They'll think I'm a fool." Chloe looked away.

"No. They'll think I'm a lucky man."

Her temper flared. "Oh yes. They'll think you have excellent luck indeed. They'll suspect you of lucking me all night long."

She'd just said it. Right out. The thing she shouldn't think about but did. She should be ashamed of imagining the heat of his skin, the exchange of their breath—

She set her jaw and glared at him, but she could feel her wants under her skin, and it *wasn't* his fault, no matter what she told herself.

"Chloe, my dear." His voice was gentle. She didn't *want* gentle. "I'll luck you anytime you wish. But I don't think anyone who has ever known you would imagine you to be so easily won. You're not easy. You never have been."

She exhaled. "No." A good reminder.

"You have *always* been worth the effort."

Her throat felt suddenly hoarse. This was unfair. It was one thing to feel a mere physical attraction. To have him talk outright about kissing and intercourse... That, she could slot in its proper box: lust. To be managed.

But this talk about her as a person? It made her feel.

She found herself yearning for things she could not have, not ever. Not with him. Because he didn't mean it. He was *him*. What did he know of value, throwing around tens of pounds as if they were nothing? If she was worth so much, why had he been gone for three years?

Enough of this indulgence. She took her pencil out from behind her ear and smoothed out the paper of her list. "Very well. Let's start with that then. You wanted a list of my characteristics so you can find a woman to marry." She must not let herself forget that. "You've now listed several. I am hard. I am prickly. I am intimidating." She glared at him. "That is what you want me to put down, yes? The qualities you want in a wife."

"Mmm. I must quibble. You're not *hard*. You're determined."

Chloe's pencil pressed painfully against her fingers where she gripped it. "I see little difference."

He ignored that. "And you're not prickly. You're *decided*. You're the last thing from hard and prickly; you're the most thoughtful person I know."

Her eyes stung for a moment. This wasn't how this was supposed to go. He wasn't supposed to take her worst qualities and turn them upside down in this way.

"You've said nothing about intimidating," she said. "I see you don't dispute that."

"Not in the slightest." He looked into her eyes. "I want my wife to intimidate me. I want to know that her enemies will all fall before her. *That's* the kind of woman I want by my side. She had *better* be intimidating."

He didn't look away, and electricity fluttered through her stomach. She had thought that his list would be disembodied characteristics, things that she could think about rationally. Things like "I prefer brunettes" or "spectacles are nice." He wasn't supposed to engage her heart like this.

"That's…" She swallowed. "That's…"

"Put that on the list," he told her.

She stared down at the blank page in front of her. It was waiting to be filled with the description of a woman who could not—absolutely *could* not—be her. For the first time, the white expanse of the empty page felt almost ominous.

"Very well." She nodded. "Let's get this over with."

Jeremy Yu, she wrote at the top, because he had never actually disclosed his real name. *List of spousal characteristics.*

Dry. All she had to do was make this dry enough and it wouldn't bother her in the slightest.

"One," she intoned as she scribed the first item onto the page. "Intimidating."

5

CHLOE HAD OFTEN PLANNED THEORETICALLY PERFECT days. As long as every task took its expected time, down to the minute, she could manage everything. In practice, this had never actually worked, for the primary reason that Chloe was not perfect, and for the secondary reason that she wished she were. She wished it so hard that she made all her lists as if perfection were a given.

Today of all days, when she needed to focus, she was distracted. She sat at a counter in the inn's kitchens, poking at a dish in front of her and trying not to let her distraction show. After all, if anyone was going to notice something was wrong, it was Naomi Kwan.

"You don't like it," Naomi said.

Wedgeford had once been on a minor stage route, and the kitchens—built to feed a horde of guests starving after hours of rattling around the roads—were so spacious that their capacity was only taxed these days during the Trials. Today she and Naomi were alone in that wide space.

Chloe looked at the dish before her—rice and a cutlet

of pork, over which a brown sauce had been ladled, served in a simple earthenware bowl.

She had put pieces of the pork in her mouth. She had scarcely tasted a thing, chewing and swallowing with her mind elsewhere.

Chloe shook her head. "No. It's not that." She took another piece and made herself concentrate as she chewed this time. Naomi had used Unnamed Sauce; she detected those rich, contradictory notes of vinegar and sweet and savory almost instantly. New peas, freshly shelled and cooked until just done through, added a hint of crunch. She shut her eyes.

"It's excellent." She nodded. "This is going to be an outright clinker of a dish."

Naomi just looked at her. "Chloe. It is *already* a clinker. I have had guests smell the sauce cooking from the back and demand it for *breakfast*. I used my last jar of your Unnamed Sauce to make this. I was supposed to have jars that I could sell at a profit. I was supposed to have little cards that would say where more could be purchased. I was supposed to have all of those a week ago."

Chloe grimaced. "Yes. Of course. This is…true."

"Where are my jars? Where are my cards? You promised me fifty percent of the profits on any sales I made. I could have sold *two dozen* jars by now."

"Yes. Well. Of course. The jars need labeling, and the cards need a name on them, and we can't do any of that until Andrew carves a nameplate in reverse for stamping…"

"Don't you blame this on my cousin."

"Which," Chloe added hastily, with a stretched, false

smile, "he cannot do until we have a name! And we do not."

"Who is we?" Naomi rolled her eyes. "You mean *you*. The Trials are two days from now, you utter clown. Name your sauce."

"I know, I know! It's been on my list for nine months. I have generated a huge number of not perfect names."

"Good." Naomi scowled at her. "Pick one of those."

"But—"

"I don't want to hear your excuses. I have as much to do as you and stand to gain less from this endeavor. I am *happy* to make a profit with a little work. I like money. But I cannot work and have you just…collapse like a bad soufflé. You need to name your damned sauce. And I want my jars tomorrow afternoon, no later. The real rush starts then when the visitors will start arriving en masse."

But I can't. It has to be perfect.

No good. Chloe had reached the end of all her possible excuses. There really was not a moment longer to put this off. She was going to have to settle for imperfect.

Chloe shuddered. "Argh."

Naomi flicked her forehead. "I love you, but you must get on with it. You're as bad as your father. How many jars are you bringing me on the morrow?"

Chloe sighed. "More than zero?"

"Chloe."

Chloe sighed again. "One hundred."

"It won't be enough." Naomi tossed her head. "I can guarantee already that it won't be enough. I'll take three hundred if you can give them to me."

"I could not! I've only got four hundred filled as it is."

Naomi just shrugged. "You purchased a thousand empties, and I know you've enough sauce in kegs out in your barn to fill quite a few more."

"But—" *But I can't,* she did not say. She didn't have *time* to fill any more jars.

If she was to succeed with this endeavor as she hoped, she also did not have time *not* to sell every jar that she possibly could. The more people who purchased their sauce, the more who would tell friends and family, the more who would write in inquiry, and the faster her father's sauce empire would grow. She couldn't possibly *not*. It was just a matter of how to fit such a task onto her ungainly list, now bulging out at the sides.

She and Naomi had planned this out nine months ago. Chloe and her father would have their booth on the green that used their sauce; Naomi would offer heartier fare in the inn that did the same. For her trouble, Naomi would split the profits on any jars she sold.

"What are you calling the dish for now?" Chloe asked.

Chloe had dithered too long and had finally printed labels and little cards with advertisements, but had left a blank space at the top of both. And now here she was, two days before the Trials would start, and she had *choose a name that Andrew can carve in reverse on a wood block, then stamp hundreds of pieces of paper with that name* still on her list.

Naomi just shrugged. "I thought 'pork in brown sauce.'"

"Brown sauce." Chloe could have torn her hair out. "Just…brown! How dare you! This is nothing so generic as brown sauce!" She frowned. "Also, it's more...reddish brown, don't you think?"

"This is why you don't have a name yet. Everything you think of is always wrong. Of course Unnamed Sauce is nothing like brown sauce. But brown sauce is familiar and people like things that are familiar. Think of White and Whistler's Pure English Sauce, for instance."

"I have thought of this so many times my head is aching. I am sick to death of thinking of White and Whistler."

Naomi didn't let that stop her. "Did they say 'sauce made by a Chinese man with Chinese ingredients according to a Chinese recipe?' No. Because that scares people."

"Technically true." Chloe sniffed. "I have said the same myself. But it is also extremely unhelpful in the moment."

"'Pure English Sauce' sounds comforting. It sounds homey. It sounds not frightening at all. Then once people have committed to trying it, you reach in and grab them with the deliciousness. Hence: brown sauce."

It was true. Chloe *knew* it was true. "Yes... But... The sauce isn't entirely brown. And the appellation is so...nondescript."

Naomi just shrugged. "Then come up with something better."

Chloe gave up. "I can't. I just keep going over the same names in my head. 'Very English Sauce.' 'Extremely English Sauce.' 'Nothing but British Sauce.' They're all wrong, and I don't know how to fix them."

"You're trying to imitate White and Whistler too

much, is all." Naomi shrugged. "And they're lying thieves, so stop doing that."

"I have two days! I have ten million pieces of paper that all need to be stamped with a name I don't have! It's not working."

Naomi raised an eyebrow. "What you need is someone to sit on you until you come up with something halfway acceptable, and then beat you until you accept it. It doesn't have to be perfect. You don't have to be perfect."

Chloe made a scalded noise. She wished her friend were…less right. But it was true; every time she sat down by herself and made lists of names, she crossed every single one off. Not a one was perfect, and she and her father had worked too long on this sauce to not have the name be perfect in every regard.

"I would do it, but…" Naomi trailed off and then looked at her. When their eyes met, the corners of her mouth turned up. "But," she continued, with a hint of glee in her voice, "you would owe me."

Oh, *no*. "I *already* owe you."

"I haven't time for this any more than you do," Naomi said. "But if you do one…no, two…little things for me, I may be able to find a little extra time to sit down with you at eight this evening to do the aforementioned sitting. And beating."

"What two things?" She was going to have to rearrange her list.

"I want two hundred jars," Naomi said, "not just one."

"Ugh." That would mean an extra hundred jars she would have to fill. Chloe had no idea how to make that happen; never mind, she'd work it out later. "Fine. And?"

Why she bothered asking, she didn't know. She knew *exactly* what Naomi was going to ask her.

Naomi smiled broadly, teeth showing. "And I want you to hide a Widgelot."

Of course. The Trials were all about hiding and finding tokens. It would have been nice if those tokens were little brass coins or a carved wooden statuette that would fit in one hand. Instead, every team had what was called a Wedgelot—a round object of unknown provenance, now almost a foot wide and extremely heavy. They were painted every year with new designs that symbolized what had happened during the year prior. Each year's cover of paint went over the last year's designs, which resulted in the Wedgelots swelling under those annual coats of paint like a tree growing rings with every season.

Each team hid their Wedgelot on the outskirts of town before the start of the Trials, and the first team to bring two Wedgelots (any two Wedgelots) onto their designated territory near the center won. In the week when the Wedgelots were being hidden, anyone who might hide such a thing was watched with the greatest of suspicion. It wasn't easy to secrete what was essentially a foot-wide rock on one's person, and so where pure hiding would not do, misdirection took place. Every team engaged in Frauds—the hiding of fake tokens.

Someone had called them Widgelots—so very like a Wedgelot, and yet not one.

Chloe had done so well at not being involved in the Trials this year. She sighed and gave in to the inevitable. "Very well," she said. "Where?"

"Anywhere to the southwest."

"The blackthorn bramble on the south side?" That, at least, was close enough to town that she wouldn't have to alter her schedule too much.

Naomi waved a hand, gracious in her victory. "That should do. I'll see you at eight then."

Chloe nodded and started to stand.

But Naomi just gave her another amused look. "Speaking of Nothing but British... Andrew says that Posh Jim is here."

Chloe sank back into her seat. She knew the expression her face must be making. Of course Naomi knew; she helped her mother and her aunt run the inn. The present reason for Chloe's distraction popped into her mind. His face. His *smile*. The things they had talked about. What an absolute mess this all was.

"Oh." Her voice sounded strained. "Is he?"

Naomi gave her an unamused look. "Andrew said that *he* said he was going to bask in your magnificence or some such excessive nonsense."

Damn it. "Andrew talks too much." She frowned. "So does Jeremy."

"The fact that you are lying about it worries me. Chloe, you know what wealthy, privileged men are like."

Chloe didn't, actually. The only wealthy man she had ever truly known was Jeremy. But she knew of White and Whistler through her father's stories, and yes, she *did* know what wealthy men were like.

"He may be wealthy," she said, "but he's half-Chinese."

Naomi just wrinkled her nose. She didn't say anything. She didn't have to. Chloe could feel her judgment, and oh, she had already earned it. In the space of one morning, she had agreed to not only make a list of the qualities that Jeremy wanted in a wife—and she did *not* want to think how that made her feel—but she'd wrangled an agreement to kiss him.

She tried to imagine telling Naomi that. *You see,* she might say, *as long as the intimacy is couched in transactions, my heart will surely not be at risk, and I will be able to protect myself from further harm.*

It was such patently foolish nonsense that she didn't have the temerity to say it aloud. She would be roundly abused for it, and rightly so.

Instead, she waved a hand. "Oh, very well. I don't need to know what wealthy men are like in general. I know what *he's* like."

He was brilliant like the sun. He made her laugh. He smiled at her. When he was in her company, he made her feel like she was the only woman on the planet.

And he left. Every year that she'd seen him, he'd said goodbye and he'd left.

"So if you *do* take him to bed, tell me everything."

Chloe blushed. "I'm—I'm not—what do you take me for?"

Naomi touched her hand. "I take you for my dearest friend. You've worked yourself to the bone for years in preparation for the launch of Unnamed Sauce. You and your father are about to succeed as long as you don't trip over your own skirts at the last possible moment."

It had been easy to say similar things to her father in the privacy of their own home. But then she had been praising *him*. It sounded rash and arrogant to agree to such a thing about *herself* no matter what Chloe believed.

"*Maybe* I am possibly going to achieve some small success."

"*Definitely* you are about to succeed. It only remains to be seen how much. I take you for someone who will realize her dreams are coming true. Who might end up celebrating and perhaps doing things during that celebration that she might think better of at a later time. And if you do, I don't want you to feel you need to hide it from me. *I'm* curious as well."

Chloe couldn't even imagine what she would say or how she would say it. Where she could start. *Naomi, I have already agreed to kiss him.* If she said that out loud, she would get talked out of it. She would talk *herself* out of it because it was foolish.

Chloe swallowed. "You're making too much of it. He's already agreed not to seduce me." There. That sounded rational and proper.

Naomi looked at her. "You've already talked about it?"

"Um."

"And did he actually agree not to seduce you, or did he put a condition on it?"

"Um."

"I'm right, aren't I?" Naomi sighed.

Chloe gave up. "How did you *know?*"

"I've known you both for years," Naomi said. "And look—I will mock you all I want about the fact that you have no name for your sauce, you ridiculous creature. But I just want you to know… I love you. And you don't have to hide."

People had talked the last time Jeremy had been in the village. They hadn't imagined he had *done* anything to her

—they had just talked. And they had teased. Mostly they had felt pity for her when he didn't come, again and again.

After that, it was almost overwhelming to know that Naomi would still love her and treat her the same, no matter what happened in the future.

Chloe put her face in her hands. "Naomi," she whispered. "You don't know what he has asked me to do."

"Has he already propositioned you? He works fast. He just arrived late last night!"

"He asked me to make a list for him." She swallowed and then went forward. "Of the qualities he wants in a wife. So he can give that list to his aunt and she can identify suitable candidates."

Naomi stared at her for a long moment. "I might feed him sometime this week. Shall I poison him for you?" She was joking. At least, Chloe thought she was.

"Probably not," Chloe finally said. "Please. Remember what you said about wealthy, privileged men. If he dies, there will be an inquest, and they'll discover it."

Naomi sighed. "Very well. We'll see to him later."

In the forty-five minutes that Jeremy spent in the common area of the inn waiting for Chloe to come out from the kitchens, he had been surrounded. At first, it had only been Andrew again, come to bring in a load of coal. Then the Master of the Reelers had arrived with a boy in tow.

The Reelers were one of three teams that Wedgeford split into for the Trials. Once the outside world had heard of the Trials—and had started to attend—each team had appointed a Master, whose job it was to assign outsiders to roles.

The alternative was that the game (and by extension, the village) would be overrun by those who hadn't an inkling how the Trials were supposed to go. For as long as Jeremy had been coming to Wedgeford, the Reelers' Master was the elder Mr. Bei. He entered the inn and looked around before his eyes landed on Jeremy. He gave a nod and started forward.

"Posh Jim! The exact person I was looking for. This is Mr. Alan Wilderhampsher." He gestured to the boy at his side.

Alan Wilderhampsher appeared a bit older than Jeremy had been when he'd first come to Wedgeford—maybe thirteen or fourteen. He was looking around the inn with wide eyes.

"Mr. Wilderhampsher." Jeremy's nose wrinkled. "That's a bit of a mouthful."

"Ha ha." The boy rolled his eyes. "You're the first person who has ever said that in the known history of Britain. How clever you must think yourself."

"I'll leave him to you!" Mr. Bei said, retreating with a haste that suggested the boy had been making similarly pleasant witticisms throughout their acquaintance.

Mr. Wilderhampsher frowned sulkily.

Jeremy just shook his head. "Eton, eh?"

"How did—" A frustrated look came over his face. "Stupid accent. How am I ever supposed to—"

"You can't." Jeremy shrugged. "It's part of where you came from, and there's no use trying to pretend otherwise.

I see why they've put me in charge of you. Your first time coming to the Trials, then?"

"Yes, but I don't want *you* to be in charge of me." He frowned. "*You're* not from around here. You don't know anything about *anything.*" He pointed at Andrew, who was laboring at the back of the inn. "I want *him.*"

"Too bad. It's your first year here. You don't get what you want."

"But—"

"Yes, I know," Jeremy said soothingly, because he knew what spoiled Eton boys were like all too well. "You're a very important person. You're used to people doing your bidding. You've read the newspaper accounts of the Trials and you thought how dashing it would be to be the one who discovers a Wedgelot and brings it back through enemy territory, winning the victory and getting your name in the permanent annals. Except that's not how it works. This is not a free-for-all. There are rules, and if you don't know how any of this works and you just run around and do anything you like, you'll be placed in Purgatory and not allowed to play at all."

"But—"

"The Master of the Reelers gave you to me to show you the ropes, and so that is what we are going to do with you. When I have a chance. And if you're very good and you follow directions now, next year they'll know you're trustworthy, and you'll get a larger role."

The boy sent a longing glance at Andrew. He had probably heard that the key to being involved in the thick of the fun was to get yourself assigned to one of the townspeople, and he wasn't wrong. After all, when Jeremy had first arrived, he'd been assigned to Chloe, and after she had put him through his paces, he'd finally won an official Trials nickname and a permanent place on the Reelers team.

"But..." He looked up. "I don't *want* to work with you. I want to work with *him* over there. You look boring."

Jeremy put a hand over his mouth to hide a grin. Of all the things to be told.

"Oh yes," he said. "I am a great bore. I drone on and on, just like an Oxford lecturer." Except for that bit about not having graduated with honors. "Like an Oxford lecturer," he amended with a frown, "except with fewer credentials."

"Oh, so like a vicar?"

Jeremy choked on the laugh that rose at this. "That's not very kind to vicars, who generally have a rough time of it. And who are far better credentialed than I am. You are entirely correct; Mr. Swan is far more amusing."

"Mr. Swan?" Mr. Wilderhampsher's nose wrinkled. "That's...that's not his name. Is it?"

Andy, on the other side of the inn, had perked up at this conversation. He now came over.

"It's my Trials nickname. I'm Andrew Uchida, but for the Trials, I'm called Mr. Swan for reasons that don't need to be discussed. This is Jeremy Yu; he's Posh Jim."

The boy frowned. "Well, if we're going to have nicknames... I'll be Strong Al."

"Ah, ah." Andy wagged a finger. "You won't be anything until we give you a nickname. You should listen to Jim here."

"Oh." Mr. Wilderhampsher blushed and looked up at Andy with something that looked like hero worship. "Yes. You—look, can I be transferred to you? Please? I rate better than a buffoon, I should think."

"Do you?" Andy grinned.

"I don't know *nothing* about the Trials," Mr. Wilderhampsher said. "I know *everything*. I tracked down accounts from twelve years past. Three years ago, you found the Wedgelot in the Minders territory and swam across a raging river to bring home victory."

Andrew just laughed and reached out and ruffled the boy's hair. "Oh, you really have studied, haven't you?"

"I have! And I want to work with you. Not..." He glanced at Jeremy and his lip curled. "Not this uncredentialed Oxford lecturer."

Jeremy laughed.

"Here is a thing the papers will never tell you." Andrew gestured Mr. Wilderhampsher in closer, and then whispered, loud enough for Jeremy to hear. "This uncredentialed Oxford lecturer is a particular friend of mine and the only reason I didn't drown in the river."

Mr. Wilderhampsher's smile died. "Oh."

"He is prone to exaggeration, but unfortunately, when it comes to himself, he often uses it to negative effect, downplaying who he is and what he does. We call him 'Posh Jim' for a reason. But he's a good egg and he's got a Trials nickname for a reason."

"You hear that?" Jeremy folded his arms and nodded. "*I've* got a Trials nickname. Pretty good for the likes of *me*, boring as I am."

"Ugh." Mr. Wilderhampsher sighed again and looked

up. "Right, then. I suppose I can tolerate you for a few hours."

"Let Posh Jim show you the ropes, and I'll bring you in on something fun during the Trials. He won't be participating as such; he'll be too busy."

"Busy doing what?" Mr. Wilderhampsher turned wide eyes to Jeremy, as if reevaluating. "Something important?"

"Busy mooning," Andrew said, nudging Jeremy with an elbow.

"Don't tease." Jeremy adjusted his cuffs with an amused air. "This is very important mooning. I've been planning it since—" He stopped.

Chloe had returned to the common room; he hadn't noticed when she did. And not only had she returned, there were two men around her. Jeremy thought at least one looked vaguely familiar—Barry Dalton, but with a mustache? But the names didn't matter, because it was obvious what they were doing. One of them had Chloe's board clip, which he was holding over his head.

She was holding a massive basket—one she could scarcely lift more than a foot off the ground. She wasn't supposed to be taking a basket from the inn; he'd seen her entire list. If she was holding a basket that size, it meant that Naomi had talked her into doing Frauds. Ha. And she called herself intimidating.

Jeremy couldn't make out what the man was saying, but his body language—that taunting smile, the way the other man with him was laughing into a hand—made the situation all too clear. Chloe was short and weighed down by an extremely heavy object. And they'd taken her list.

He straightened. "Speaking of mooning. I've some business to attend to." He crossed the room in a flash.

"Now, now," Barry Dalton was saying, "Miss Lists, don't be so huffy. Just one afternoon on the verge of the Trials. There's no need to be so cold and calculating. Just allow yourself one afternoon to take a moment to rest with old friends. I'm back from London for only three days. Set aside the tasks and sit a spell."

Her nose wrinkled. "Give me back my list."

"You're no fun. Don't you want to be fun?"

A muscle twitched in her jaw and she looked away. "My list is fun," Chloe said. "My list is very fun. Now give it back." Her hair had stayed in her perfect bun, pinned into place. The golden tassels of her earrings swung as she reached above her abortively.

Barry's friend burst into laughter. "Her list is fun, she says." He looked around the room as if for support, and his eyes landed on Jeremy. "Posh Jim! You're back. Tell Miss Lists here to stop being so stuffy."

"But of course." Jeremy smiled as he walked up to Barry. Barry was a little taller than him, but the disparity was not so great as with Chloe. He reached up and plucked the board clip from that man's hands.

For a moment, Chloe's eyes met his. There was a second—just one second—where her nose flared and her shoulders fell in what looked like resignation, as if she actually *expected* him to keep on teasing her. And, well. That was fair. He loved teasing her.

Just not like this.

"Miss Lists." He bowed and handed her the board clip

and the lists that had given her that Trials nickname. "Fun lists for a fun lady."

She let out a long breath. That look of resignation vanished for one second, only to be replaced by another, more wistful look of somewhat deeper resignation.

"Aw, you're no fun either," said the man Jeremy didn't know.

"Haven't you heard the rule?" Jeremy said in response.

"The rule? What rule?"

"Nobody takes Miss Fong's lists," Jeremy said. "Not ever. That's the rule."

Barry frowned suspiciously. "Since when has this been a rule?"

"Since September the first, in the year of our Lord eighteen hundred and sixty-five."

Chloe blinked. She probably hadn't realize that he remembered her birthday.

"Jeremy Yu," Barry Dalton said, staring at him. "You gigantic hypocrite. You tease her all the time."

Chloe clutched the lists to her chest and looked up angrily. "He does, but it's different because I like it," she shot back.

Jeremy had just one instant to look at her in delighted surprise, before she realized what she'd said and blushed furiously. If they'd been alone, he would have teased her then, and without mercy. But as it was, they had an enemy to defeat.

"I know," Jeremy said, reaching out and clapping a hand against Barry's shoulder. "It is very sad. Chloe has a lot to do right around now; she doesn't have time to put up with your inferior sort of teasing. I would consult with her on a good time to bother her so she can put it on her list."

"But doesn't that defeat the purpose?"

"What's the purpose?"

"Is it even teasing if she allows it?"

"I don't know," Jeremy said with a smile. "Tell me, Chloe. Am *I* on your list?"

She swallowed. Her cheeks were still red. "Yes. You are on my list. I am to spend the next hour and a half with you."

"Have I ever *not* teased you?"

She looked thoughtful, as if she were actually going to consider the question.

"You see?" Jeremy interjected before she could answer. "You're too late, gentlemen. You have to be swift if you're going to get time to tease Chloe here; she is much in demand. Goodbye; we shall see you when the list permits." He looked beyond them to where Mr. Wilderhampsher was watching. "Later today," he called. "Around three—meet me here."

"Wait," said Mr. Wilderhampsher. "I want to know—"

"This seems backward," Barry was saying. "Entirely backward. If she consents to being teased, can it actually be any fun?"

Jeremy took the basket from Chloe. "Farewell!" He waved cheerily and then conducted her out of the inn. As they left, she cast a look at him, one of narrow-eyed suspicion. Then she shook her head and settled her bonnet atop her head, tying it in place. It was almost noon now; the village green looked so very verdant in the bright sunshine, dotted with pale pink and bright yellow cowslips here and there.

The basket was heavy; he hefted it up to get both hands on it.

She just frowned at him. "Where are you dragging me off to?"

"You'll have to tell me. What does the list say?"

"And what nonsense were you spouting in there?" Chloe demanded, turning to him. "You know very well that you stole my list on one memorable occasion. Barry was right. You're the worst sort of hypocrite."

He *had* stolen her list, which was why he'd intervened so quickly this time. In his defense, he'd been fourteen—an age that had described the number of brain cells he had as well as the number of years he'd spent on the earth. Stealing her list had seemed like a brilliant idea.

It was not. She had cried. He had never seen her cry before, not even when she'd broken her arm the year prior. She'd been angry about crying too—swiping at her cheeks in a fury—and that was the point when he realized that Chloe liked her lists, and he liked Chloe. Stealing a list to make her pay attention to him was counterproductive. If he made her believe he didn't like her lists, she'd think he didn't like *her*, because one didn't come without the other.

"That was a mistake," he said. "I never make the same mistake twice."

She gave him a dubious look.

"Let me rephrase. I only make the same mistake twice if I intend to do so. I didn't *intend* to make you cry. I felt terrible about that."

"I'm sure you did." She rolled her eyes.

"You must give me credit. Look at how much more effective I am at gaining your attention as an adult." He gave her a sly look. "And you like it. You said so yourself. Never tell me you're taking that back."

That furious blush returned. "Well, so?" She shrugged as if she could give the lie to the brilliant red spreading across her cheeks. "You're very personable, and I do like to laugh. Especially at you."

"You see." Jeremy waggled an eyebrow. "I *am* good for something."

She sighed. "If you were more like Barry Dalton, I wouldn't have this problem. Why am I even talking to you about this?"

"I'm easy to talk to. And we're old friends even if you are...rather rightfully...angry at me at the moment. Besides, you know I'll never be anything like Barry Dalton. I work hard on that last point."

"Shocking." She glanced at her board clip. "I had no idea you had any kind of self-discipline."

"That's because I have absolutely none. If I'm going to tease you, it will be by telling you that you are wonderful and lovely and perfect because it makes you blush— exactly like that. And, as you said. You like it." He grinned. "You admitted it. You like it."

Her nose, a delightful pink, scrunched. "Agh. Jeremy. Stop reminding me!"

"If I tease you, it won't be by telling you lies, like saying you're boring and cold. That would make you feel bad, and where's the fun in that?"

"What did you think—?" Chloe cut herself off,

shaking her head. "Ha. Never mind. Why are you here in Wedgeford anyway?"

"I told you. I want you to make me a list."

"Rubbish. You may be disorganized, but you're capable of scrawling out a set of adjectives without my assistance. Why are you *really* here?"

For a moment, Jeremy thought about just saying it outright. *I want to marry you.* Therein lay the problem. Saying "I want to marry you" would necessitate other statements, like "by the way, I own your house and my solicitor would like you to know you've never paid rents." She was already ready to stuff him headfirst in a barrel of sauce.

Instead, he winked at her. "What do you think? You made a request of me earlier this morning when we spoke. I'm eager to get started."

Her eyes met his. For a second, he was transported back to the moment on the rocks when she'd admitted that she read...something (novels, he suspected; not, alas, pornography) and wanted him to kiss her. If he had thought of swooning on command at that point, he would have done it, just for dramatic effect. Alas that he'd only thought of it now.

"Ugh. That." Her tone suggested that the kiss was nothing; only the little blush that spread over her face made him think that she remembered this morning's conversation with anything other than annoyance. "In any event, I...may just have agreed to...do more work?" She didn't look at him. "A great deal more? So before we do anything at all, I must rearrange my list."

6

CHLOE HAD EXPECTED JEREMY TO COMPLAIN WHEN she plonked herself on a bench halfway between her home and the village green and set her list on her lap, ignoring him completely. She had taken off her gloves to write, and put on her spectacles to see the page. She chewed the end of her pencil, frowning. It was almost noon; how was it almost noon, and she'd only crossed off a tenth of her tasks?

The sun was hot overhead, and her bonnet scarcely covered the back of her neck. Somehow she needed to fit more tasks in this day.

"Can I be of assistance?" Jeremy asked after about five minutes.

"No." The answer was reflexive. She sighed, remembering the conversation with her father, and gave in. "Maybe. I have a minor problem. Two of them, in fact."

"Go ahead. I'm listening."

Chloe glanced at Jeremy. His outline was made fuzzy by her spectacles, and just as well, because she didn't need to actually be distracted by him at the moment. She was going to have to admit the dire place in which she'd found herself. "You see, after more than a decade of work, we aim to introduce my father's sauce as a commercial product at the Trials this year."

Jeremy nodded. "Yes. You mentioned it as a possibility when we talked about this three years ago. Clever strategy."

"*Obvious* strategy." She waved off the compliment and refused to examine what it meant that he remembered such a detail. "There is one last minor hurdle that must be cleared before we can offer the sauce for sale."

He was watching her from six inches away on the bench. Close. Too close. She looked ahead of her, staring resolutely at the stone wall on the other side of the road. She could almost hear Naomi's invective: *You utter clown.*

"A minor issue," he prompted. "Go ahead."

"We have not yet named the sauce."

Out of the corner of her eye, she could see his lips twitching in amusement. But he somehow did not take the obvious route of teasing her for the foolishness of labeling the issue minor.

"And," she said, "this *morning,* I was supposed to decide on a name while I was walking to the green. I was going to give the name to Andrew, and he was going to carve a stamp so I could finish the labels for the sauce and the little cards explaining where to obtain more..." She trailed off. "Which I was supposed to do this afternoon. But I didn't have a name and so I won't have a stamp and—"

"I see," Jeremy said. "I distracted you, so it's my fault."

Chloe wished she could agree. But she'd talked to her father, seen the butcher, spoken with Naomi about the sauce... If she'd *also* spent time with him on the green in lieu of naming Unnamed Sauce, it had been because she had procrastinated the naming for so long that the very prospect of proceeding filled her with terror.

She let out a sigh. "Not everything is your fault. I've been supposed to think of a name for the past nine months."

He looked over at her. There was nothing particularly moralizing in his expression, but she still felt a wash of shame come over her.

She hid her face in her palms. "I *know,*" she moaned. "You don't have to tell me. I *know.* It's the most important thing, and I haven't done it precisely because it's so important."

It made no sense, yet still he nodded as if she had said something logical.

"What?" she ventured. "No comment on how my lists have failed me?"

"We've already established that your lists don't fail you."

"You're right." Chloe sighed. "*I* failed my lists." Then she flushed; she couldn't believe she was whining to him.

But he just smiled at her. "Ah, Chloe." He said nothing more.

"What?" she snapped.

"I'm thinking. It feels wrong to disagree even though I'd castigate anyone who spoke about you that way. *I* don't want to fail you."

She stared at him in befuddlement. She didn't think he

was teasing, so why did it feel that way? That same sense of expectation, that same rush of heat…

"You can't fail me," she finally said. "You have no duty to me. You're here for a list, and once you have it, you're going to leave." There. She'd said it. Her voice hadn't trembled; she had stated facts rationally.

"Am I?" He reached over and took the pencil from her, rubbing his fingers over the end where she'd worried little toothmarks into the wood. "You're a little more observant than that, Chloe. Do a little better."

"You've always left."

He handed her the pencil again. "How curious. I feel as if I've always been here. I'm trying not to fail you right now. You have things to do. What's left on your list?"

Her list. Too many items. Too little time. She shook her head.

"Breathe, Chloe. What *most* needs to be done? Start with that."

She let out a long exhale. "Naomi browbeat me just now about the naming of the sauce." And for good reason. "I'm meeting her and Andy this evening at the inn, and she's sitting on me until I pick a name. She'll hold me to it even if what I end up with is terrible. Nothing happens without a name."

"Good," he said. "Next on the list."

"Unfortunately…" She sighed. "In return, I've promised to give her two hundred jars of Unnamed Sauce instead of just one, and to…do another thing." She didn't meet his gaze. "That thing I said I wasn't doing? I'm doing it now. I don't have an extra hundred jars to give her, so somehow those must be filled."

Jeremy nodded as if this were nothing. "Right. How long does it take to fill jars?"

"*I* can fill jars at the rate of thirty an hour. So it will take me approximately three hours and then some, if I can work without stopping, which I can't. I'll just have to sleep less tonight."

"Or I can assist you, and then we will each only miss an hour or so." His face crinkled, and he gave her a mischievous smile. "Perfect. I've always wanted to spend the night with you."

She exhaled, looking away from his beaming face. But it had already burned into her, that knowing grin. And now she was thinking of how he *might* spend the night, filling something other than jars. He hadn't been this overtly wicked last time he had been here. He'd flirted, yes —he flirted without ceasing—but he'd never come out and said such things. Something in her chest coiled, something that was half longing, half fury. He was going to leave.

"*You,*" she said, pointing a finger at him, "would fill jars at the rate of five an hour. You'd scarcely make a difference."

He put a hand on his chest. "Are you accusing me of incompetent filling?"

"You have no experience." She glanced at him. "Posh Jim, have you ever done any sort of manual labor in your life?"

"Um. I care for my own horse? My uncle insisted. He said it builds character."

Chloe sighed.

"And it worked! Look at me. Do I not have excellent

character? I think you underestimate me. I could manage at least *six* jars an hour."

Chloe shut her eyes. "I hate to ask my father." He would do it, of course, without hesitation. That was precisely the problem.

"Would he balk?" Jeremy asked.

"Of course he would not. But... It's his hands." She said it so casually when it had been the source of so much consternation on her part. "He has wet wind inflamed joint disease; dampness collects in his hands. They get stiff and cramped, and when that gets bad, it stops just being his hands. Then it's headaches and flashing lights. It's probably worse even than that, but he won't admit how bad it is because he doesn't want me to worry. Sometimes it happens with no reason, but if he works too hard, it can be particularly bad."

Even the word *cramp* could hardly describe the pain he went through. The way his hands constricted, the muscles stiffening of their own accord. The last time he'd helped her fill jars, he'd barely been able to hold so much as a pen for days.

"He's seen the acupuncturist in London. The treatments have helped, and there's an herbal formula he takes that helps clear blood stagnation and strengthen his kidneys to manage the worst of it. But she said that his condition was not curable. Just manageable."

Here she was, spilling out all her fears. She cut herself off. None of this was Jeremy's problem, and she hated seeing him look at her with that heightened scrutiny.

"So." He spoke after a long while. "Miss Kwan asked you to provide a hundred extra jars, and you agreed. She's tasked you with hiding a Widgelot, which of course you will also do. You're still not done with your own preparations—you've jars to label and suchlike, and tomorrow I imagine will be entirely taken up with preparing to feed the throngs the day after. On top of all that, you've agreed to help me construct a list of qualities I want in a wife. Miss Fong, do you do *everything* that people ask of you?"

"Not everything. Not even fifty percent."

"Fifty percent is a lot of percent." He looked at her. "You forgot to add one thing to your voluminous list. We'll be kissing often over the next few days. We shall have to be efficient about that."

Her lungs felt like fire. How could he say it so matter-of-factly? *We'll be kissing often.* That verb tense. It implied ongoing activity. Kissing often…over the next few days? How long did he think it would take to kiss her? She was afraid to ask even more afraid of the answer, and most afraid of her own response.

"We should put this on the list I am constructing for you," she said, trying to match his matter-of-fact tone. "You don't want a wife who overdoes things. She'll get in over her head and start panicking just because she can't say no."

Jeremy gave her a little smile, before he reached out and took the hand that was unencumbered by her board clip. He turned it over, gently swiveling her wrist so that her palm faced up. He took off his glove, and she could feel the heat of his fingertips against her own, gently rubbing. Could feel her own breaths coming shorter and shorter.

"You heard Mr. Dalton," she said, because it was easier

to pretend he was not touching her in any way, and she didn't want to pull away. "I'm cold. I'm no fun. I have things to do all the time."

His thumb ran down her palm, and she let out an exhale.

"That's silly." He smiled. "You're the furthest thing from cold. You're very interesting. You're fun. You have things to do, and that makes you more fun."

He leaned down and placed a kiss in the palm of her hand. She sat frozen in place, her fingers curling, heat rising in her belly, unsure what to do.

"What are you doing?" The words came out trembling.

"I'm being efficient," he replied. "You're remaking your list, so I'm getting on with the kissing part while you do that."

"But I—that's—I thought—"

"You thought I was going to kiss you on the lips? Well, of course." He brushed his mouth against her thumb. His breath was warm. He moved on to her index finger. She should pull away. How could this be happening?

"What are you *doing?*"

"Oh?" He looked up at her, a half smile on his face. "Can you not tell? I suppose the sensation must be too subtle, then. Thank you for letting me know." He sucked the tip of her pinky finger into his mouth. She felt one second of wet heat. The sensation seemed to travel up her arm, making her yearn for his mouth there, following that electricity up, up—

It was too much. She yanked her hand from him. "That will be sufficient for now."

"Of course." He smiled at her. "Later."

"We're in public." True, nobody was about—not that she could see. Nonetheless. "And I had not anticipated *that* as part of kissing. That *hand* thing. It's unnecessary."

"All the more reason for me to offer it, then. You said you wanted to experience kissing. You didn't mean that you wanted me to buss you on the cheek once and go my merry way, did you? You wanted to experience it the way it could be done. I'm merely trying to be effectual about your request in light of your packed schedule."

"Well, thank you for your efficacy." She glared at him. "But I'm trying to focus, and you are not helping in the least."

"No, but I am. Let's go through the options, shall we? You need a hundred or so jars filled. There are four options. You can fill the jars yourself, but you do not have the time."

"I could choose not to sleep."

"You really can't," he shot back, "not and be pleasant to hundreds of people wanting your food and your sauce on the day of the Trials."

"Ugh." She hated that he made sense.

"I could fill the jars," Jeremy said, "but it would take me until the end of the week, which is of little use to you. You could hire someone in Wedgeford to fill the jars—"

"But there isn't anyone," she said. "The only ones with nothing to do are layabouts like Barry Dalton, who would make more work for me than they're worth. And going to Dover to hire someone would take more time than it would save."

"Then it's your father."

She didn't *want* to ask her father. He would say yes,

and he would have such a difficult time screwing the lids on, and his hands would cramp, and…

"He stands to gain equally from the enterprise, does he not?"

"Of course!" She frowned at him. "It's *his* sauce. He's spent years refining it to perfection. But I promised my mother he wouldn't stand alone. I can't just…toss him out there like that."

Jeremy looked at her. "How would he feel if you *didn't* ask him?"

He would be upset. Jeremy was right; she had to ask him, and of course he would say yes.

"All my options are terrible," she moaned.

"Alas." He tapped the paper. "Put it on your list. What else must you do?"

She filled out the rest of her day all too easily and sighed when she finished. "There." She gestured at the page. "Today's list is a mess, but it's reconfigured. Tomorrow is now officially impossible." She stuck out her tongue at Jeremy.

"You're welcome. By the way, one correction from our discussion earlier." He grinned at her. "I don't mind at all having a wife who takes on too much and panics when she realizes what she's got herself into. Not if she's like you."

She exhaled and looked up. He was trying to goad her, trying to make her imagine herself in that position. Which was ridiculous. That was impossible. She could still feel the echo of his lips against her fingers. It was…all too tempting.

Chloe shook her head. "This is going to be a long day."

IT WAS JUST PAST NOON BY THE TIME JEREMY accompanied Chloe back to her home. From a legal standpoint, calling it *Chloe's* home was inaccurate. She lived on the edge of Wedgeford. Many decades ago, his ancestors had occasionally kept horses here to change on their voyages to the seashore for their health.

Chloe and her father lived in what had once been the quarters for occasional grooms: a tight, cramped building close to an abandoned barn, with a rudimentary kitchen and common area, and a few nooks for beds. Jeremy had gone to his solicitor's office when he was fifteen and locked himself up in a room with the records just to see if the townspeople's gibes about the Duke Who Didn't had any merit.

Surely he couldn't own *everything*, could he?

He did not. There were four houses and several pastures that belonged to the Church of England. The rest? His.

It was an awkward thing to bring to mind at a time like this, facing Chloe's father for the first time in three years.

"How many more jars does Miss Kwan think we should have?"

Mr. Fong looked precisely the way that Jeremy remembered. He was a full eight inches shorter than Jeremy and some indeterminate number of years his elder. He did not give the impression of either in the slightest. There were maybe a few tiny lines at the corners of his eyes —scarcely visible—and something that might have been an age spot, but was probably a beauty mark, on one cheek.

In other words, he appeared to have aged only slightly more than Jeremy's more dissolute classmates from Oxford. The only real sign of his age was his demeanor—cold and lofty, to Jeremy at least. He had given Jeremy a faintly unimpressed once-over the moment he stepped inside their tiny house—one that dismissed him as trivial pointlessness, a pest to be tolerated simply because throwing him out was too much of a bother.

"I thought we could produce fifty more jars? Maybe?" Chloe didn't *seem* to be terrified of her own father. Then again, that air of *hurt my daughter and I will destroy you* probably felt welcoming to her.

"Mmm." Her father looked at her suspiciously. "I didn't ask you what you *thought*. I asked what Miss Kwan requested."

Conversations in Wedgeford were always a bit of a language exercise. Chloe and Mr. Fong spoke Hakka fluently, but a dialect different from the other Hakka people in the village, and Jeremy had only a few words he'd picked up from Chloe. Jeremy and Mr. Fong spoke Cantonese fluently enough to converse, but Chloe's Cantonese was more rudimentary. Hakka and Cantonese were similar enough that Jeremy could sometimes understand the gist of what was being said…but only sometimes. English was—often—the primary common language.

Chloe's hands fidgeted in her skirts. Maybe she wasn't as immune to her father as she had appeared. "One hundred." It came out as a mutter.

"So she wants one hundred. And you think I can't do it?"

"Ah Ba, your hands."

He shrugged. "My hands are my hands."

"But you're going to have to cook for the Trials. You know I'm not as good as you are. It doesn't make sense for you to—"

"My hands," he repeated, "are *my* hands. I'll make the decision. You were already taking on too much."

"Not *too* much," she said stubbornly, as if she hadn't been on the verge of tears half an hour ago. "Really, barely even enough."

Instead of answering her, Mr. Fong held out an arm, pointing rudely at Jeremy where he stood. He didn't look at Jeremy. It was, in fact, his first acknowledgment of Jeremy's existence. "Posh Jim," he said, "tell my daughter that she is taking on too much."

"Um." He'd *just* had that exact conversation with Chloe. On the one hand, he couldn't disrespect her father. On the other, he didn't want to pit himself against her. There was no winning here; any action he took would annoy Chloe, and he was trying to only annoy her in the ways *he* chose, not the ones her father picked out for him. "If I may humbly choose not to involve myself in the matter, I would be most obliged to both of you."

"Hmm." Her father didn't sound displeased. He didn't sound pleased either. "That may be wise of you."

Ha. He'd successfully navigated that one, then.

"But it's cowardly," the man added on.

Damn it. Jeremy looked upward. Mr. Fong had always intimidated him, from the day he met him. He'd always looked at Jeremy, sizing him up in short glances, before looking away dismissively, as if to imply that Jeremy was absolutely nothing. There had never been a way to win with the man. Not when his daughter was involved.

"Right," Chloe said loudly, reaching for the basket. "Well then. Don't feel obligated to fill a hundred jars. Just do as many as you want! Be careful. Don't hurt yourself. We'll be off."

That scowl on her father's face grew. "Where are you off to, without having eaten lunch?"

"Ah Ba, I don't have *time* for lunch."

"So you have time to collapse of hunger?" He frowned at Chloe. "Is that on your list?"

"Oh my God." Chloe put her head in her hands. "I'm not going to collapse of hunger. I had a perfectly good breakfast! And I ate at Naomi's!" Jeremy hadn't seen it, but given how long she'd disappeared from sight, he suspected it had been a few bites at best. "I will eat dinner when it is time. What was it you said? Oh, right. My hunger is *my* hunger."

"No." Her father glared at her. "You are my daughter. Your hunger is also my hunger. It won't take long. Help with the noodles."

"This is why I can never finish everything on my list," Chloe groused. "Because nobody ever lets me. It's always 'eat dinner, Chloe,' or 'go to sleep, Chloe' or 'take a break and talk to me, Chloe.' Do you know how much I would get done if other people would just *stop?*"

"Stop caring about you?" Her father rolled his eyes. "Hmm. Tell me how much you'd get done if you were starving. Start from the beginning."

"Hmph." Chloe stuck out her tongue at her father. "Boo." But she had a smile on her face, and Jeremy thought she seemed fond. Indeed, she hummed happily as she rinsed her hands from a pitcher in the room.

"I'll just…wait outside," Jeremy said, gesturing vaguely behind them.

"No," said Mr. Fong. "You will also eat. You are rich, which means you are weak. You do not have the necessary fortitude to go without meals."

"I—that's—" Jeremy bit his lip. "Really unfair. I've skipped meals before, and it only killed me twice."

Mr. Fong ignored this attempt at levity. "Chloe does not have time on her list to care for a stubborn fool who collapses of hunger, and she is too kind to leave you lying in the dirt where you belong."

"We can fix that," Jeremy shot back. "Chloe, you have my permission to leave me lying anywhere I collapse. You see? We *do* agree on something, after all."

Mr. Fong met this with a level, unamused gaze, and Jeremy refused to look away.

"Ah Ba." Chloe sighed after thirty seconds of this. "Jeremy. Behave. Both of you."

"Who is misbehaving?" Mr. Fong said, his gaze sliding away. "The person who rejects the meal, I think."

Jeremy glanced at her father. He wasn't *smiling*, not as such. But the corner of his lip quirked up.

"Ah Ba." Chloe sighed again. "Stop antagonizing him."

"Why?" Mr. Fong countered. "Have you seen his face?"

"Ah *Ba.*"

"Thank you very much for the offer," Jeremy said, so politely that he could see Mr. Fong's teeth grit. "I accept."

They worked together swiftly at the table and mason-work range at the back of the room, where the windows were open for ventilation. The last time Jeremy had eaten with them, Mr. Fong had chopped the vegetables with a knife that flashed so quickly that Jeremy couldn't follow its path. This time, Chloe cut the greens, while Mr. Fong lit coal in the range, set a pot on to boil, and retrieved a round white mound from beneath a cloth. Chloe finished the vegetables, and they traded places without speaking. Mr. Fong set the wok over a fire; she rolled out the dough and sliced it into thick strips. She worked without wasted motion, hand-pulling the dough into wide noodles and tossing these into the boiling broth.

Jeremy watched, feeling almost…jealous, maybe. After his father had died, he and his mother had gone back to his grandparents' house in Guangzhou. Watching Chloe and her father brought back memories of that time—his mother and grandmother folding dumplings at a table together. Or, perhaps, his grandmother deftly pulling strips of dough into thin, even noodles while his mother chopped vegetables.

Chloe pulled noodles differently than his grandmother —holding one end of the dough strips in each hand and shaking them longer and longer. Still, Jeremy felt an intense homesickness just watching.

By the time she fished the noodles out with a mesh spider, her father was sliding vegetables into the pot, adding pinches of this and that, cracking eggs and stirring them with chopsticks before pouring them in the wok to make a thin crepe.

They operated together like a single entity, Chloe stepping out of the way as her father passed, getting bowls without a single word being said. Noodles, vegetables, fish poached in the same broth, were all set in separate bowls. Without speaking, her father filled one of those bowls with broth, then another, topping those with chopped scallions and a swirl of oil.

He started to reach for the third bowl, then stopped. He contemplated the remaining broth in the pot and lifted his head and met Jeremy's eyes. There was an intensity in his gaze that Jeremy didn't understand, a look that he might almost have called hatred.

What had Jeremy ever done to him? Well, admittedly, Jeremy was planning on kissing his daughter later that day. Which…would explain a lot, but it wasn't as if Mr. Fong knew that.

Did he?

While still looking him in the eyes, Mr. Fong took out a covered jar. He did not look away from Jeremy as he unwrapped twine from the wax paper around the top, lifted the paper, and scooped out dried red flakes into his hand, measuring by feel. He held Jeremy's gaze as he upended a generous palmful of those flakes—dried scotch bonnet, Jeremy suspected—into the final bowl of broth. And he smiled.

Jeremy exhaled. Well. Then. Smashing. Mr. Fong finally looked away and set the serving bowls on the table —a wide bowl of noodles, another of vegetables, and a third with thinly chiffonade egg. There was a bowl of broth for everyone, but Jeremy's bowl was bright pink.

"Enjoy," he said. There was a hint of amusement in his voice.

What was Jeremy to do? Say, *No, I can't possibly eat that?* It was a challenge, of course.

Jeremy nodded. "Thank you very much, sir."

Mr. Fong handed him a thick ceramic spoon and a pair of chopsticks. "Of course."

Jeremy waited for Mr. Fong to add the best bits to Chloe's bowl, then for him to serve himself. Finally, Jeremy reached out and added noodles and greens to his own soup.

There was nothing to do but go straight in. He took a spoonful of broth. He wasn't going to back down. He'd spent years of his life in Guangzhou. He had no fear of hot food.

He sipped. It wasn't that bad. In fact, it was almost reasonable—just a hint of heat. The noodles were perfectly, beautifully chewy, and the vegetables were both crisp and tender. He could taste a hint of soy sauce, a touch of anise... Beyond that, there were so many subtle seasonings that he'd never be able to identify them all. They gave the broth a glorious flavor, savory with a hint of sweet and sour, so utterly unlike the long-boiled British fare that was served with the accompaniment of salt and maybe pepper.

He could understand how Mr. Fong had been snapped up the instant two Englishmen in Trinidad had tasted his cooking. One sip, and he almost wanted to throw himself on the man's mercy and beg that he do nothing but cook for the rest of all time.

Then the heat—the heat he had at first thought a mere tickle—kicked in. It started gradually, a rising near-pain in the back of his mouth as Jeremy chewed. It came on inexorably, consuming his senses. Jeremy could feel his nose begin to run. He swallowed the flaming mouthful, looked at what remained in his bowl, and wiped the little bit of water that had begun to run from his eyes.

Chloe looked at him sharply, then peered into his bowl. Her breath sucked in. "Ah Ba, what did you *do?*"

"Why bother asking?" Mr. Fong said, his mouth twitching. "You already know."

"Ah Ba. Stop terrorizing him."

"I am not terrorizing him. We are having a little conversation over a meal. Aren't we, *Mr. Yu?*"

Jeremy took a swallow of water. It didn't alleviate the pain in his mouth; in fact, it spread the heat to new and interesting places. Down his throat. Into his belly.

"Yes," he said. "We are having a conversation. Although I do think that words might have allowed for a little more specificity." But he took another bite of the noodles.

"We are having a conversation in general," Mr. Fong replied. "Specifics are not necessary."

"No, why would we use specifics to express ourselves, when we could instead strike fear into the hearts of our enemies with a handful of dried plant material?"

"Besides," Mr. Fong said with a shrug, "neither my English nor my Cantonese is as good as my cooking. I don't know how to express this particular sentiment any other way."

"Do you want me to switch with you?" Chloe whispered at Jeremy's side.

Calling this a test was probably not accurate. Calling this a punishment...was also probably not accurate. But Jeremy looked into Mr. Fong's eyes. He knew how he must appear. He was a spoiled, wealthy man, one who had sauntered into town after a three-year absence, and immediately attached himself to Chloe. Whom he had attempted to kiss the last time he had been here.

This was a warning. Mr. Fong wanted to protect his daughter.

It brought to mind a long-ago memory. Jeremy had been on board a medium-size junk, still docked at the harbor in Guangzhou, ready to take him to Hong Kong where he'd take a larger steamship for England.

He had been eleven years old and his aunt Grace had been at his side. She had come all the way to China to make her argument. It had been well and good for Jeremy to be with his mother when he was a child. But he was the Duke of Lansing, and he needed to be prepared for the task of duking. That meant he needed to go to school in England, be trained in British manners, and be introduced to British society.

His mother was her parents' only remaining child. Jeremy had understood two things at the time: He could not ask her to leave with him, not when it meant leaving Ah Poh and Ah Gung on their own. And it was his duty to return with his aunt to England.

"Don't worry, Ah Ma," he'd said, as bravely as he could

manage. "It will all work out, and I'll be back before you know it." It had been a lie. Years at Eton and then Oxford lay before him—longer than his entire life had been thus far.

"Who will protect you?" she'd asked, switching to Cantonese while his aunt watched. He'd understood by that that she did not think his aunt could—or perhaps, that she *would*.

"You will." He had said it to reassure her, and when tears had started to form in her eyes, he knew he had to act. If she cried, *he* would cry. "Send me letters," he'd said cockily. "If anyone's a problem, I'll give them paper cuts."

It hadn't been that funny, but she had laughed instead of cried. And so had he, until they were far enough out to sea that the shore was no longer visible. Looking at Mr. Fong brought back to mind his mother's expression on that day—that moment when it had balanced between mirth and misery, when he'd said her letters would protect him.

Who will protect her? he imagined Mr. Fong thinking. *I will.*

Paper cuts and jokes and letters and the right advice at the right time… Jeremy's mother *had* protected him.

So it was simple now. "No," Jeremy said. "There's no need to switch. This bowl is mine, after all."

And Jeremy ate the soup. Every searing, painful drop of it.

7

In at least two ways, Jeremy was glad that Naomi had browbeaten Chloe into participating in this year's Trials even if in such a minimal fashion.

First, figuring out how to hide the fake Widgelot that Naomi had given her distracted him from the burning in his throat. The item Naomi had given them was a ball around a foot in diameter, painted in multiple shades of greens—much like a real Wedgelot would have been—but for the white words that said "Not a real Wedgelot" on one side.

They'd tried putting it under Jeremy's hat, which definitely had not worked. Jeremy suggested under Chloe's skirts; she'd glared at him and demanded to know how she should walk.

Finally, they'd given up and put it back in the same basket Chloe had brought it in.

"It's a picnic," she declared. "We're having a picnic."

"Won't we look suspicious if we avoid going near the green while lugging the world's heaviest basket?" Jeremy had asked as she took them on a route that cut through a field of cows, back behind a hedgerow, before returning to the banks of a little stream.

There was a trick to hiding Widgelots. Of course they were fake, and of course the point was to mislead people into thinking they were real. But if you were too obvious about hiding them, people would assume they were fake, defeating the entire purpose.

Jeremy had taken said heavy basket shortly after leaving the house, and his arms already ached with the effort of carrying it. At first, the track they followed started almost level, but all too soon, it sloped up the hills, away from the village. Just the sort of trail one wanted to traverse carrying a basket that felt like it contained a baby goat.

"Everyone is already going to be suspicious," Chloe said. "I've spent the last week declaring how busy I am, and now I'm taking a picnic? None of this makes sense, and this is the time of year when suspicions run high. But if we were attempting to spend some time together in private, we wouldn't want to be seen either. So we are going to pretend that we enjoy each other's company."

"We do," Jeremy said. "No pretending needed."

"We don't."

"Very well. You pretend; I'll just act like I normally do."

She wrinkled her nose and didn't say anything in response.

"We should take the time to converse," he said after he'd followed her up the little track next to the stream for five minutes, all while shifting the basket from one hand, then to the other. "Didn't you say we must be efficient?"

She gave him a look over her shoulder. It was late spring on the downs, and that meant that the fescue grass on the hills was littered with a profusion of buttercups, interrupted only by the darker yellow of cowslip. Chloe fit into this scene so perfectly—the dark, forbidding slash of her eyebrows, the fringed gold of her earrings in counterpoint to the gold of the fields. The wind picked up the ends of her sash, blowing it behind her.

"It would look suspicious if anyone were to observe us and we *weren't* talking," Jeremy said. "And besides, you're busy. We might as well do more than one thing. We're supposed to be making a list of all your qualities. Why don't we discuss that in greater detail?"

She put on her spectacles, shifted her board clip out from under her arm, flipped through a few sheets of paper, and wrinkled her nose. He'd always marveled at her ability to walk and plan at the same time. "At present, we have only one quality on your list: intimidating. You are correct. We are behind."

"No, there's been more than that," Jeremy pointed out. "By my recollection, I want a wife who makes me sign contracts to pay for lists, a wife who agrees to do too many things and then falls into a panic, and a wife who has at one point in her life told me to stick my head in a river and swallow. You must admit that those few items alone exclude a substantial number of women."

She gave him a level look. "You are not seriously going to put those things on a list you give your aunt."

"Technically, you are correct."

"Then we have one quality: intimidating."

"But it's *such* a good quality. It counts treble."

"Hmm."

The corners of her mouth turned down and she increased her pace as if she could outrace him up the hill. Which she could, weighed down as he was. He huffed, ignored the strain in his shoulders, and followed.

"Shall we talk about physical properties, then? I imagine you have an acceptable range of female frame that you are considering, and so as to not limit your options, we should make the parameters as wide as possible."

"As wide as possible? There's no point, given that I am exceptionally particular in my tastes."

"I am only trying to be of assistance. Shall we start with the basics? How do you feel about tall women?"

He pretended to contemplate this for a moment. "I like a woman of your height. I think you would snuggle against me very well. I like the idea of being able to wrap you up in my arms and keep you safe and warm in the winter. Or of being able to lift you up so that I could kiss you."

"Mr. Yu." She spoke his mother's family name in tones of great exasperation. "I beg of you to remember that we are making a list of general properties for a woman *out there*. We are not talking about a woman from Wedgeford. We are very much *not* talking about me."

He looked at her, one eyebrow raised. "Are we not?"

She stopped walking, her cheeks pinkening under the sun. Her eyes met his. For the barest moment, he thought she might ask. Or, better yet, realize.

Instead, she shook her head firmly and started striding

ahead again at an even more accelerated pace. He raced to keep up.

"Stop that," she said in a low voice when he had caught up with her. "Stop trying to fluster me with your stupid, stupid jokes. Do you not think of how this makes me feel?"

Jeremy took off his hat and scrambled to keep up. "The entire point of this bloody exercise is that I am not making a joke. I am—not. Very much not. I have not told you a thing I did not mean with my entire heart since I arrived."

She didn't say anything for a moment. She kept walking, her eyes fixed straight in front. She gave her head a little shake, as if trying to dislodge what he had just said. "Moving on to the next physical characteristic. What think you of hair colors? You seem like the sort to prefer blondes. Do you?"

He couldn't help the exasperated noise that escaped the back of his throat even had he wanted to do so. "Chloe, are you blond?"

She actually reached up and pulled a little strand from her bun, examining it, before tucking it behind her ear.

"You are not. Therefore, the answer is no. I must have failed to communicate this to you in the beginning: My list has *all* your characteristics. Not just some of them. *All* of them. It does not differ from you in any particular. Not a single one."

Her jaw worked. She looked straight ahead. "Brunettes it is, then." She somehow managed to write this down in sloppy hand as they walked.

"Brunette? I would never insult you with such a bare

description. I want a woman with hair that's black in the shade and that shines like silver in sunlight. I want her to keep it in a perfect bun, careful and tidy, except at night, when I want her to take it down. How far do you think her hair will fall when she brushes it out?"

"It will depend on the specific lady."

"How far does yours go?"

Her cheeks were almost crimson now. "Jeremy. Please stop."

"No, let us, by all means, be specific. How far does your hair reach when it's down?"

"It's not down." She straightened her back. "It's not coming down. I agreed to make a list of characteristics for you, not provide you with intimate details about my person."

"Well then." Jeremy nodded at her. "Don't tell me. Just put that—that I want a woman whose hair is as long as yours. Exactly as long as yours; not a finger's breadth longer."

She let out a long exhalation. She did not write anything down. Instead she looked up at the sky as if begging for celestial intervention. "Talking about physical characteristics is not proving productive. Let us move on to something else—ambitions for the future."

He couldn't shift the basket to his left side, not and walk by her side without striking her on accident. He ignored the growing ache in his arm. "By all means," he gritted out.

"Despite what you say, you're a wealthy man. You're going to need a wife who…" Her nose wrinkled. "I don't know what a wealthy man's wife does. Sees to charity? Eats bonbons on the sofa? Makes friends with all the wealthy neighbors? She likely has ambitions in some direction even if it is simply to taste every bonbon available in London."

"Well, you tell me." They came to a stop. The slope of the hill evened out here for a space, and the stream formed a little pool. "What are *your* ambitions?"

She looked him in the eyes. "I want revenge for my father. Revenge is not a suitable ambition for your wife."

He just smiled. "I was already aware of that ambition. What part of 'does not differ from you in any particular' makes you think that my list will differ on so fundamental an aspect of your character?"

"Jeremy. Your wife should be pleasant. I want Mr. White and Whistler and their stupid, stolen sauce to lose favor. I want them to weep that they never allowed my father to perfect it. I want them to feel badly. I also want them to lose a great deal of money. You cannot marry a woman who wants such things."

She was trying very hard not to understand, Jeremy thought. He just shrugged. "Very tepid, as far as revenge goes. There's neither death nor dismemberment present. Put that down—I want a wife who specializes in mild revenge."

She balked mulishly. "Wouldn't you rather have one who makes friends with your very wealthy neighbors?"

"Chloe, my dear, I am half-Chinese. Being wealthy does not stop me from being half-Chinese. My wealthy neighbors will always know that I am half-Chinese. A wife who took their side over mine would be intolerable. I could not live with such a person. A wife who is committed to mild revenge on my behalf, however, who makes the neighbors feel that they have no choice but to treat me with respect? *That's* who I want."

"Oh." She swallowed. "Well. Actually. That does make sense." After a pause, she wrote this on the list: *mild revenge acceptable.*

"You see? I am not just having fun at your expense. I really do want someone who possesses your characteristics. Tell me more about your ambitions and desires."

She looked ahead. "I want recognition," she said softly. "My father… He is brilliant. You know this."

Jeremy nodded. He'd had Mr. Fong's food before today's mouth-blistering version. *Brilliant* could hardly describe it. His cooking had been a revelation the first time he'd tried it. He had not known that food could have such flavor, such expression.

"As for me…" Chloe lifted her head. "I know people mock me, and I understand why. I'm hard and no fun at all. But I am a very capable woman. If I had been old enough, I would never have allowed White and Whistler to do what they did. We would have had contracts that spelled the deal all out and made it enforceable. I would have had records of all that my father had done. I would have brought the matter to the courts and demanded just compensation. We work well together, and I want people to respect us."

Jeremy grinned at her in helpless admiration. "You cannot possibly imagine that I want an incompetent wife who tolerates injustice."

"I want my father to be able to rest," Chloe said. "He's worked so hard to make a life for me. He should have a chance to sit back and allow others to work in his stead."

That, Jeremy could understand. "Hence the sale of Unnamed Sauce."

"Precisely." She looked away. "I don't know if you can possibly understand—you're wealthy—but we've had a fair bit of luck for the last fifteen years, making our way to Wedgeford. We have it rather easy here. You see…" She paused, her lips pursing, before she continued. "No. You've heard about Wedgeford, I'm sure, from everyone else here. The fact that we don't actually pay rents here has been an unqualified blessing. At any moment, His Grace Good Riddance could die and some foul cousin could inherit, and that person might try to squeeze out what little extra we have. Think what it means: We have not paid rents in all the years we have lived here. If we had to pay all that back…"

You will never have to, Jeremy wanted to say. His foul cousin—and truly, James was excessively odious—would never inherit Wedgeford. Jeremy had already made *that* change with his solicitor. But he couldn't tell her that. What could he say instead?

"Well then," he said, and he pitched his voice to jovial, as if this were the least consequential of his questions. "While we're on the subject of your wants and desires, I might as well ask. What do you want in a husband? Maybe you should look for someone rich. If only you knew such a fellow."

Her breath sucked in. She ran one hand along the edge of her board clip, and looked down at the ground.

"I haven't given it much thought. I have so many of my own worries right now; there's no time to plague myself with thoughts about another person."

Jeremy reached out and gently set his fingertips atop the hand on her board clip. Her cheeks pinked, and she cautiously looked up, as if afraid to be caught glancing at him.

"Please," he said, raising a hand to her cheek as she turned away. "Don't shy from me. This is the most important question, you know. Because if I find a woman who has every one of your finest qualities, you *know* the difficulty I will face. It seems almost insurmountable."

"I do?" She glanced toward him. "It *does?*"

"I will have to convince her to marry me," Jeremy said. "And she will be so splendid. So wonderful. Likely she'll say no." His finger trailed against her jaw. Her face was sun-warm; her eyes were sun-bright. He never wanted to let her go, and he didn't even have her yet.

"Oh." She frowned.

"So tell me," he whispered. "Chloe. Tell me what you want in a husband."

"Someone who supports me." Her head tilted slightly, nestling into his palm. "Someone who..." She swallowed, her eyes slitting for a moment.

"Can you think of anything in particular that you would want?"

She drew in a deep breath, looking over his shoulder at something unseen. "There was," she finally whispered, "someone. Once. Who I thought..."

He could almost taste the bitter vinegar of jealousy.

"My feelings were entirely childish," Chloe said. "But you have noticed that I have some flaws. He always made my heart feel lighter anytime I was around. He was charismatic." She looked away. "The kind of person who makes friends with everyone, which is exceptionally convenient as I'm very bad at that sort of thing."

Jeremy hated him already, both because he'd had her heart, enough to make her look this sad, and because he'd made her sad. It took him a moment to wrestle his covetous resentment into place. He had no claim on her, no right to be jealous of her past liaisons.

"He wasn't right." Her eyes glistened with some long-forgotten memory. "He was never going to be right, and I was a fool for not seeing it when it was so plainly obvious."

"Chloe." He reached up and set his other hand under her chin. "Tell me. What was it he did that was so disqualifying?"

She looked up at him. "You asked what I wanted in a husband."

He nodded.

Her nostrils flared. She put a hand on his chest and pushed. "I want someone who stays." Her voice cracked on the last syllable, betraying a depth of sadness that took him unawares. She stared at him resolutely.

It took him a moment to understand what she had just said. She hadn't talked about *any* person or about some *other* liaison. She was talking about *him*. He'd left. It had never occurred to him that he had the capacity to hurt her; it seemed impossible that she had cared for him a tenth as much as he had for her.

He'd hurt her.

"Chloe."

She looked away. "You left, Jeremy." He almost wished she were angry instead of this sadness. "Every year, you came. You charmed me. You made me feel as if I were the center of your universe. And then—five days, a week later, it never mattered—you left. I wouldn't hear from you again, not until the next year. For three hundred and sixty days out of the year, I didn't exist to you. And yet I was here, waiting."

"Chloe." He took a step toward her. "Sweetheart. I thought of you. I always thought of you all year."

"Maybe. But you weren't *here*. I don't know what you're trying to do now with your list. You've come to indulge your childhood whims, I think, where you imagine that you can simply swoop in and turn my head and collect whatever you wish from me. But you're going to leave. You're always going to leave, and I'm going to be left here."

Not this time, he wanted to say. But she wasn't completely wrong. He was holding a part of himself back from her, and with good reason. *I'm the Duke of Lansing,* he thought about saying. *I never wanted to leave you. I just didn't know how to keep you safe in my world.*

His reasons didn't matter. He had hurt her. He had come here and made her feel things simply because he also felt things. And then he'd left her alone with those feelings, alone to feel hurt, alone with no way to reach out to him even if she had wanted to.

Jeremy didn't have a list. He didn't have a plan. He wasn't good at that sort of thing. But she'd just told him plainly what he had to do.

I must never let you feel alone again. He didn't know how. He just knew he had to do it.

"Well then," he said, stepping back from her. "I

shouldn't kiss you. A kiss is for hope and you've told me there is no room for hope on your list when it comes to me. I have to change that first."

She shook her head. "A kiss is for closing the door on old memories. A kiss is for goodbye."

"Not mine." He leaned over her. "Not mine. If I kiss you, it's a beginning."

"Stop it." She prodded his shoulder. "Did you hear what I said? You're leaving. You're *always* leaving, and no matter what happens between us, it will always end. I *know*. I'm better at planning for the future than you."

A bird called from somewhere in the grass. Another answered. The lazy hum of insect wings seemed to swell around them as she stared at him. Despite the look in her eyes—that mix of anger and uncertainty and fear—something about the moment, about being here on the downs with Wedgeford a tiny miniature below, seemed right. He'd left, but he'd stayed. Some portion of his heart had always remained here. He'd been clever enough to know he needed her, but he'd needed her to push him to this as well—to the understanding that it wasn't Wedgeford that belonged to him, no matter what property records said.

He belonged to Wedgeford, whatever that meant, and if she needed someone to stay, he was going to stay. He didn't know how. He just knew that he must.

"Well then." He took a step closer to her. "We seem to be in complete disagreement about what a kiss would mean. We are entirely at odds."

She looked up at him, bristling and angry and also sad, so sad. He wanted to soothe away the angry line between her eyebrows. "You're right." But she didn't pull away. "Our meaning is utterly irreconcilable."

He didn't know how to solve anything. But he did know one thing—one thing that seemed obvious here, on this hill, with the wind blowing around them, with the heavy basket weighing him down.

"Our goals for kissing are antithetical." Jeremy shrugged. "Let's do it anyway." And so saying, he dropped the basket containing the Widgelot with one hand, released his hat into the wind, and leaned in.

8

CHLOE SHOULD HAVE PUSHED HIM AWAY, BUT SHE had regrets from last time—too many of them, all piled atop each other. Instead, she stepped into his arms. He made a soft sound of surprise as if he hadn't expected her to allow it. But she took hold of his waist, gripping the rough fabric of his jacket, and his arms came around her, pulling her in.

His lips were soft and teasing. It felt like too much, the way his mouth moved against hers, and yet too little all at once, his breath warm against her lips. The scent of him made something not so deep inside her, something she'd never quite been able to suppress, shiver in want. She wanted him to open up his mouth and devour her; she wanted him to crush her against his chest until she had no choice but to melt against the solidity of his body. She wanted him to push her beyond her limits, fast and hard, so she would know what this was: him taking, her giving.

He did not do that. His breath touched her lips,

coaxing her. His fingers stroked down her spine, tiny little gestures as if he were painting characters against her back.

He mostly spoke Cantonese; she mostly spoke Hakka. The Chinese they primarily had in common were characters, identical in meaning if different in pronunciation.

Those gestures could not have been characters. She was fooling herself, imagining messages where there were none. Still, she felt as if she could detect them anyway.

Everything, she thought he wrote with the tiny strokes of his fingers. He paused, then added two strokes. *Gold.* His hand flattened against her back. She knew it was her imagination; the fine strokes of Chinese characters were impossible to detect when she herself was the medium. Still, his fingers made little almost-circles against the fabric on her back as his lips danced with hers. If she pretended —and she knew she was pretending—she could pretend he was scribing those above the thing that might have been a field radical.

She knew what character she wanted him to have written: *Stay.* But he hadn't. It was her own wants she was indulging, wanted so hard that it was as if she'd shouted, as if she now heard the repeated echo of her own scream floating back to her through his kiss.

I'm staying, she wanted this to mean. *I'm staying.* She couldn't let herself believe it. She'd deluded herself on this point before, and every time it had hurt too much to discover she was wrong.

Still, she pushed closer to him. Opened her mouth just that barest inch. She could feel the groan he made reverberating against her. Then the warmth of his tongue swept in to greet her.

He could not stay even if he'd wanted to do so. It was not in the realm of what was possible for him. For *them*.

He had an entire life outside Wedgeford. There were people who knew him and demanded his presence—like the aunt he had mentioned. He'd referred to his wealth before, but wealth came with the weight of responsibility. Somewhere he had a home and servants and land in an amount that would dwarf Wedgeford into insignificance. He had people who depended upon him.

I'm staying, she wanted to hear.

He pulled away from her. "Chloe." His voice was hoarse. "You must know—I may not be serious about anything, but about you? I am."

I'm staying, she wanted him to say. But even if he did, even if he believed it down to the tips of his toes... That wouldn't make it true.

He'd never once been purposefully false. She'd given him her youthful confidences, whispering all her ambitions for the future to him one night as they'd sat in the forest by the lake, yearning for one another and never touching.

So she kissed him again to stop more words from coming out of his mouth.

On some level, she knew this wasn't just lust, not for either of them. He was hungry, he was lonely, and she was here. He would never *intend* to harm her.

But intent or no, he'd done it before, and he would do it again.

He wasn't staying. Wedgeford was too small for him. He was not staying, and she was not leaving.

It could not work. This kiss was goodbye—goodbye to

girlish dreams that she'd held too long into adulthood. Goodbye to his boyish infatuation. In the future, there was no intersection to be found between them—none at all.

She pulled away first. He blinked at her, his hands sliding from her back down her shoulders to her elbows, before he realized what she was doing and tightened his grip.

"You see?" she said.

He looked down at her, his eyes dark, his breath coming swiftly. His hands tightened around her arms, and he reached back in to kiss her once more.

She was so bewildered that she let him do it. She let their mouths meld. She let his tongue touch hers, tender and sweet; she did not object when his hand slid up the side of her neck. She did not swallow the gasp or try to tamp down the feeling that settled inside her.

He pulled away again, flushed, and gave her a broad, delighted smile. "I *do* see."

Oh. The realization sank like a shot of lead in her stomach. He had *not* seen. If he understood how impossible anything further was, he would never smile at her that way. He had not heard what she was saying, only what he'd wanted to hear.

She was going to have to say it with words. She wiped the answering smile off her face. Ordered her eyebrows to furrow and straightened her back. Then she said the words: "Jeremy. That was goodbye."

He looked at her uncomprehending for a moment, before he finally shook his head. "I am no linguist, but I do not think that was goodbye in any dialect on the face of this planet."

"Jeremy, you turnip. *Think.* How would it function out there? You and me? With what you are and what I am?"

He scrubbed a hand through his hair and finally shrugged. "I have no idea. To be honest, *out there* doesn't always work so well even when it's just me. I don't know how to bring you into it."

She looked at him. His head was bare; his hair was straight and blowing in the wind. His eyes were fixed on hers with a determined light.

"But I hurt you," he told her. "It never occurred to me that I could." He seemed bewildered by this. "I did. And I don't want to do it again."

What if, her foolish hopes whispered. *What if this time he was serious?*

She'd thought it so many times. It had never been true. Nonetheless: *What if?* she thought, *what if what if?*

"Please," she finally said. "We have a Fraud to hide. Can we…" She couldn't complete the sentence; she didn't know what she was asking. *Can we do that again?* Maybe. *Can we pretend this never happened?* Also maybe.

But perhaps he did know, because he just nodded at her. He walked off a few paces, retrieved his hat, dusted it off, and set it back on his head.

"Let's." He nodded at her, as if they'd come to some sort of agreement, before bending and hoisting the heavy basket.

And that was that. She'd had her kiss. She'd said good-bye. Surely now she could begin the process of forgetting him.

Inside the barn, it was dark. A broad stripe of sunlight spilled from the door providing the only illumination. Jeremy was used to barns smelling of hay and horse. But this one made Jeremy think of street corners in Guangzhou, aromatic and delicious.

"Mr. Fong?" he called.

"Back here." The response came in Cantonese, a sure sign that Mr. Fong knew it was him.

He and Chloe had hidden the Widgelot at the edge of an impenetrable thicket of blackthorn, pushed in far enough that the long thorns had scraped his shoulder through the wool fabric of his jacket. She'd excused herself quickly after they'd returned, as if wanting as much distance between herself and that kiss as she could get.

"Go," she'd said, shooing him off. "Talk to people—other people—people who are not me. You're impressively good at that."

It was probably just as well. Jeremy needed to think, and if he did it in her vicinity, he would probably do something ridiculous like demand that they practice kissing again, just to see who was better at it.

So he'd gone back to the village green, met with Mr. Wilderhampsher, explained the rules, and introduced him to some other young people his age. All the while, he'd been contemplating.

He'd kissed her. God, he wished he could just crow about that. Spend an afternoon wandering around with a dazed expression on his face because he'd kissed her and she'd kissed him back and they'd kissed, oh, God. He *wanted* to be giddy with joy.

But. He'd hurt her. He'd imagined that she would be angry, annoyed… anything, really. But hurt? Just because he left? He'd not realized he had that kind of power. Whatever he did, he had to *not* hurt Chloe. Not ever again.

So instead of basking in the memory of the kiss and making exuberant plans for more, he'd gone to see her father. And here Jeremy was, eyes straining in a dark barn that he technically owned, wondering how to make things right.

He made his way back around the dark silhouettes of various obstacles toward Mr. Fong's voice. His eyes adjusted slowly to the dim illumination. Black blobs were scattered around, seemingly at random, waiting to stub his toes, resolved into wooden kegs placed at regular intervals, marked with Chinese characters in white paint.

Mr. Fong was at the far north corner of the barn, sitting on a tall stool, a keg open in front of him. The barn had been fitted with a mobile Chinese-style cooking range —used for applying heat to vinegars and sauces when necessary. It was in the back, where a few boards had been removed for ventilation. At the moment, steam rose from a lidless pot atop the range. Near that, an array of glistening jars had been set to dry.

Mr. Fong reached for one of those jars with metal tongs. The grip of the tongs was unsteady; the jar bobbled momentarily, but he nonetheless managed to bring it toward him. He set it on a cloth, then filled it with a brown liquid ladled from the keg in front of him. He transferred this jar to a toweled hand, wiped the threads, and then, with care, screwed on a lid.

He did not look up as Jeremy arrived but continued working in this fashion—dipping a ladle into the keg, scooping up a generous amount of brown fluid, pouring it into a jar, wiping it down, then putting on a lid.

"Chloe is off. She said something about seeing to the ovens with Mr. Tanner." Jeremy also spoke in Cantonese.

"I know her schedule." The reply was curt and uninviting.

Jeremy squatted down to be near his level. "I'm here to help."

"I don't require your help." Mr. Fong wiped another jar and picked up a replacement with tongs.

"It will make Chloe happy nonetheless. So I'm here."

"You've never filled a jar in your life. You'll make a mess. You're not worth the trouble."

"I can help you go faster. I can hand you jars and wipe them down and put the lids on after you've filled them."

Mr. Fong paused. After a long moment staring at the jar in his hand, he looked up to meet Jeremy's eyes. "Keep up then." He didn't say anything else, but that was permission, and Jeremy would accept that.

It took a while to get into the rhythm of the work. Set a sterile jar in front of Mr. Fong with the tongs; take the one he had just filled, wipe it with a cloth and put the lid on, carefully and yet swiftly enough that he could hand Mr. Fong the next empty jar. Take the filled jar and repeat. It didn't seem like hard work, but the steam had made the barn humid and hot, and after five minutes, Jeremy found he was working up a sweat, trying to keep up.

After ten, he'd found a rhythm. And after twenty, his muscles had learned the cadence well enough that he thought he could start a conversation.

"I understand why you don't like me." His words seemed to ring loudly in the barn.

"I have never said I don't like you."

Technically true. "I wouldn't like me much either." He'd thought it over, turning it in his mind. "It must look pretty horrible from your end of things. I toyed with Chloe's affections. I disappeared every year after making her no promises. And there would be no further communication until the next time I arrived. I left for three years without a word. I wouldn't think myself trustworthy if I were her father."

Mr. Fong handed him a filled jar. "All of that is true. But you've neglected to mention the fact that you're the Duke of Lansing." Those last three words were said in English, with an almost mocking emphasis on the English intonation.

Jeremy nearly dropped the jar and its lid. As it was, he was a second late to get the next empty to Mr. Fong, and the man huffed in impatience.

"Wait a minute." His heart was pounding. It was humid, so humid his head swam. He could scarcely breathe through the clouds of steam, and yet his mouth felt dry. It was foolish to whisper—nobody else was about —but he couldn't manage to speak at a regular volume. "How did you know that?"

Mr. Fong shot him a long wide-eyed look before he shook his head. "You *are* aware that I obtain additional funds by serving as a chef on occasion?"

Jeremy exhaled. "Chloe mentioned it."

"People talk," Mr. Fong said simply. "I'm Chinese. They think that all Chinese people know one another. More than half a dozen have asked me if I know the half-Chinese Duke of Lansing."

Holy hells above. This was not a complication he'd expected. He didn't know what to think. "What did you tell them?"

Mr. Fong shrugged. "After we had met the first time? I told them yes. Did you expect me to lie?"

Jeremy's head whirled. He'd been coming here for more than a decade, thinking himself entirely anonymous. Here in Wedgeford, where half the population wasn't white, a half-Chinese person fit right in. He was part of their fun, part of their jokes, even if they knew he did have some money outside the community.

Mr. Fong had known the truth for…how long now? Well, Jeremy thought grimly, at least it explained why the man had never warmed to him.

Another thought occurred to him, one that shot horror through his veins. He had to remind himself not to break the rhythm of the work—handing over jars, wiping, putting on lids.

"Have you… Have you told Chloe?"

He couldn't have done. Logically? If Chloe known, all throughout his childhood? She would never have bossed him around the way she had in the beginning. She would never have been so free with him. It was an impossibility.

Mr. Fong looked over at him. For a moment, he stared as if seeing into Jeremy's soul. Then the corner of his mouth twitched, as if he were suppressing a smile. "I see what you're hoping for. *You* should have had this conversation with Chloe years ago. Now you wish I'd done it in your stead. But I haven't finished the conversations *I* should have with her. There's no need for me to assist with yours."

Jeremy winced. It sounded...a lot harsher coming from her father's mouth.

"Was I supposed to tell her, 'by the way, that boy who has turned your head—he is not just rich and handsome, but also powerful'? That would hardly have the effect I hoped for."

Jeremy passed over another jar. "In my defense," he muttered as he wiped, "I'm not that powerful. It's not like being a *regular* duke. I don't get the same deference. I'm half-Chinese. It's...odd. It's all odd."

"That is what you say in your defense? That the government you must participate in by virtue of your birth hates you?" Mr. Fong gave him a scornful look as he passed over a filled jar. "That is not *odd;* it's harmful. Chloe is English; I haven't been able to stop that from happening. But *she* doesn't have to take part in a government that imposed the Unequal Treaties on our people."

Jeremy let out a long breath. And Mr. Fong likely didn't know the half of it. "I—that's—I can't help that I was born into this." He was not making a stellar case for himself. "I know you must doubt my feelings, but I really do feel genuine affection for Chloe. I have for years."

"You are foolish." Mr. Fong shook his head. "But fool as you are even *I* think you understand how precious my daughter is. I'm sure you have a dozen reasons you tell yourself why you have not had this exact conversation with Chloe. Whatever those are, you are lying to yourself. You know how hard it was for you, for your mother. And you know she will be better off not marrying you. That's why you haven't spoken to her about it."

It was a pretty damning indictment of Jeremy. It was also...largely accurate. His mother had left England as soon as she could; she'd wanted to protect him from it. When he'd gone back to talk to her, she'd told him to ruthlessly prune out every poisonous vine.

The problem was, all the vines were poison. Parliament. The dukedom. The friends he'd made at Eton and Oxford. Even his aunt Grace, who loved him and wanted the best for him... Even she had urged him to marry *the right sort of girl,* in that tone of voice—a reminder that he was not, and would never be, the *right sort,* no matter what he did.

"Uncle." He bowed his head.

Just to make sure that Jeremy understood, Mr. Fong delivered the killing blow. "Her mother would never have picked you as a son-in-law. You don't deserve her."

There was nothing to say to that. He *didn't* deserve her. If he'd been Chloe's parent, he wouldn't have picked himself either. His chest squeezed.

The *easiest* part of why he'd come to Wedgeford was convincing Chloe that he was serious, and he'd still not yet managed that. The hard part was going to be convincing her that he was deserving. And he wasn't.

"I agree with every word," he finally whispered out. "I don't. I *don't* deserve her."

Mr. Fong didn't say anything. The stack of filled jars

grew, and after another fifteen minutes, by mutual agreement, they took something of a rest. Mr. Fong rolled his
shoulders and flexed his wrists, stretching out cramping
muscles, before pressing into points on his palm while
biting his lip.

Jeremy carefully moved the stack of filled jars into the
empty crate nearby. He found another wooden crate that
contained another set of empties.

"That's one hundred so far by my count," he
commented. "Do you think we should stop?"

"If Naomi thought she could sell an extra hundred, we
should have more."

"Chloe said she didn't want you to hurt your hands."
He glanced at where Mr. Fong was still pressing his thumb
into a palm.

"Chloe isn't here," Mr. Fong said almost sharply.

"I am," Jeremy replied. "Chloe would want me to
remind you."

"And I don't. Are you going up against me on her
say-so?"

There was no right answer to that one; he lost either
way. Jeremy sighed and just let out the truth. "Yes."

Mr. Fong exhaled softly. "Then maybe another one
hundred, and we'll stop there."

They set the jars in the hot bath and stoked the flames,
not speaking until the steam billowed out. Mr. Fong
nodded after they'd removed them and allowed them to
dry. "Now we can start again."

They got into the rhythm of it again, passing jars back
and forth.

"You're not wrong about me," Jeremy said eventually.

"I'm like... I'm like White and Whistler's Pure English Sauce. I'm not English at all, no matter what it says on the label. I'm an unrefined fake, falsely labeled. Chloe deserves..." He swallowed. He wasn't quite sure how to extend the metaphor. "She deserves... Something that's not British sauce. Something like this, whatever she names it."

Mr. Fong made another noise. "You don't know *anything.* This is British."

Jeremy made a small noise of confusion.

"It's extremely British," Mr. Fong said. "I didn't have qu after White and Whistler tossed me out, and no way to get it from China."

"You didn't have...qu?" Jeremy didn't know if the word was Hakka, or if it was one he'd never acquired in Cantonese.

"Kuk," Mr. Fong tried, and when Jeremy shook his head blankly: "The...thing used in fermentation?" He said this in English, before switching back to Cantonese. "I didn't have any. That meant I had to cultivate my own. This sauce *is* British."

"I don't understand."

Mr. Fong looked at him, as if wondering about the quality of his education, before sighing. "You see, qu grows everywhere. We cannot see it, not with our eyes, not until we've given it time to grow into molds, to know whether it will become poison or leavening or an agent of fermentation. People have known this since the dawn of civilization. The things that cause fermentation... They exist everywhere, as long as you give them a place to grow."

"I...see."

"But they are not the same everywhere." Mr. Fong looked over at Jeremy in the dark. "Nothing I have cultured anywhere will ever taste like it was made with the qu from Look King, the village where I grew up. Nothing here in England has ever tasted like Guangzhou or Nanjing or Trinidad. And the culture that grows here in Wedgeford tastes just a little different too. This sauce *is* British. This taste has been here all this time, waiting for Britain to discover it."

Jeremy wasn't sure what to say to that.

"The place you are," Mr. Fong said, "is not permanent. Stop waiting. Work with what you have and who you are to make what you want to be. I am waiting to see what you will discover."

Jeremy took in a breath, then another, and still yet another. He wasn't sure what he'd expected coming here, talking to her father, but this felt startlingly...kind.

"I haven't talked to her about who I am." He sighed. "You'll tell me I should do it right away, I'm sure."

Mr. Fong gave him a long, unreadable look.

"Ghost without courage, hmm?"

Jeremy flushed. "That's the *exact* insult my mother used when I told her about the situation. But I'm not a coward. Just...trying to be practical."

"Practical." The corner of Mr. Fong's mouth twitched, but whether it was a smile or a grimace, Jeremy wasn't sure. "Chloe is busy," Mr. Fong finally said. "If you wait until after the Trials, you will have her full attention. After twelve years, a few more days won't matter."

Stay, Chloe had told him. *Grow,* her father had

admonished. *Stay. Grow.* Those two words seemed the clue to not hurting Chloe again. They weren't answers. They weren't even questions. They felt closer to a beginning—like the first drops of water falling on parched soil.

"Thank you, Uncle," he finally responded. "I needed that advice."

"Don't wait too long." Mr. Fong sighed. "It gets harder the longer you put it off."

9

THE SUN WAS DEEPER IN THE SKY—NOT QUITE orange yet—by the time Jeremy left Mr. Fong's property. His shoulders ached and he felt exhausted already.

Weak was what he had expected Mr. Fong to call him. But the man had nodded at him in something like thanks and retired rather abruptly. It was still early evening, which meant Jeremy had a little time before he could meet up with Chloe at the inn.

He found Mr. Wilderhampsher on the edge of the green, sitting on a rock and kicking his feet in the air, a frown on his face.

"You know," Jeremy said, coming up to him, "with your preoccupation about being accepted in the Trials, I expected that you would go talk to people. Make friends and so forth."

Mr. Wilderhampsher scowled. "No good. Why do you think I was so insistent on being assigned to a *real* Wedge-fordian?"

"What's no good?"

"Me. Talking to people I don't know." He gestured widely at the green, as if that were sufficient explanation, and then huffed and hunched up in a little ball on his rock. "This was all a silly idea anyway."

"Probably," Jeremy agreed and sat beside him on the rock.

Mr. Wilderhampsher cast him an annoyed sidelong look. "You're an adult. You aren't supposed to *agree* with me. You're supposed to pat me on the back and say, 'there, there' or some similar platitudes. 'It'll be all right' or some such."

Jeremy shrugged. "I'm not *that* much of an adult. And you've been extremely rude to me; I'm just returning the favor."

"You're *old*. Twenty, at least. Probably as old as twenty-two."

Jeremy huffed at this assessment of his age. Not that far off, but the tone… "As old as that, do you think?"

"Ancient," Mr. Wilderhampsher agreed. "Someone old like you can't call someone my age silly. It's the rules."

"Why not? It was a silly idea when I came here too." Jeremy looked out over the green, at the children playing. "The first time I came here wasn't because of the Trials. At least not directly. I was supposed to go to some distant relation's house for a 'visit.'" He rolled his eyes on that last word. "It was arranged by my aunt, who thought that I should get to know that fatuous windbag—"

He had almost been going to say, *that fatuous windbag, James Etheridge,* but using the name *James Etheridge* to someone who maybe knew the workings of polite society would have been like scribbling his title in red paint on his forehead.

"Who happened to be a distant cousin," he said instead.

Aunt Grace had, in fact, thought it would be good for little James to help little Jeremy become substantially more English.

Yet another reason Jeremy had not been looking forward to the visit.

That must have come through in his expression because Mr. Wilderhampsher pursed his lips. "You don't like your cousin then." He frowned. "What a waste. I always wanted cousins."

"Have mine, with delight. He's prissy and full of himself. The first time we met, he made snide comments about my mother. I retaliated by making fun of him. He'd needle me incessantly when the adults weren't around, order me to do things, and tell me it was only the natural order that I obey him. I didn't. We hated each other. If I told anyone what was happening—my aunt, his parents— he would deny it all in innocent tones. And they'd always believe him. My cousin is a—" He cut himself off. No need to curse around the children.

"Oh." Mr. Wilderhampsher looked at him, as if reassessing. "One of *those*. Ugh. I didn't know they came as cousins."

One of those, indeed.

"So I had just got into Paddington Station and was supposed to transfer—"

Mr. Wilderhampsher blinked at this. "And they let you travel? All alone?"

Jeremy shrugged. "Technically... I wasn't supposed to be alone. But I was rather tired of being followed around everywhere. I had already told the valet who accompanied me to take a holiday, and he didn't like me much better than I did him, so... In any event, I saw Andrew Uchida."

Mr. Wilderhampsher leaned forward. "You did? Did you know each other? Even then?"

"Not in the slightest." Jeremy shrugged. But he'd had a letter from his mother in his pocket, one that he'd read over and over.

You don't have to do everything they want you to, she had written in response to one of his complaints. *They want to make you English, but you need only be yourself.*

He'd seen other people of Asian descent in England before—most often, people in the civil service. But this had been his first time seeing another boy—one who also seemed to be half.

"Andrew was with his mother. He saw me, and he ran over and asked if I was coming to the Wedgeford Trials."

Jeremy hadn't known what the Wedgeford Trials were back then.

"He assumed I had some connection to Wedgeford because I'm half-Chinese—obviously someone who should know about Wedgeford, he seemed to think. There was some confusion as we dithered outside the train platform; we talked at each other, and he apologized for assuming I'd belong in Wedgeford simply because of my race, and that's how I figured out that there was an *entire village* where people looked like me. I thought about spending time with my cousin, and..."

And he'd thought about the letter in his pocket. *You*

don't have to do everything they want, his mother had written, and he'd thought of how he'd joked with her on the docks, how he'd said her letters would protect him. What better protection could she provide than to give him permission to avoid his odious cousin?

"So I sent a telegram to my horrible cousin's family with my regrets, saying I would be unable to visit, and I went to Wedgeford with Andrew instead."

Mr. Wilderhampsher was watching him with surprise in his eyes. "What did your family do when they found out? Were they angry?"

"They…didn't find out." Jeremy made a pained face. "I…somehow managed to convince them, every year thereafter, that I was…staying with friends? I suspect my cousin helped with the ruse—he didn't want to see me either. My aunt and uncle were happy enough to see me socializing with what they imagined was high society. And it wasn't entirely false, because I *do* have friends here. Now I'm too old to punish, so look! It turned out for me."

"Huh." Mr. Wilderhampsher nodded. "That's… That's a good strategy. Never telling anyone."

Belatedly, Jeremy realized that he'd inadvertently told this boy to lie to his parents. "Wait—no. That's—it really isn't. I don't think—"

"In any event, why *is* Wedgeford like this?" Mr. Wilderhampsher gestured around at the green.

It wasn't that there were *no* white people in Wedgeford; the village of hundreds was maybe half white, by Jeremy's estimation. But only half white, in a small village in rural England, did make it something of a rarity.

"Where did they all *come* from?" Mr. Wilderhampsher asked.

"Ah, ah." Jeremy shook a finger at him. "That's against Wedgeford rules."

"There's Wedgeford rules?" The young man squinted. "Are those about the Trials?"

"It's more general manners. One of those rules is that you don't ask prying questions. People will tell you what they wish you to know, if they want you to know."

The boy's forehead scrunched. "But why?"

"Look at it from their perspective. It would be exhausting if everyone who was white kept asking you things like 'where are you from?' and 'how did you get here?' Nobody ever asks *you* that, Mr. Wilderhampsher, and you're not actually *from* Wedgeford."

"Oh."

"Now think of it from our perspective." Jeremy smiled at the boy. "The perspective of us Wedgeford outsiders. Think how inconvenient it would be if someone asked *you* where you were really from."

"But *I'm* from England."

"So am I." Jeremy let a little exasperation show. "Mr. Wilderhampsher. Use a little imagination. Where are you *really* from? Where are your parents right now? Why are you here alone? Do you have money? Should we contact the authorities? What if I told your guardian that you were here?"

"Ugh." Mr. Wilderhampsher made a face. "Ugh, ugh. You've made your point."

"I've hardly started. What if I asked why you couldn't

get along with other boys? What if I asked why you didn't want your parents to know where you were? What if I—"

"Ugh, stop, stop, be quiet!" Mr. Wilderhampsher put his hands over his ears. "You don't need to beat it into me; be quiet, stop mentioning it."

"You see? There are some benefits to being somewhere that doesn't believe in asking prying questions, after all."

Mr. Wilderhampsher nodded, and opened his mouth to ask another potentially prying question. But they were interrupted.

"Ah, it's Posh Jim!"

Jeremy scarcely had a chance to look around before someone punched his shoulder, pushing him off-balance.

"Brother!" Jeremy caught himself before he fell, turned, and jumped to his feet, grinning. "Brother, how dare you! Three years I haven't seen you, and the way you greet me is with assault?"

After Andrew, after Chloe… Kam Ming, who used his Chinese name, family name first, had been the third person Jeremy had become friends with in Wedgeford, and the first person he'd met who spoke the same Yue dialect of Cantonese as Jeremy's mother. They had got along immediately, despite the fact that Ming was a shepherd's son and Jeremy was a very wealthy boy pretending he wasn't a duke.

Jeremy had spent years wishing that Ming were his actual cousin instead of that gigantic knapsack of actual flatulence that was James.

"Ah, but I'm *good* for the assault now." Ming postured. "You should have seen the lambing last season. You could not believe the number of lambs we had. I bet I'm almost as rich as you now." He said this with a sly grin. "You could have me in your courts of law or…whatever it is you posh people do when people smack you. You could fine me, and I'd pay it with money to spare. It would be worth it to beat you when you've absconded for so long."

"That *is* a fine new coat."

"Isn't it? And you should see the one I bought my mother."

"Your honored mother is well then, I hope?"

"Very well, and very comfortable. That's what happens when you graze all your sheep for free on the fucking duke's land." Ming let out a little laugh. "A fine thank-you to the Duke Who Didn't—he can't trouble himself with us at all, and his stupidity has made such a lovely present in his very long absence."

Jeremy swallowed his unease and the memory of his conversation with Mr. Fong and nudged the man in the elbow. "Good for you. No reason you shouldn't get that duke's money." In for a penny, in for a pound. "What an absolute fool he is. Fuck the duke!"

Ming laughed long and loud. "You're always a good one, Posh Jim."

He wasn't. He so wasn't. At some point—some point extremely soon—Jeremy was going to have to tell his friends the truth, and…that was going to be intensely painful. *Don't worry,* he wanted to say, *I can promise you the duke will never expect you to pay back what you owe him. He's a fool, but not* that *big a fool.*

So he said nothing. The Duke Who Didn't—it was a more fitting appellation for him than any of them actually knew.

"So you're in on the Trials this year?"

"Ah, just showing young Mr. Wilderhampsher here the way it's done." Jeremy sighed and looked up. "Mostly I'm assisting Chloe with her booth."

"Chloe." Ming made a sympathetic noise. "She's a tough nut to crack. But you always did prefer a challenge, brother."

Jeremy bristled. "She's not a nut."

"You're not denying that she's tough, I see."

"It's a bad analogy. Nuts aren't tough. At most, they have a brittle exterior."

"Ah. My apologies then. How would *you* refer to the most intimidating Fong YiLin then?"

"Well," Jeremy said, thinking of her list, "intimidating will do for the likes of you. I'd say more, but if you talked about her the way I talk about her, I'd have to assault you too."

"Ha." Ming's smile flashed at that.

"And that would be very inconvenient, because *you'd* take *me* to the courts of law, and you'd be twice as wealthy, and I'd be poor."

Ming cackled at that. "No! We can't have that, not at all. What would we call you, if you weren't Posh Jim? You'd need some *other* title. Does anything else come to mind?"

Jeremy hid his wince. If only Ming knew. Wedgeford had already given his other self a regular handful of other nicknames. "'Posh Jim' would still do—I will still be stuck with this stuffy accent no matter what my bank says of me."

"True." Ming clapped him on the shoulders. "Very

true. And on that, I must be off. I've got some strategizing to do with Naomi. I'll see you around."

"Sure." Jeremy reached out and tapped Ming's back in farewell, then watched his friend go. There was a weight, heavy and dark, in his chest. This was the last friendly conversation they might ever have. After Ming found out how many duke jokes Jeremy had laughed at while withholding the truth… Well. Jeremy wouldn't want to be friends with himself either. Maybe if he was amusing enough when he admitted to the truth, it would all work out.

His heart clenched. *They want you to be British,* his mother had written in that long-ago letter, *but I want you to be yourself.*

He'd taken it a little too literally. It had seemed like permission to have friends and fall in love—not just with Chloe, but with all of Wedgeford, with a place that opened up to accept him without asking dangerous questions like *are you a duke?* And *shouldn't you be more stuffy?*

He'd wanted to be himself. He'd wanted to be a *different* self than his aunt had wanted. And either he was going to lose all of this… Or…

Stay. Grow.

Or he was going to be himself. Himself, but better, however that turned out.

A clearing of a throat interrupted this reverie. Mr. Wilderhampsher was watching him with an odd expression on his face. "So." He frowned. "Do you know everyone here? And do they all speak…that language?"

"It's 'Yue,'" Jeremy said. "A dialect of Cantonese. Not 'that language.' Wedgeford is a village of two hundred and thirty-ish people. And I think there are at least five separate languages with multiple dialects, including three versions of Hakka that are only slightly mutually intelligible."

Mr. Wilderhampsher sighed. "That's the difference between us. I'm no good at talking to people even in English. I just…walk up to them and by the time I've thought of something to say that *isn't* rude, they've left already."

"That sounds rough." Jeremy came to sit on the rock beside him again. "I never realized how hard it was to be surly. But I can make some introductions, if you want, and that should ease the way."

"Really? You'd actually do that?"

"No," Jeremy said, rolling his eyes. "I only made the offer to get your hopes up so I could crush them."

Mr. Wilderhampsher looked at him with such a distraught expression that Jeremy immediately gave up his teasing. He reached over and gave him a friendly cuff at the back of his head. "Don't be silly. Of course I'll do it. It doesn't cost me anything, does it?"

Mr. Wilderhampsher shrugged, but when Jeremy stood, he stayed on his rock, biting his lip.

"Can I ask…" His frown deepened. "I don't want to violate Wedgeford rules. But how did a place like this actually come to be?"

It should have been amusing. Jeremy's solicitor had stored the answer away within his dusty files. Jeremy had uncovered it and then wondered whether to tell anyone else.

Wedgeford had once been on a minor stage route. Like

most villages on such routes, the residents' life had revolved around the stage and the post. There had been a handful of stables for changing horses. A tiny church had made Wedgeford the central gathering point for the local shepherds.

Then one of the stage routes ended, killed by the railways, followed by the other. The post and stage companies took their horses and their grooms; the inn's patronage fell precipitously. The shops closed, and families who had lived here for centuries began to leave too, searching for work.

The vicar in the local church on the corner reported this all to the then Duke of Lansing. Houses went empty; that duke had stopped collecting rents. The vicar's living was evaluated, and it was decided that upon his death, it would remain empty. Wedgeford's demise had been diagnosed; the only question of interest was the precise time of passing.

Then Mr. Bei and Mr. Pang had arrived. This, Jeremy had heard from friends over ale. Mr. Bei had been in service with a merchant, but a shoulder injury prevented him from working his way home. They'd been wandering the countryside, looking for work.

Most places had taken one look at them and sent them on, citing poor laws and the potential drain on the parish.

But Wedgeford had been mostly empty. Its aging vicar had looked about, shrugged, and said that there were houses and there was land, such as it was. Mr. Bei and Mr. Pang were Hakka—a people that had been farming desolate hillsides in China for longer than the Church of England had existed.

After that, once Wedgeford had been established as a

place of refuge when someone would end up stranded in England for some reason—nursemaids brought from foreign countries and tossed out after the children went away to school, or sailors pressed into service and let out in Bristol—they'd sometimes hear of Wedgeford.

That had been all it took for Wedgeford to flourish once again: Nobody had demanded that they leave, and nobody had required that they pay rent.

Mr. Wilderhampsher frowned at him. "You don't know the answer. You don't know how it came to be."

Wedgeford rules were Wedgeford rules for a reason.

"I'm not answering because it's a silly question." Jeremy stood, brushing off his hands. "Wedgeford happened the same way every other village in England ever happened. People stayed. That's all. Now let me introduce you to the other children. You'll make friends easily enough. Just give it a chance."

———

THE SUN HAD SET BY THE TIME JEREMY REJOINED Chloe at the inn. The subtle roll of his shoulders did nothing to alleviate the ache that had set in. He could feel the aftereffects of the work he'd done with her father, from the soreness in the tips of his fingers up through the ache in his shoulders. If *he* felt like this after the afternoon's labor, he hoped Mr. Fong was faring well.

But Chloe was here too, slumped in a chair, her eyes half-shut. Her board clip was clutched in her hands; he could see the items that she'd crossed off with dark, bold lines (many) and the ones that remained to be done (still a few).

"Chloe." Naomi Kwan came to crouch beside her. "Chloe, wake up. It's not bedtime yet."

"Noooo." Chloe stifled a yawn and burrowed her head into the unforgiving wood of the chair. "I'm exhausted. Don't talk to me."

Jeremy stifled a smile. She was adorable even when she was complaining. Her nose wrinkled, and for a second, he thought about what it would be like if she were his, avowed and acknowledged by all. He could pick her up and carry her home, and she could rest her head against his shoulder instead of that hard wood. She could complain to him the entire way about her exhaustion, and he could make sweet noises the entire time. And once he brought her home...

"You can't be exhausted." Andrew Uchida had come to kneel on the other side of Chloe's chair, rudely interrupting Jeremy's domestic fantasy. "You can't be exhausted because you need to pick a name for Unnamed Sauce."

Chloe's forehead scrunched. "No."

"Have some compassion. I need to carve the stamp tonight. I'm already going to be up late as it is."

She made a pained noise. "Let's just call it Unnamed Sauce forever. There. We've agreed. We're done. Let me sleep."

Jeremy stood up. Naomi sent him a questioning look, but there was no point in him staying around; the two of them would badger her into something like wakefulness. He could either sit in place, fantasizing about things that were not happening, or he could take action and make something else happen instead. So he wandered back to the kitchens and charmed Mrs. Kwan and her sister into setting up a tray for him.

By the time he came back laden with his goods, Chloe was sitting upright, her list in front of her. "Why didn't you wake me sooner?" she was moaning. "I have so much to do. I need to paste the labels on all the jars tomorrow and make the dough. I haven't even stamped the name on the labels, and I'm going to need to do five hundred of them."

"Six hundred," Jeremy said, setting his tray down.

"Six hundred!" She straightened. "No! Ah Ba said he was only going to make a hundred more."

"I helped."

She put her head in her hands. "Ugh. Don't help him overdo it."

"If I *didn't* help, he would have done them anyway."

Chloe sighed. "You're probably right. *Probably.* But I will still blame you if his hands cramp up so badly those flashing headaches come back."

"That's fair." Jeremy took the teapot off the tray and set out a cup and saucer on the table between them.

"Chloe," said Naomi, "stop blaming Posh Jim for everything as a method of procrastination. You need a *name.* You need a name *now.*"

Chloe's nose wrinkled stubbornly. "In my defense," she muttered, "he is so very blamable."

"Yes, yes," Jeremy soothed and set a black sesame cake on the edge of the saucer. "I am."

Chloe blinked blearily and finally seemed to notice his tray. "Ooh."

He poured the tea. The tea served in Wedgeford's inn was good green tea, with the kind of delicate aroma that one rarely found in Britain—a little grassy for his taste, but good tea nonetheless. Good enough that adulterating it with milk and sugar would be a crime. Chloe's eyes followed the cup. She looked at him once, opened her mouth as if to ask if he had really obtained tea with only one cup for himself.

Then she squeezed her lips shut and sighed, looking away. "Right. A name for Unnamed Sauce. We haven't much time."

He handed her the saucer. For a moment, she blinked at it in confusion.

Jeremy mimed lifting a cup to his lips and drinking, and she followed suit. Her weariness seemed to fall away with the first sip. Unfortunately, it just turned into frustration.

"Sauce. Names." She lifted the cake. "I've been pondering this forever, and I have absolutely nothing to show for it. Argh." She took an angry bite. Jeremy tried not to focus on the dark crumbs flecking her lips; her tongue darted out, capturing them.

"It is because you are so very picky, and so very unreasonable," Naomi explained.

"Well." Another angry bite. "It is the very best sauce. It must have the very best name."

"There you are," Jeremy offered. "What about 'The Very Best Sauce'?"

Chloe's nose wrinkled. "That's not distinctive enough." The last bit of cake disappeared into her mouth.

"Very Delicious Sauce," Jeremy tried again.

"Not distinctive enough."

Naomi sighed and looked upward. "You see, Jim? We have tried every combination of words under the sun, and she has rejected every single one. There are three dozen perfectly adequate names that we have all come up with, and yet none of them are good enough."

"True," Chloe interjected, "but would *you* purchase 'Perfectly Adequate Sauce'?"

"Oh, as if *your* names are any better. The only ones you've considered for any length of time sound like 'Excessively English Sauce,' and that only because you want to sound like White and Whistler."

"Mmm." Jeremy shook his head and slid another cake onto Chloe's plate. "That's no good. Nobody wants *excessively* English sauce. Trust me. Even foods that have the regular amount of English in them are...not particularly appealing."

Andrew dropped to the floor beside them, cross-legged, and made a face. "Urgh. Mushy peas."

Naomi rolled her eyes and looked upward. "Those dreadful beans. Why? Why beans? Why overcooked when you could ferment them and make them delicious or sugar them and use them in desserts?"

"Or," Jeremy offered, "the way they just cook massive chunks of meat. Just chunks of meat. With salt. A great deal of salt. Cooked until chewy. I *hated* that at Eton."

"Bubble and squeak," said Andrew. "Rather more like bubble and spew."

Naomi shook her head. "Toad-in-the-hole."

"Now wait a minute." Jeremy frowned at her. "I draw the line right there. Toad-in-the hole is actually good."

Three faces turned to him in unison. They all frowned. Finally, Chloe shook her head. "He's wrong, but he can't help it."

"It *is* good!" Jeremy stared back at them. "You've just never had good toad-in-the-hole."

"He went to fancy schools," Chloe said in extremely sorrowful tones. "His taste is permanently marred."

Jeremy straightened. "I did not come to this inn just to have my taste abused so mercilessly."

"And yet you knew I was here." Chloe finished her tea; he gestured for her to hold out her cup and refilled it. "Your protestations strike me as highly untruthful."

Jeremy grinned. It felt almost like old times. She was finally teasing him back.

"Jeremy," Naomi said in dire tones, "are you helping Chloe procrastinate by listing terrible foods?"

"Ah." He gave a conciliatory smile. "No? Maybe? It happened on accident."

"On accident!" Naomi raised a hand as if to smack him.

"I can't help it!" He cringed from her but smiled broadly. "I went to fancy British schools! I plead guilty by reason of ingrained poor taste!"

A smile twitched across Naomi's lips but disappeared.

The second cake had also disappeared from Chloe's plate; Jeremy replaced it with a third and then topped up the tea in her cup.

"But to come back to the point. I keep coming back to 'Excessively English' or 'Very English' or 'Brutally British' or the like," Chloe said. "Mostly because I want something that makes White and Whistler know that I'm aware of what they've done. They ought to harbor the requisite amount of dread."

"Dread is good." Naomi reached over and stole a cake from the tray herself. "But surprise is also good."

Jeremy just shrugged. "I don't understand why White and Whistler are relevant."

Chloe raised her head, the last of her weariness vanquished. "I have told you the story before." Her tone brooked no argument. "More than once. You *know* why they are relevant. They stole my father's recipe and threw him out without a reference or a single shilling. This is *revenge* sauce. It must be named adequately."

"Must it?" Jeremy shrugged. "It was made for revenge, but once you put them out of business, they'll be gone. You'll be left with your name. Every single time you see the success of your sauce, you'll be reminded of how angry you once were. Do you *want* to be reminded of them long after you've prevailed?"

"Mmm." Chloe reached for another cake. "I had not thought of that. On the one hand, I do love the idea of remembering our triumph every time I hear the name. On the other hand, a name that brings to mind White and bloody Whistler is a reminder of failure, not of triumph."

"You see?" Jeremy shrugged. "You're going to have to hear the name for a very long time. You might as well name it after something you love. Something that this sauce represents."

Chloe nodded and looked off into the fire, her head tilted.

"What about 'Butterfly Sauce'?" Naomi offered. "You like butterflies."

"That sounds as if it's got butterflies in it," Andrew interjected. "I'm not really good at names, but nobody wants to eat insects."

"I meant it figuratively. But what about…cake sauce," was Naomi's next offering, as she gestured with the cake in her hand.

"Ew." Chloe made a face. "Disgusting."

"Cakes aren't disgusting," Naomi said, "and if you think my mother's are, you can give back the one you're holding in your filthy little palm."

"It's the idea of *sauce* on cake that I was rejecting, not the idea of cake in general. Stop poking me!"

There was a long pause. Andrew sighed.

"Wedgeford Brown," Chloe said. "If it's to be about something we love."

Beside her, Andrew blinked. Naomi straightened and leaned forward.

"Wedgeford Brown?" Andrew asked.

"Well." Naomi pursed her lips. "Hmm. It's not terrible."

"It tells everyone where we are, where the sauce is to be found. It says where we are from. It makes it that much less likely that the name will be absconded with; nobody could possibly think that Wedgeford Brown would be manufactured somewhere like Northampton."

"True," Naomi said slowly.

"And it's from Wedgeford," Jeremy put in. "It couldn't ferment anywhere else and still taste the same."

Chloe gave him a look. "You *have* been talking to my father. Or, rather, he's been talking to you."

"Wedgeford Brown," Naomi repeated. "I rather like it."

"The only issue," Andrew said, staring determinedly at the tea set, "is this: What if the Duke Who Didn't makes a claim? He owns more than half of Wedgeford. Might there be some kind of title associated with the village? Dukes have a tendency to get odd about things attached to their names."

Wedgeford was *not,* in fact, one of Jeremy's titles. Nobody cared about piffling little hamlets in southern England, certainly not enough to entitle someone over them. But it wasn't like he could volunteer that information, not without having to explain that he was intimately acquainted with all the lesser titles of the Duke of Lansing.

He let out a pained laugh instead. "Does it look like the duke actually cares about any of this?"

Andrew raised his head to look at Jeremy. "He might. Just because he doesn't care now… You never know. People change. In five or ten years when the sauce is famous and people are asking him about it? He might."

"That's a point," Chloe said with a deflating sigh. "Drat it."

Jeremy gritted his teeth. "No, it's *not* a point. It's a *terrible* point. Fuck the damned duke. After fifty-some years of neglect, you could use his *actual* name, and he'd have no right to object."

Andrew raised an eyebrow. "Please, Posh Jim. Enlighten us, as you are so well-versed in the subject. How *do* powerful dukes think about these things?"

Jeremy froze in horror. How was he supposed to answer that? He found his mouth drawing up into an uncomfortable smile. "Me? Know about dukes?" He let out an uncomfortable laugh. "I…went to school with one." Technically true even if he was the one.

This earned him an additional roll of the eyes. "Did you then. Tell us more."

"They're humans, just like the rest of us."

"*Unlike* the rest of us, they have better lawyers."

"This is ridiculous." Jeremy took a cake for himself. "Nobody cared about him until now; why should any of you start? Mr. Fong says the sauce tastes like it came from Wedgeford. It wouldn't be Wedgeford Brown if it came from anywhere else. I want to sleep at some point tonight, and all of us seem to think the name has merit."

"And if the duke *does* someday care?" Andrew pressed.

"Oh, for God's sake." He'd managed to trip over his own feet, and this wasn't even his fault. "If you need lawyers, I'll promise to fund them out of my own pocket. If you have to pay damages, I'll pay them myself. Satisfied?"

"Well…" Andrew seemed to consider this.

"And it won't come to that," Jeremy said, "because you could just bribe him, if it came down to that."

"With *what?*" Naomi demanded. "He's a duke. He has everything."

He most certainly did not.

"He's eaten far too much British food," Jeremy muttered. "He'd probably trade half his dukedom for two jars of sauce and a smile."

"Dukes get lots of smiles," Chloe pointed out. "He doesn't need any more of those."

Jeremy sighed and put his head in his hands. "I'm talking about one of *yours,* obviously. Those are different."

This was met with silence. It took him a beat to realize what he had said—to realize that he'd said it out loud, to Chloe's best friends in the entire world. He peeked out through his fingers. Chloe was looking at him with a light in her eyes—something hopeful and worried, all at once.

No, really, he imagined himself saying. *I really am prepared to give half my dukedom to you. But I should warn you—it's no fun.*

That would go over…extremely not well at all.

Chloe was blushing and very pointedly not looking at Naomi.

"Right," she finally said. "I'm convinced. Wedgeford Brown it is, and if the duke objects, I'll throw the jars right at his head."

"Your aim is terrible," Naomi pointed out.

"But his head is so very large," Chloe responded, and everyone but Jeremy burst out laughing at that.

10

"I CAN'T POSSIBLY GO TO SLEEP." THE PROBLEM WITH that statement, Chloe realized, was that she was teetering between half asleep and half tipsy, her face flushing even in the cold air of the night. She would be dragging herself home, barely coherent, if Jeremy were not with her, lending her his arm to lean on.

"Yes, you can," he said patiently.

She was aware that she was tired and cranky. Still, she went on. "I can't. There are still four things on my list. I can't."

At least the question of naming was behind her. Andrew had carved her nameplate after they'd decided on "Wedgeford Brown," and she'd taken the opportunity to have more cakes…and, at Naomi's suggestion, some beer. As celebration. The beer had either been a brilliant idea or a terrible one. She'd been delightfully warm after the first few sips.

"Sleep is good. You have too much to do tomorrow

and the day after to skip sleep now. Sometimes, you can't do everything."

"I am *aware*." She reached out and jabbed his side. "People keep telling me this! Why do people keep telling me this?"

"Um." There was a long pause. "Possibly because you do not behave as if you are aware."

She frowned mulishly. "Just because I *want* to do everything doesn't mean I think I can."

"Chloe." He let out a sigh, then wrapped his arm around her. "You don't have to be perfect."

She was tired, so tired. Somehow that made it easier to say the thing that had lodged in her heart all day. "Isn't that on the list?"

He just sighed and kept her moving in the direction of home. "Of course you put 'be perfect' on one of your lists, and now you're badgering yourself because you can't cross it off."

He was warm, so warm next to her. And nice. So nice. He was supporting her with a hand at her arm and another at her waist. He smelled nicely too. He smelled warm, like hay. No, not like hay. Like sunshine. Like something she would be able to identify, if she could just push this numbing mind-fog away…

"I meant your list. The list of qualities you want in a wife," she explained to him. And then, because she wanted him to know she knew his evil plan, she leaned in. "I figured it out. I figured out what you want."

"Did you?" He sounded amused. "Did you come to this brilliant insight after your second pint of beer?"

"*You* want someone who is perfect," she told him.

"Because you can *have* someone who is perfect. So if you want a list of *my* qualities...and I am not perfect...your list will be wrong. That is why I have to finish *my* list. For you."

She turned to look into his eyes. He was looking down at her with an emotion that she could not quite place.

He sighed. "Never before has someone been so wrong with so few words. You're an intelligent woman. I think you know the answer, after all."

"Pffft." Somehow they had arrived just outside her home. A lamp was still lit in the window, but nothing else. Her father had already gone to sleep, and that meant nobody was watching.

She wound her fingers around his arm and tilted her face up.

For a second, his lips hovered over hers. His face seemed to take up the entirety of her vision. How, then, was it that she could see the stars spangled across the sky behind him? An entire field of stars, the arm of the Milky Way, splashed around them.

He was close, so close. He'd kissed her once. He should kiss her more, so that she'd have more memories once he'd gone.

"Jeremy."

He pulled away. "Your father is *right* there."

"He's asleep."

"I'm still afraid of him."

"Afraid?" Chloe heard herself giggle. "But he's...soft. Like a bunny rabbit."

"Yes, sweetheart, that's because he's *your* father. I'm trying to get on his good side."

Chloe wrinkled her nose. "Incomprehensible. He only has good sides. And *you* don't need to worry about what he thinks. You're *you*."

That was precisely it. He was *him*. When did Jeremy ever have to worry about someone else's good opinion? He already *had* all the money. And the things. He had things.

"On the contrary," Jeremy said, sounding amused. "I care very much about what your father thinks of me. And he has informed me of my shortcomings in excruciating detail."

"I don't understand." She looked up at him. "You are so very likeable."

That was the worst part of his coming back, she realized. When he was gone, she could dislike him excessively, because he wasn't there. She'd forgotten how very likeable he was in person. Now he was here, and she remembered. She remembered how he told her she was lovely and how he genuflected to her list and how he brought her cakes.

She was supposed to hate it, and him, and she couldn't. Not even after three years away. What was the point of being rational if she was just going to feel absurd things anyway?

"It's not hard to understand why I care about your father, Chloe. Same reason as the list. Think on it in the morning, and it will all come clear."

"I have *things* to do in the morning. I haven't any time to think."

"I know," Jeremy said. "I'll help. But you don't need time to think. You already know the answer."

She couldn't look away from him. She was aware, vaguely, that had she not had those beers, she might have stood a little farther apart from him. Still. "The answer is…you don't want to kiss me?"

"You're drunk and you're exhausted."

"Tipsy and tired." She smiled at him. "Doesn't matter. Here's a secret: I *always* want you to kiss me." Maybe she shouldn't have said that. "I like you. I shouldn't, but I do."

He inhaled and pulled her closer to him. "Chloe."

She looked up. Somewhere, perhaps, she remembered that this was not a good idea. That he was only here for a handful of days, that he wouldn't buy her tea and cakes next week. But his fingers burned into her arms. And he was so close and so warm in the cool breeze of the night.

"If I already know the answer," she told him, "and you already know I know the answer…it seems to me you should be kissing me more, not less."

He exhaled, and she felt his breath, warm and shivery, waft over her face. She tilted her face up toward his, pushed up onto tiptoes, pressing in. He leaned down an inch, then another, until he was so close that her eyelashes shivered against his lips.

But his mouth landed on her forehead—a kiss, but a chaste one, a sweet press that made something hot boil up inside her. His thumb came up to brush the top of her ear, then slid down, down the rim, spreading little tingles of want. For a second—just a second—his fingers ran down the tassel of her earring.

Then he pulled away. "Go to sleep, Chloe." So saying, his hands left her side. The cold night air rushed into the warm imprints remaining from his fingers.

He touched a finger to his hat in a salute, dropped his head in something like a bow, and turned away.

By the time Chloe checked that her father was asleep in his bed, and retreated to the little alcove on the other side of the main room, she was exhausted. If she had been one bit less weary, she could have drifted immediately into sleep. Instead, she was tired and aching in every inch of her body. And the events of the day still cycled through her mind, holding on to her.

The sauce in the morning. Seeing Jeremy again after so long. Having him look at her, touch her. That kiss at the top of the hill. The way he'd held her hand on the way home from the inn. The way he'd said *you already know the answer.*

She didn't know anything. Even with her eyes screwed shut and her mind focused on the question, she could not figure it out. It was a puzzle, and she had no time for puzzles. She needed to let go and sleep.

Letting go took energy that she did not have.

After five minutes spent willing herself to sleep, and failing, she gave in and let her thoughts wash around her.

She'd kissed him. In the cold light of morning, it had seemed a rational thing to do. In the sunshine of the day, it had felt like a memory she could create—one she could take out when she wanted, and lock away in a steel box wrapped with chains when she didn't. The kiss would always be there, but she'd imagined it could be cordoned off from the rest of her life.

Now at night, when she needed to place that kiss in its box, she realized that it had infected everything—her mind, her heart, her skin, all the places where she could still feel the echo of his touch. She remembered the taste of his mouth against her lips, the feel of the fabric of his jacket on the tips of her fingers.

It was a good thing he'd left so often. Year after year, he'd left; year after year, she'd expected it, had smiled when he said his farewell and had tried not to imagine him returning early. He'd come when the Trials arrived, no sooner. It was a good thing she had become so practiced at watching him go, because now she knew what to expect.

This hope of him lingering, this thing she felt in her body? It was an illusion born out of longing. Men like him did not stay for women like her. And oh, she could come up with answers to that—she could tell herself that she was important, that she was clever, that she had any number of sterling qualities. She was, after all, making a list to that effect.

None of those things would outweigh the fact that she was some Hakka girl from a village. Her class alone would horrify anyone in his orbit; if they excused her race, they'd decry her manners, her speech, even the earrings she'd received from her mother.

Hoping for more was a fantasy. Jeremy was kind and clever and sweet in so many ways, but if she let him have more than a kiss, he'd take it, and still he'd leave.

So when she finally gave in to the memory of his touch, she made sure not to imagine too much. There would be no sunlit proposals for her, no protestations of an undying love that would last their entire lives. It would happen, if it happened, in secret. If she were just a little stupider—or perhaps, to be honest, a little less busy—they might arrange a tryst.

She was not so poorly trained as to arrange that tryst in her own home in reality, with her father present. But she *was* apparently naive enough to let herself think of it. To imagine that she could hear the soft pads of his footfalls as he tiptoed in the dark to where she lay.

They wouldn't be able to speak under the circumstances, and so she didn't have to fool herself by coming up with protestations of love on his part. He'd make himself comfortable on her narrow bed—well, technically, there was no room for him—but all the more reason for him to lie on top of her.

In the dark of the night, she could imagine the weight of him. The touch of his lips against hers, again and again, the kisses he hadn't given her at their last parting. She often felt as if she were coiled into a tightly wound spring, holding on to inconvenient and shameful urges that she dared not let loose. She could imagine what would happen if she let go of all that control.

That was the problem with giving in to one kiss. She had wants, wants that were not susceptible to the regulation of lists no matter how hard she tried, wants with nowhere to go, no outlet but the press of her fingers against her inner thighs and the free rein of her fancy.

Images came to her in increasingly heated patches—the flash of his smile, the feel of his tongue, rough against her lips. The imagined heaviness of him, bearing down into her, pushing, pushing.

It took a few moments to hike up the fabric of her night dress, to press her fingers between her legs. To imagine what he would feel like *there,* as he slid inside her.

In her imagination, he was silent; that was how she

knew it for a lie. In reality, he would never stop talking. He would whisper things to her, things that would make her blush. He would tell her she was good and sweet; he would tease her about the wants she could not conceal. He would say everything to her, everything except the things she most wanted to hear.

I will never leave.

You will never doubt me.

Her heart felt almost ragged, at odds with the desire racing through her body. She came quietly, her feelings swallowed up in the pure electric race of pleasure in her veins. For a moment, everything she wanted seemed close, kissing close.

Then she returned to the heave of her breath and the rational function of her mind. The silence of the night loomed around her like a reprimand. It was dark; the hand between her legs was sticky. She'd been ridiculous, but—thank God—she'd been ridiculous alone. She got up, poured water into a basin, and washed as best as she could while her breath slowed to its normal rhythm.

If it were only the kiss. If it were only his smile that set her stomach aflutter. If it were only those few things…

Chloe had always been an awkward child, and moving about from place to place interminably for the first years of her life hadn't helped. On the outside, she was determined—cold, people sometimes said. It had always felt strange to be judged so when she knew she was so hot inside.

But it had always been that way. She warmed to others slowly, and the barriers that race and language had created when she was a young child had only heightened the effects of her natural shyness. She'd been self-conscious of her speech for years.

Then she and her father had come to Wedgeford, where nobody teased her for the way she spoke—just for the spectacles she needed to read, for the way she dithered and stepped back to think before she acted. (*Responsible*, the adults had called her, as if her reticence somehow meant that she could handle heavier burdens.)

She'd always wanted to play with the other children, but she hadn't known how, and while she'd made a few tenuous friendships and been put in charge of younger children by parents eager for the help, she often found herself watching at the edges of a group of her age-mates, envious, yet not knowing how to break in.

Her first lists had been born out of watching those groups, watching how the other children asked to play. She'd made herself little guides so she could join the fun.

1. Ask if I might be allowed.

2. Smile. People like that.

3. Remember to laugh occasionally.

4. Answer questions when asked instead of jumping like a frightened cat.

No matter how often or how carefully she made the lists, it always took her a little too long to remember what she was supposed to do. By the time she brought the specific item to mind, the awkwardness had already set in. Never laughing was bad, but laughing five seconds too late was worse. Chloe had almost given up. She *had* friends—Naomi, for one, who she'd looked after so often she felt almost like a sister.

Then Jeremy had arrived. He'd joined in a game with a

merry wave, and she'd felt a flush of jealousy that an outsider—a complete outsider!—could take part without even thinking.

But the first time he'd done it, he'd turned to look at her where she stood a few paces away on the green when everyone else had been on the verge of scrambling off to hide.

"Wait," he'd said. "Chloe wants to play."

Kam Ming had scoffed. "Chloe? No, she never does."

All their eyes had been on her. She knew she should say something—anything—but words had been hard. She'd fumbled, trying to remember one of her lists. But none of them had been written for this precise situation.

"Chloe?"

Chloe had looked at Jeremy, tongue-tied and furious with herself. And maybe he'd seen something nobody else had, because he winked at her.

"Just nod, if you want in," he had said.

It had been that simple. She had given him a nod.

And he'd smiled as if she'd handed him the world. "You see?" he'd told the others. "She can't resist me."

That had been it for her: the moment at which return had not been possible. It hadn't been love. It had just been the knowledge that he'd seen her and done her a kindness.

"You're the *worst*," she had told him. She had meant that he was the best.

He had laughed, maybe misunderstanding. "I am," he'd said, taking off his cap and bowing at her in the English manner. "The absolute worst, at your service."

Over the years, her painful shyness had given way to

something more like confidence. She no longer needed to make lists to know how to talk to others.

But one thing hadn't changed. Jeremy's smile had lodged itself deep inside her, so deep she did not think she would ever get it out. She did not think she would ever *not* respond to him, body and soul, when he looked at her the way he did. It seemed as natural as breathing.

And he had never stayed. He could not; he would not. She couldn't even make herself blame him for it.

She sighed, set down the cloth she'd washed her hands with, and went back to bed. She wasn't going to stop thinking of him. If she hadn't figured out how to eradicate the memory of him over the course of the many years of their acquaintance, she wasn't going to figure it out now.

She couldn't save herself from being hurt; all she could do was hope the knife wouldn't sink too deeply. She just had to make sure that she kept most of the heat of her feelings to herself, to examine only at night, only when it wasn't real.

11

WHEN JEREMY ARRIVED THE NEXT MORNING, CHLOE was all business. She was, in point of fact, too much business, bustling about with an air of frenetic energy that made him think she was purposefully attempting to rebuild the wall between them. She directed him to leave his shoes near the door, then took him into a side room, where a table stood, one side liberally festooned with flour.

"Here," she said, gesturing. "You're just in time to knead the dough."

He approached. "I don't know how to knead dough."

"It's not hard. I'll show you." She motioned him to come stand by her; he did, and his hopes of being shown with her hands on his died as she moved two feet away, not even subtle about her desire to put distance between them.

Today the silk tassels of her earrings were green, swaying against her cheeks with every move of her shoulders as she manhandled the dough. Jeremy's mother also wore earrings, but hers were jade drops or wrought gold flowers or the like. He'd asked Chloe about her tassels once, and she'd said only that they were from her mother.

He'd liked them ever since the first time he'd seen them, drawing his eye with the subtle flick of their movement.

She *must* remember their conversation last night. He hadn't been able to judge her sobriety, but apparently, she'd been tipsy enough that she now regretted what she'd said. Apparently, *I like you* had been too much to admit; now she wanted to pretend she'd never said it and it wasn't true.

"Like this," she said, earrings swishing. "This motion, see? Over and over. Keep at it until the dough feels like your ear lobe. This is the third batch."

He reached up and touched his ear tentatively.

"Wash your hands," she told him sharply. He did. When he returned from the basin, she went to wash her own hands, and then retreated to the other side of the table, setting out a row of small, printed squares of paper. Andrew had given her the finished stamp last night before she left the inn; she proceeded to dab the wood in dark blue ink and press it against the first paper.

These must be the labels for the jars. He could see a sunrise between two hills, and the words WEDGEFORD BROWN in all capital letters beneath some smaller type, illegible at this distance.

"What are you waiting for?" she asked, and proceeded to line up five of the labels. STAMP STAMP STAMP STAMP STAMP.

"Nothing." The amount of dough was truly staggering —a lump larger and heavier than the Widgelot they'd hidden yesterday. He gave it a tentative shove with the heel of his hand. "Just a little sore from filling jars with your father yesterday. Don't worry about me."

"Soft," she said in a scornful tone of voice, and he didn't think that this *soft* was meant the way she'd spoken about her father last night. *Soft like a bunny rabbit.* Ha. For him, she probably meant *soft like a worm.*

"I'm just unused to this particular activity." Jeremy gritted his teeth. "Don't worry. I'll become accustomed."

"After you've kneaded the dough, you'll be even more sore tomorrow. Not that it matters to me how you feel."

STAMP STAMP STAMP STAMP STAMP. Another set of labels finished.

It took him a few minutes to get into the rhythm of the work, to feel the squish of the dough as he pressed his palms in a rolling, pushing motion.

STAMP STAMP STAMP STAMP STAMP came from the other side of the table, an angry counterpoint to the gentler action of his kneading.

After a few minutes, Jeremy spoke. "This is actually rather satisfying, come to think of it."

"Then we aren't doing enough," Chloe snapped. "While we're working, you should tell me what intellectual capabilities you are looking for in a wife. We have too much to do to dillydally on your list."

STAMP STAMP STAMP STAMP STAMP.

Jeremy waited until she was finished with the row of labels before her, until she was gently testing to see if the ink on the first row had dried, before he answered.

"I want someone clever. I'd like her to be stubborn." The corner of his lip turned up. "I'd prefer if she was grumpy when tired. Tired and…slightly hungover?" He flashed a grin in her direction. "On two glasses of beer? You truly *are* efficient."

Chloe let out a long sigh and straightened, one stained hand going unconsciously to the small of her back. Then she realized her fingers were dark with ink and hastily pulled them away. "Please don't speak of last night."

"Why not?" Jeremy focused on the dough in front of him, grinning. "You were cute. You reminded me of a kitten."

She lined up another row of labels and slammed her stamp down. "I am *not* cute," she said between stamps, glaring at him. "I am *mean* and *harsh* and you will *respect* that."

"Yes. Absolutely. Anything you say." He winked at her.

She looked down swiftly. If anything, the sounds came even louder: STAMP STAMP STAMP STAMP STAMP.

He let her frown at her papers. The fact that she was frowning meant she was thinking. And the fact that she was thinking… Well, she was very clever. She'd figure it out. She'd figure it out at any moment.

After more minutes of working in silence, the dough had begun to take on a silken resistance to his touch. "Is this done yet?"

She washed her hands—the ink stains did not quite come out, but they faded to a lighter blue—and rubbed the dough between her fingers. "Five minutes more."

"Right." He went back to kneading.

Despite the soreness in his arms, his shoulders, he felt a sense of accomplishment. The dough had transformed from something pasty and insubstantial into a thing that would be bread with the addition of time.

"I think," Chloe said, after yet another round of angry stamping, "you are doing this on purpose."

"I'm doing *what* on purpose now?"

"You're making me think that you're making a list about *me*. It's not about who your aunt will find."

"Clever girl," Jeremy said. "It *is* on purpose, and I'm doing that for a reason. Now guess the reason."

"It's *not* me, though. You don't mean me."

Jeremy took his hands off the dough and gave her his best unimpressed look.

She simply met his eyes and shook her head. "It doesn't make any sense for it to be me. Why would it be me?"

"You make *perfect* sense to me."

"You're done," Chloe said abruptly. "Don't overwork the dough. Put it back in the basin, cover it with the cloth, and put it in the cellar."

"Why the cellar?"

"It's cooler there. We need the dough to rise, but slowly—*very* slowly. It needs to not be overproofed tomorrow morning when we use it for the buns."

He wasn't sure what it meant for dough to be overproofed, but he would take her word for it. At least going away would give her time to think.

But she didn't watch him as he folded a blue-checked cloth over the dough. She kept stamping away. He could hear her stamps as he came out of the side room where they'd been working into the main room where the cellar door stood.

Her father was there, mixing a giant tub of what must be filling for the dumplings. Jeremy felt his shoulders freeze. The man didn't look up even though he must have heard Jeremy come in. He kept working, stopping to taste the mix before shaking his head and adding in a handful of something else.

"Good morning, Uncle," Jeremy essayed.

"Is it." It wasn't a question. Mr. Fong still did not look up.

Soft. Like a *bunny rabbit.* Ha. Maybe like a feral rabbit wearing battle armor while manning a cannon.

"It's a busy morning, that's for sure. I'm just going to…um, put this dough. In the cellar."

Stamp stamp stamp stamp stamp. The sounds of Chloe stamping out labels were a little muted in here.

Mr. Fong made no answer, and Jeremy slunk past him with his massive basin of dough.

On his way back, he tried again. "Have a nice day, Uncle."

Not a hint of an acknowledgment.

With a sigh, he left. When he returned to Chloe, she had set down the stamp and was rolling her shoulders.

"You're sore too," Jeremy stated.

"Nonsense." But she flexed her fingers, then her wrists.

"What would you do if your father's hands were sore?" he asked.

"I'd massage his hands, and—wait!"

She stared up at him as he stepped in front of her and took her hands in his.

"Just for a moment," Jeremy said. "You'll be able to do so much more if we work the little knots out."

That was it. Talk of work. Her hands were stiff in his for a minute, and then relaxed as he worked them gently in his own, rubbing them knuckle by knuckle, flexing each finger. He was close enough that he could breathe her air. The room smelled like sweet yeasted dough and India ink, an odd mixture of scents. He turned her hand palm up and dug his thumbs into the meat of her hand, and she made a little noise of pleasure.

"I can't let myself think it's me, Jeremy," she said as he pressed his fingers into the joint of her thumb. "Don't be cruel."

"Chloe, sweetheart. I never want to be cruel to you."

"I let myself think it could be me years ago, and you disappeared. It made me…" She inhaled loudly. "Please don't hurt me like that again."

He looked up from her hand into her eyes. They were dark and begging, and it hit him again how much those years had harmed her.

"I'm so sorry," he said. "I left because I was *trying* to be serious for you."

She gave him a questioning look.

"I'll tell you about it sometime soon. I wanted to come back and tell you how serious I'd been. I didn't become more serious, but I came back anyway because I missed you."

Her lips parted. She looked at him, her eyebrows furrowing in question.

"You—"

The door opened behind them. Chloe gasped, yanked her hand from his, then turned to face the door.

"Ah Ba!" She pasted a weak smile on her face.

Mr. Fong smiled at her, and yet somehow simultaneously gave Jeremy the fiercest look possible over her shoulder.

"It is breakfast time," he announced. "It is no longer time to hold hands."

"Ah Ba! We weren't holding hands. He was just... helping me with my hands being sore."

It was not even slightly convincing. Jeremy felt himself blush.

"Oh," Mr. Fong said. "I see. Posh Jim, what a self-sacrificing, noble, and convenient reason to hold my daughter's hands."

That, Jeremy thought, *and the fact that I'm trying to marry her.*

Mr. Fong passed his daughter a bowl and a spoon. "Do you know what will also help with your hands being sore? Eating."

"I don't think that's how it works."

"Here," Mr. Fong said, handing a bowl to Jeremy as well.

"There was no need to trouble yourself..." Jeremy started to say, before he took a look in the bowl. Chloe's bowl contained the beautiful yellow of a millet jook, speckled with little additions—scallions, bits of fermented tofu.

His was bright red.

Chloe saw it the same time he did. "Ah Ba! What are you *doing* to him?"

"There *was* a need to trouble myself," Mr. Fong said. He wasn't smiling, but there was a satisfied tilt to his chin that made Jeremy think he was being laughed at. "There was *definitely* a need to trouble myself."

"Jeremy, you don't have to eat that."

Mr. Fong held his eyes. There was an intensity to his stare, as if he were daring him to back down. And Jeremy hadn't told Chloe the truth yet.

"Of course I do," Jeremy said with a smile. "Of *course* I have to eat it." How bad could it be? He lifted the spoon, took the first bite, and suffered.

———

IT TOOK ANOTHER TWO AND A HALF HOURS FOR Chloe to finish stamping out labels and cards. There was only the one stamp; Chloe monopolized it, mostly because she wanted to have an excuse to not have Jeremy too close by.

Instead, she set him to pasting labels on jars. The first few he'd managed had been crooked, with paste glopping out under the edges, but he'd taken to the task with a surprising dedication.

It made no sense. The business was not his own; it belonged to the father of a woman he'd seen only once a year…and lately, not even that.

Chloe didn't want to think about his dedication to her tasks at the moment. She didn't want to think about what he'd told her. It wasn't that she *wanted* to avoid whatever the truth was. It was simply that she didn't have any time. If she stopped to piece together what he meant, it all turned into a jumble. If he wanted *her*—

No. There it was. Confusion in her heart instead of the

certainty she needed to finish her tasks for the day. And there were so many tasks. Instead, she gathered up the jars as Jeremy finished applying the last of the labels, sorting them back into wooden crates for transportation.

In the kitchen, she could hear her father's knife working. He wasn't as fast with it as he'd once been, but she could imagine his work nonetheless—quick, precise cuts, slashing the most stubborn of vegetables into identical shapes. If the progress she'd glimpsed during the morning continued to hold true, the filling should be done by now, so he was working on…

Lunch, probably. He took the business of feeding her very seriously.

So far, his hands hadn't stiffened up from his efforts yesterday. That was the important point. It had been a foolish risk to fill all those jars, but he'd taken the risk on his own stubborn initiative, and it had worked out. She let out a covert sigh of relief.

It *had* worked out. She had too much to do today and tomorrow, but her father's dream felt closer than it had ever been before. She had jars of sauce—hundreds of jars with names and labels—and if people bought them and liked them, she would have a business, and if they continued to like them very well, she would have her revenge.

"There," Jeremy said, pasting one final label in place. "That's done."

She looked over at him. His tie was loose and his jacket was unbuttoned. The snow-white cuffs that peeked out beneath brown sleeves had little bits of drying paste on them. There was another smear of paste across his cheek, as if he'd swiped messy hands unknowingly across his face. She wanted to get a cloth and wipe it away. To tell him to hold still as she swept the fabric over his cheek.

She glanced at her own hands, fingertips stained an uneven blue. She was probably as messy as he. She couldn't touch him; he would get ideas if she did. And Jeremy tended to act on his ideas. So if *her* thoughts went from fabric to fingers, *his* would...

Chloe took a deep breath, shaking her head, and crossed to the basin. Scrubbing didn't get the ink from her fingers. It would certainly not remove the bits of dark ink that had stained the brown cuffs of her gown. She pulled away from the water, holding dripping hands up, and caught the wavering reflection of her face on the surface. Sure enough, there was a smear of ink right on her nose.

She managed to scrub that one off. When she looked up, Jeremy was right behind her.

"Go ahead." She nodded at the basin. "There's more water in the pail."

He probably thought washing his hands with cold water from a pail was quaint and burdensome. She didn't know how people like him lived. She couldn't even imagine it. He likely had servants to fetch his water. He might even have water pipes; she'd read about those in a newspaper.

He had just set aside a towel when the door to the kitchen opened.

Her father came through, holding bowls of rice—one in the crook of each arm, and a third in one hand. He looked around briefly, saw the jars in their crates, and gave an approving nod.

"Here," he said, putting the dishes down. "Lunch."

The work had left Chloe starving. She could smell whatever he had made wafting through from the kitchen —something with pork and ginger and garlic.

He disappeared for another moment and returned with serving dishes. He set these down, and made a motion with his hands. "Eat."

She picked up the best-looking triangle of nyong tofu with her chopsticks, one where the creamy tofu was stuffed to overflowing with minced pork and fish and green onions, and set it in her father's bowl. Then, she reached for another one.

"Something's wrong," Jeremy said, frowning at her father. "You didn't spice my portion."

Her father looked down at his bowl, picked up his chopsticks, and... Chloe felt the bottom drop out of her stomach. His hand had the slightest tremor to it. And now that she was looking, the mince of the pork was slightly uneven—just *slightly,* but...

"Nothing is wrong," Ah Ba said calmly.

"Ah Ba." Chloe pulled back from the table. "Your hands are cramping again."

"Nothing is wrong," he repeated stubbornly. "Every-thing is exactly as I expected."

"You have to take care of yourself."

He made a dismissive noise. "It's no problem. I'll be fine for rolling the dough tomorrow. I just need to rest a little later."

"Is there anything we can do to help?" Jeremy asked.

"He won't be fine," Chloe said mutinously. "He *won't*

be fine. That's not how it works. If you're cramping today, it could be worse tomorrow."

"I can push through."

Chloe's appetite had vanished. She set her chopsticks on the table. "That's not what this is supposed to be about. I promised I wouldn't leave you to stand alone. Am I supposed to just ignore your pain?"

Her father shrugged. "I do."

She took in a deep breath. "You're supposed to rest. Have you taken your herbal formula yet today? I'll make it."

"I am out of herbal formula," her father said, almost conversationally, as if this were a minor matter.

She stared at him. "What do you mean, we're out of it? Madame Lee told you to take the formula every morning, and if your hands started stiffening, in the afternoon too. I asked two weeks ago when you were going to London how much you had left, and you said—"

"I said I had enough." He met her eyes. "And I do. We needed to use the money to print labels. Under the circumstances, I had enough formula."

Chloe felt a rebellious anger surge through her. She gritted her teeth, trying to push it away, but it caught her up. "Ah Ba. Zero is not enough."

He shrugged carelessly. "There's nothing to be done now. I have no formula, and there is no time to go to London and obtain more."

He said that as if he were picking off one of her discarded tiles to make a winning meld—with an unerring sense of confidence that the game was over, and that he'd triumphed.

"No." She glared at him. "You shouldn't ignore what you need. I won't have it." She'd made a list for the day... Well, she'd have to rearrange everything again. Literally everything, because she refused to accept this. "That's it then. I'm going to London this afternoon. I'm getting you the formula."

He simply looked at her, then at Jeremy. Then he shifted into Hakka. "With what money?"

"You have reserves. I know you do."

He shook his head. "Not that I'm willing to risk on this. And not enough. What if everything goes wrong with Unnamed Sauce? What will we do next winter?"

"It won't go wrong."

"It won't go wrong if you run off to London, with the Trials tomorrow?" He raised an eyebrow at her. "Listen to what you're saying. There is no choice. There is too much to be done, and I will not risk our savings on anything so frivolous. I promised your mother you wouldn't starve."

"Well." She gathered herself up. "So what? *I* promised my mother you wouldn't have to stand alone any longer."

"I promised first." He sighed.

She balled her fist on the table. He knew she was at a disadvantage in Hakka; she hadn't the fluency needed to make the arguments that popped into her head. She touched the bracelet at her wrist for comfort, and then more tightly for courage.

"If money is the issue," she told him, "I'll sell my bracelet."

Something flared in his eyes at that, something hot and angry. "You mustn't." He looked almost alarmed. "That bracelet is from your Ba. I can always rest; you cannot get that back. You have enough to do, Ah Lin. Worrying about me is not on your list; you must stop doing it. This is the end of the conversation." He nodded as if that settled everything and picked up his chopsticks.

"It isn't. I'm your *daughter*. I should—"

His eyes glittered for a moment. "The only thing you should do is *stop worrying*."

"But I—"

"I promised your mother you would live up to your name." He stared at her over his chopsticks. "Now stop this nonsense and do what she wanted for you, YiLin."

She stared at him a moment in pained silence. Her head was ringing, echoing with the sound of her own name. YiLin… What sound did feathers make? No sound. It was as good as telling her to shut up.

With that came a sudden clarity. He'd been resistant to her helping with the sauce at first, always telling her to do other things instead. But it had meant so much to him, and so it had meant much to her. After a few months of work and research and making lists, she'd begun to love the idea for herself—the challenge of the thing, the strategy, the hope.

She hadn't realized what it had meant to love what she was doing. She'd worn him down—the opposite of what he'd wanted. He'd resented her help after all.

She should have realized. She'd seen his moments of uncertainty. She had thought it was just his perfectionism, his incessant drive to do his best. She hadn't realized he was uncertain about *her,* that she had fallen so far short of his standards.

Chloe hadn't been born in China. She didn't

remember her mother. Her Hakka would never be as fluent as her English; there would always be a gulf between the two of them.

No matter what she did, she would never live up to her name, never allow him to keep the promise he'd made. She felt fragile and strangely shattered. The sound of feathers was silence, and—for now, for once—that was all she could manage.

Beside her, Jeremy watched, his eyes wide in confusion. Chloe didn't know if he had followed the conversation at all. He knew a little Hakka—enough to greet her father, to say yes and no. She didn't think he understood what her father had just said, and she wasn't sure she wanted him to know.

"Ah Ba."

Her father looked away from her dismissively. "Stop worrying about me."

She knew he loved her. That made his dismissal all the more painful. His obligatory familial love didn't feel enough, not when she wanted to give so much in return. She'd put everything into his sauce, to prove that maybe feathers could make noise.

It hadn't been enough. No amount of list making could fix what was never going to happen.

She felt her eyes sting, but she wasn't going to cry. Not here; not in front of Jeremy.

"This conversation is over," her father said. He looked at her plate—at the untouched rice and tofu—and shook his head. "You're not eating enough. You have a long day ahead of you. Finish your food."

12

CHLOE COULDN'T BRING HERSELF TO SPEAK THROUGH the end of the meal, couldn't bring herself to do more than give curt instructions to Jeremy afterward. He loaded up the wooden crates of jars that she still needed to bring to the inn. It wasn't until the crates were all put into the handcart, and Jeremy had taken up the shafts and set a reasonable pace toward the village center, that she finally managed to arrange her emotions to the point where she could speak of them.

"My apologies that you had to see that," she said as brightly as she could manage. "It was just a minor disagreement. He doesn't like accepting help."

He glanced over at her, one eyebrow raised. "The two of you seem to have that in common."

Chloe frowned. She wasn't like *that*. Surely not?

"In any event," she continued, brushing this off in a tone so cheerful it felt as fake as garishly dyed fabric, "he reproved me for wanting to drop everything and obtain his herbal formula, that's all. Surely nothing to talk about any longer. Look at all these jars. Isn't this nice?"

Jeremy's gaze slid to her, his expression taking on an unsettling combination of pity and knowledge.

"He said some things," she said breezily, "but he didn't mean them."

"Does he often say things he doesn't mean when you argue?"

No. That was the worst of it. He never did.

Stop this nonsense and live up to your name. It hurt as much in her memory as it had on delivery. More, now that the sheer shock of the moment had passed.

"Well, no matter! The jars are filled and labeled, the dough is made and proofing, the pork for the filling is cooked. We're well on our way to finishing. What is there to be unhappy about?"

"I don't know," Jeremy said in a warm, patient voice. "Maybe you could tell me what there is to be sad about?" He said it so calmly that it slipped under the thick shell shielding her emotions and lodged in the tender ache in her soul.

Chloe let out an involuntary gasp and inhaled swiftly, trying to hold the tears at bay.

"What is it?" he asked.

"Nothing."

"Nothing?" He just looked over at her. Of course he looked at her with disbelief writ across his features. He'd been there. He'd seen it all even if he hadn't spoken the language.

"Nothing," she repeated, "except—except—" And then it burst out. "This isn't how I wanted these days to go." Her eyes stung; she pulled a handkerchief from her pocket and swiped all evidence of her feelings away.

The sun was annoyingly brilliant overhead; the weather seemed determined to hit the pinnacle of perfection, just to make it clear how far Chloe had fallen short.

"No?" He tilted his head. "How did you want it?"

All her dreams. All her lists leading up to this moment. All her imagination, thrown full tilt at this problem, all her work. It was worth nothing if her father thought she was failing him.

"I wanted him to be able to celebrate. I wanted us to be together. I wanted us to make bao while the Trials went on. I wanted him to be happy."

Jeremy nodded as if this was all reasonable. "I can fold dumplings," he offered. "Are your bao that different?"

She glanced over at him, wrinkling her nose in disbelief. "*You* can fold dumplings. I thought we had this conversation about you and manual labor."

"No, I really can. When I went back to my grandmother's house in Guangzhou last year, she and my mother and I would sit and fold dumplings and talk. I really could."

There was so much in those few sentences—he rarely talked of his family, let alone his family in China.

"Oh." She swallowed. "Well. These…are not exactly dumplings. And…"

"And that doesn't answer for any of the other problems," he said. "So go on."

"Well." She took in a deep breath. "Nothing is perfect, I suppose." She had wanted the day they introduced their sauce to the world to be perfection—all sweet victory.

She'd have to accept bittersweet instead. Maybe more bitter than sweet. "That's that." She bit back tears.

"Chloe?"

She wouldn't look at him. She couldn't. If he saw her crying…

"Chloe, sweetheart. This is a matter between you and your father; I don't want to get between you unwanted. But it sounds like you need…" He trailed off.

She needed to be a different person; that was what she needed. She fixed her gaze forward, willing herself not to cry. She couldn't speak any longer, not and maintain her composure.

"Chloe," he said, "nod if you want me to help."

She inhaled. That offer was so like that first year he was here that it sank deep into her before she could stop it. She could feel tears forming in her eyes. She knew she should say no. She knew she should put him off. But she didn't.

Instead, without looking at him, she gave one short, sharp nod.

"There we are," Jeremy said, as if that settled everything. "I suppose we have to get more of the herbal formula. I didn't catch most of what you said, but you get it from London? Do they sell it at the Chinese mercantile exchange near the docks?"

"No." Chloe exhaled. "Madame Lee has her pharmacy near there, though. But Ah Ba is right. It'll be ten miles to Dover on foot over the hills, although that's faster than taking the stage road that goes the long way around. From there, if we're lucky with the timing of the trains, it's an hour and a half to London. Then an hour to the shop and another hour back to the station, and then the return journey…" She swallowed and shook her head. "It can't be done. We will miss the last train."

Jeremy glanced at the sun in the sky and rearranged the cart shafts before continuing on. "We need to deliver these jars," Jeremy said. "That *can* be done within the hour. What else must we do?"

"We need to set up the booth and decorate it for tomorrow. We need to move the mobile cooking range from the barn and reconstruct it on the green so we can steam the buns."

Jeremy looked at her. "None of that sounds particularly difficult, just laborious. What if we hired someone?"

She made a noise. "Who? Everyone is busy for the Trials; you know that."

"Someone from Dover, I'd imagine. It shouldn't be hard to find someone, if we paid them enough. With me and one or two others working, we could handle all that early tomorrow morning."

Chloe made a scalded noise. "I can't afford that! All of this is pointless. I can't afford the herbal formula unless I sell my bracelet, and he'll never speak to me again if I do. I can't afford the journey to London. I can't afford to miss any time at all. If I could throw money around the way you can, maybe this would all be different."

He just looked at her. "There's a telegraph station in the Wedgeford post office."

She frowned at him. "Yes?"

"Let us suppose," Jeremy said, a faint blush spreading across his nose, "that I telegraph ahead to my, um, employees in London. They can bring it here—oh, um."

He frowned. "No; I wouldn't want to trust that they could find Wedgeford so easily. I'll go to Dover; my horse is here, after all, so the ten miles won't be much. I can meet my...person at the station. We can hire someone to help you. And you can sit and not worry about whatever else it is you have to do. You've done enough."

She scoffed. "I can't let you do all that."

"Can't you?" He looked over at her. "Can you truly not? Knowing what it is like to see your father not allow you to help, will you make me feel the same way?"

"That's different," she snapped. "I love my father."

"Chloe." There was a hint of reproach in his voice.

Chloe looked away. "All of this is irrelevant for another reason." She inhaled. "I don't have any money. I couldn't purchase what I need or pay someone to help."

"You could," he said bullishly. "With my money. You could easily do so."

Oh. That was right. He'd offered her the ungodly sum of ten pounds. "I suppose." She frowned dubiously. "I hate to ask for any sum in advance, but there is what you will owe me once I finish your list." Her frown deepened.

He sighed. "The list is finished, Chloe."

"It's not. It's not very thorough."

"I'm going to telegraph my aunt when I'm in Dover." He looked up. "The list is finished. I know what it is going to say. Besides, the money I'll give you for the list is *your* money. I said *my* money."

"I couldn't possibly accept that degree of help."

He tilted his head. When he spoke, his words were mild—too mild. "Well. You wanted my help..." He sighed. "Tell me, Chloe, how is this going to work? I'm not much for planning, but I do have some…questions." He enunciated that word, as if it were not actually questions he had. "How exactly are you going to build a sauce empire all by yourself? You're already exhausted and overworked, just preparing for one day with some hundreds of jars that fit in a single hand-cart. Is that your plan? To be exhausted for the remainder of your life?"

She blinked at him. "No. My Ba will…" She trailed off.

"You learned it from him," Jeremy replied. "The two of you are equal in this regard."

She fell silent. She couldn't accept his help. She had any number of reasons. She didn't want to be beholden to him. She didn't want him to think she was unable to care for herself. She didn't want to admit that she needed help. All of these seemed horribly flimsy.

"Is that what you think of me?" she finally said in a small voice. "That I need help?"

"*Everyone* needs help from time to time, Chloe. *Especially* women who want revenge through sauce empires. Even I'm aware you're not perfect." There was a hint of amusement in his voice when he said it. "I've been your friend long enough to know your worst flaws. You're good at planning, so you keep doing it. You're good at executing, so everyone just lets you go on. You don't put 'take a breath' on your list because you don't think it's necessary. Do you think your father is the only one who refuses to take his own needs seriously?"

"There isn't time for me to take a breath."

He looked over at her. "You're the genius list maker," he said. "And maybe this is foolish on my part, but do you think your father would ever give himself what he needs when he knows you won't either? He loves you; he would never."

She swallowed, her tears coming up. "He..." She knew her father loved her, but the thing he'd said—it had left her feeling so unworthy. "He... That's what you think?"

"He loves you," Jeremy said. "Take it from someone who has been eating very spicy food for the last twenty-four hours. So what if you told him that you needed to come to Dover with me?"

She stared at him. "I don't have time. Did you hear nothing I said?"

"I heard it all. My mare's strong enough to take two a mere ten-mile journey. Come with me. Have a few hours in the sunshine. We'll stop at an inn and take a little refreshment while we wait for the train to arrive. And we'll hire someone to handle everything else on your list, first thing tomorrow morning."

She turned to him. "Why are you doing this?"

"You said you wanted someone who will stay," Jeremy said. "I haven't been here for you for three years. If I had been, you wouldn't be worrying about a matter that I surmise comes to maybe three pounds. Maybe this is all my fault in the first place because I should have been here and I wasn't."

"That doesn't make any sense," Chloe said. It did make sense; the problem was the implication behind it.

"It makes perfect sense," Jeremy said. "You asked me to be serious. You don't *seriously* think I would let someone I care about struggle when I could fix the problem, do you?"

"Why?" Chloe asked again. "Why are you doing this?"

"The question has never been who my list is about," Jeremy told her. "It's been about whether she'll have me."

She had felt on the verge of tears the entire walk; they threatened to spill out at this.

"Look your list over," Jeremy said. "The woman I want is intimidating, determined, intelligent, ambitious… Why would that woman have *me?* Just because I'm rich? Just because I'm powerful? She wouldn't. She *didn't.* I've been grappling with a lot." He looked away. "There's much I still need to tell you. There's much I'm not proud of in my own conduct. But I'm *trying*, Chloe. I want to stay. I want to grow. I want to be who you need, and if that means helping knead dough, I'll do that. If I judge that you need someone who will put together a booth so you can take care of yourself and your father, I'll find you that person. Right now, I judge that you need someone who will help you put down burdens, not take on more of them."

"But…"

"When your father hurts, you hurt, yes?"

She nodded.

"When you hurt," he said, "it's not your hurt alone either. It hurts me too. I can help, if you'll let me."

If she let him help this once… She could be hurt. She could be hurt very, very badly. She was used to thinking that. The thought that *he* could be hurt if she *didn't* let him help seemed odd and impossible.

"Ah Ba said no." It was her final, desperate plea.

Jeremy just looked at her. "He said no because you're both terrible at accepting help. You'll have to convince him to say yes. Don't you think you can do it?"

Her chin rose. Then she turned to him and narrowed her eyes. "You're doing it. You're challenging me on purpose."

"I know." He grinned at her. "And it's working. Tell me, Chloe. Can you accept my help and take a rest, or are you too much of a coward?"

THE CURTAINS HAD BEEN DRAWN, LEAVING CHLOE'S home dark even in the bright afternoon sun. This was a sure sign that her father's symptoms were growing worse—that the cold and damp in his meridians had gone beyond making his hands cramp and stiffen. It was now so bad that the excess had spilled over into the rest of his system. She could smell that odor, almost of a sick-room. If it had gone far enough that light was hurting his eyes, and she could scent it on the air...

Chloe found him in the kitchen, still sorting and preparing vegetables for tomorrow.

"Ah Ba."

In the gloom, it seemed that he looked toward her. But his eyes were dark, hooded things in the dim light.

"Ah Lin. Did you deliver the jars?"

"I did. How are you?"

One hand went to his head, and he let out a sigh. "Not good."

Not just *not good*, not if he was actually admitting it, if he wasn't asking if she'd eaten. Answering like that was a sure sign that he'd lost his English, a thing that happened only when he was very tired or very much in pain.

She took the light knife from his hands. "Let me clean up here. Go rest."

She caught the shake of his head, felt him try to pull away from her.

"No," he said stubbornly. "There's too much to do. Stop worrying about me."

Live up to your name, he had said. The words had seemed so final, so decisive. They'd been a knife through her heart. And yet Jeremy had been right: her father loved her. She could not doubt such a thing.

Her throat felt scratchy. "How do I stop worrying? Do I stop loving you? I cannot. I'm doing this all *because* I love you. Because I want the best for you."

She could feel his pulse beating in his wrists, hammering against his skin as if it were looking for a way out. Slowly, Chloe took one of his hands in hers and pressed her palms together. Just as slowly, she started massaging his hands. Fingers first. Gently moving each joint.

He made an abortive movement to pull away. "I can manage."

"You don't have to. Jeremy is going to help."

He let out a little sigh at that.

"I know you don't trust him, Ah Ba. I know you've been…" She didn't know how to say *setting his mouth on fire* in Hakka, so she'd have to go for the understatement rather than the overstatement. "Putting pepper in his food."

Another sigh. "The pepper is a reminder. Not a punishment."

She felt her lips curl into a sad smile. "So it's going to be pepper forever?"

"Not once he's remembered what needs to be done. It's between the two of us. Ask him; he'll agree."

She sighed. She was dancing around the real point—that sharp, lancing thing he'd said, so painful that she didn't want to touch it. Chloe didn't live up to the promise he'd made her mother. Maybe she didn't have to talk about it. He was the issue here: his pain, not hers.

She moved her gentle massage up to his palms, pressing at the meridian points as Madame Lee had taught her. "Let me help you. We have a plan. We can get your formula and hire someone to handle the rest."

He didn't say anything.

"Please," she said. "I know I'm not the best daughter. I'm too English. Too loud. I'm too—everything, getting in your way. But I am trying. Please allow me to help you."

His breath sucked in. "Completely wrong." His hands clutched around hers. "That isn't why. You are the very best. Always. I am…" A long pause. "I am ashamed to ask so much of you."

"I was not ashamed to ask much more of you when I was a child."

There was a long pause. "It's different," he finally offered.

"Ah Ba." She took hold of his left hand and began the pressure again. "It's not different. I love you. I want you to be happy. If we can do something for your pain, we should try. I know that I'm not entirely what you promised Ah Me." It felt scary to broach what he had said, but she could be brave. For him. "But in this matter, please let me be your daughter."

He was quiet for a very long time, before he spoke again. "It is not a matter of what I'll allow. I am ashamed to allow you to act as my daughter because you are not my daughter."

She stared at him in the darkness, her heart hurting, uncomprehending. But he didn't pull his hands from hers.

"NyukMin was my sister," he said. "She was not my wife. You are not my daughter."

Chloe's mind went blank, everything she had believed suddenly coming to a full stop. His *sister?* Her mother was his sister?

But...

Every time she'd begged him for a story about himself, he'd given her that look. That stubborn *look* that said he wasn't going to answer. He'd told her a story about her mother and her mother's younger brother instead. No— not *instead.* In *answer.*

Every word he'd said about that little brother— hapless, he'd called him once. *Not as smart.* Or: *She outdid him in the imperial examinations,* he'd proudly proclaimed.

Once when Chloe had asked about the war, he'd said only this: *She protected her brother.*

Chloe felt her throat close with emotion. "That..." Her voice scratched out. "That was you? *You're* her little brother?"

He gave a jerky nod of his head. "I tried. I tried to protect you as well and as selflessly as she protected me. To allow you to grow into the name she gave you..."

Chloe swallowed. "I know I don't meet her standards, but—"

"No." His hands tensed under hers, and she had to press into the palm of his hand before he relaxed. "When have I said that? I'm the one who has never been enough."

For a moment, she stared at him. She could only see his silhouette; her heart was thumping wildly.

"Ridiculous," she finally managed. "I've never been quiet as the sound of feathers. That's *my* fault."

"Quiet?" He looked over at her. "That's not what your name is for. She knew you were shy from the moment you were born. You were careful around new people, cautious until you warmed up. But shy doesn't mean servile. She didn't want you to *be* quiet. She just knew that you would be."

"Oh." Chloe frowned. "But… What does my name mean, then? If she didn't want me to *be* quiet…"

"The sound of feathers—quiet, yes, but ascending on wings. Free. Not weighed down by anything that we went through. That's what she wanted for you."

Chloe swallowed. Her heart felt as if it were beating in her throat. All her life, her name had seemed a little… inapt, a misnomer given to the wrong daughter with hopes that she would become someone else. To know that her mother would have approved of her if they'd met? It made something deep in her heart catch fire.

"I promised that you would fly free, yet here you are, tangled in my petty revenge. If I'd been better, if I had been able to let go… You would be choosing your own path in life."

Chloe squeezed his hands in hers. "No."

"I had no idea what I was doing when I had to take responsibility for you," he explained. "I didn't know anything about babies. I made so many mistakes... There was so much she wanted for you; she would never have wanted you weighing yourself down with my schemes."

"Ridiculous." That she was sure of. She had been so certain that he'd told her nothing of his family, but... "You've told me dozens of stories about your childhood then." Her mind was still reeling, trying to process that.

He let out a breath.

"My...father then." She said the word in English, unfamiliarly. She felt adrift. She had no idea what to call the man who must have sired her; the name Ah Ba would forever be reserved in her heart for the man in front of her. "Who was he? What was he like? What happened to him?"

He shook his head. "I have only guesses about your Baba. Your mother returned to our childhood village alone with some jewelry near the end of the rebellion. She had enough for the two of us to bribe our way to Guangzhou, and from there, to leave the country on an indenture. I asked, but she said it was too dangerous to speak of her husband at the time."

"Dangerous?"

Her father exhaled. "It was the end of a long and bloody war. I assumed he had been involved in the military in Taiping Tianguo, but I thought she would tell me when she was ready." He sighed. "She was never ready, and when she passed away with fever, she had still not told me. I've had years to regret that I have no name to give you, almost no direction to point you in. I'm ashamed that I took his place instead."

"Ah Ba." She swallowed. "So... The two incense sticks."

He exhaled. "Yes."

She looked at her wrist. "The bracelet..."

"It's from him," he said. "You can't sell it. It was all we had left, at the end. He gave his family jewelry to your mother to protect her and keep her safe; he would want you to have what remained now."

Chloe didn't know what to think. She didn't know how to proceed or what to say. Jeremy had the right of it: they'd never make a sauce empire like this, afraid to weigh each other down, afraid to seek help even from the person who loved them best.

If she was going to live up to her name the way her mother intended, she was going to have to learn to put down burdens.

Her life seemed suddenly uncertain, but one thing she was certain about.

"You've told me story after story about my mother and her little brother. I know how deeply she loved you. I know how much you love me. My mother would never believe that her beloved lau tai was a weight for my shoulders. You are not. You will never be."

In the dark, her father raised his head. He must be looking at her.

"Let me help," Chloe said. "Let me protect you as much as you have protected me. It will not weigh me down to love you. It will set me free."

He exhaled and shut his eyes. "Very well."

13

JEREMY'S BLACK MARE MOVED AT A CANTER, BRISK enough to make good time but not so fast as to wear her out. Chloe sat behind him, her hands on his waist, just above his hips. He tried not to think of where her fingers lingered, where they might move. The heat of her touch felt as if it were branded into him.

It was not quite evening, but late enough in the afternoon that the shadows were long and the occasional hoot of an owl signaled the coming of night. Ever since Chloe had met him on the green after her conversation with her father, she had seemed...quiet, maybe. Determined. And yet somehow luminous. Those three things were at odds with one another, and yet they seemed to coexist.

"You've never told me much about your parents." Her voice was tentative. They came over a hill several miles yet from Dover.

Jeremy tried not to stiffen. She knew pieces of his past. She knew his mother was Chinese and well-to-do, that his father had been British and wealthy. That his father had died when he was nine and that his British aunt had looked after him while he went to school in England. He had to tell her everything…and soon. Perhaps this was a place to start.

"My father was the fourth son of a third son," he said. "He wasn't expected to inherit anything. He married my mother."

Her hands shifted against his waist, as if she were drawing closer so that she could hear him talk against the wind.

"He worked for a trading company that settled in Guangzhou; my grandparents owned a piece of land that the company wished to obtain. My father was tasked with making that purchase."

He could feel her leaning into him. "Hmm. So they met over land negotiations."

"Not…entirely." The corner of Jeremy's mouth turned up. "My mother's parents had no intention of selling. They couldn't be *too* rude, though, but they often stopped just short. My mother was sent to put the English off…not exactly gently. Her father would be happy to enter negotiations, she would say, but at the moment he was engaged in a frantic game of Go. Perhaps later?"

He heard an appreciative chuckle behind him.

"'Oh,'" he said, mimicking his mother's voice, "'how unfortunate that you have made the journey at such an inconvenient time. My father has an urgent appointment to wash rice. I hope you have not been inconvenienced too greatly.'"

"Is that your embellishment of events, or did you

inherit your teasing streak from her?" Chloe sounded amused behind him.

He had never thought of it that way—that he was like her. He tilted his head. "I suppose I do take after her. After four months of being put off by my mother, my father quit his position and they eloped. I believe he was quite reviled by his countrymen for it. He planned to stay in China the rest of his life, England be damned."

Her hands sank into his hips, holding on more tightly. "What happened then?"

"He was so far away from any real inheritance at the time. He thought he could get away with it."

"'Get away with it,'" she repeated behind him. "What a thing to say of a love match."

"Sometimes," Jeremy said dryly, "I wonder if he *wanted* to get away. Wanted to marry someone everyone around him thought was unsuitable."

"'Unsuitable.'" She mimicked his word again; he could almost envision the look of distaste on her face. "What a terrible word to use for a human being."

It had to be much on her mind. Chloe wasn't stupid; by now, she must know what he meant. And, not being stupid, she would know how society would see them. She would never be suitable, not to them. She wasn't accustomed to the inevitable superciliousness. Jeremy, on the other hand, had been unsuited for his title his entire life. He'd grown used to accepting it.

"What my father didn't know was that his family back in Britain had been stricken with cholera while he was eloping. The message came shortly after he returned: My grandfather and my eldest uncle had perished, and the heir had been debilitated. They asked him to return to help his family, and he could not say no." He sighed. "He promised my mother they would return to China when his brother got well. My parents came to England; I was born. Over the course of the next nine years, there was a horseback accident. Pneumonia. Two different heart attacks, separated by six years. A ship sank. I can't really keep the calamities straight. Uncles, grandfather, cousins…so many of them perished over the space of a decade. Typhus took my father, and here I am now."

Her palms pushed into his ribs. "How horrible for you."

Jeremy wasn't sure if she meant the loss of his family or the inheritance that he'd come into. She would have meant both equally, if she had known the scale of it.

"The only surviving member of my father's generation is my aunt. She and her husband had charge of me while I was here for my education."

"And she made you think you were unsuitable."

Jeremy's nose wrinkled. Not to put too fine a point on it, but…yes. Without his mother's letters and assurances, he might have believed it himself.

"She helped me understand that everyone *else* thought I was unsuitable." It was, maybe, an overly technical distinction. "Without my mother…" He trailed off.

It had not been *only* her, not even only his grandparents, who had helped him hold on to some sense of self. Wedgeford had played an enormous role as well.

"She was afraid for me when I went to Britain by myself for school. But her parents were elderly, and she could not leave them or ask them to live somewhere so different. We always joked that she would protect me with her letters. I had a letter from her in my pocket the day I encountered Andrew in the train station and decided to come to Wedgeford on something that wasn't really a whim. So I rather think she did. Protect me, that is."

He thought she was resting her head against his shoulder. He couldn't see, could only feel the warmth of her, so different from the warmth of the setting sun.

"My aunt has tried to do her best, by the standards she believes in, so that I, unlike my father…"

"Will be more suitable?" Chloe finished.

"No. Not possible." He shrugged. "She hopes I will one day have children who are more suitable than I."

"Jeremy." There was a hint of reproach in her voice.

"My aunt wants me to marry. The right woman, she has told me, is respectable and well positioned. Likely in a bit of financial distress, and so willing to think about someone who would otherwise be unthinkable."

"Jeremy." He did not mistake the clenching of her fingers against his jacket. The slide of her hand down his lower back in the hint of a caress.

"According to my aunt, when my wife and I procreate, which we will need to grit our teeth and do, our children will look much less…"

"Chinese."

"Yes. She's done her best to undo my father's mistake. That's what she sees as her duty."

The horse continued down the track, into the valley. It was darker down here, the sun catching on the rims of the hills surrounding them, and yet the sky was still blue as day above. He slowed to navigate a stream, and then another, before starting up the slope on the other side.

"According to my aunt, if I do everything right," he finally said, "in a few generations, my mother will disappear entirely, and I will be forgotten as an anomaly."

"Your list." Chloe breathed into his back. "For your aunt. *This* is that aunt? That's what I've been making for you? My list needs more invective."

"You asked me to be serious." His hands tangled in the reins. "I wanted to be serious for you. I *tried* to be serious." For a moment, he wasn't going to say any more, but he was going to have to put everything on the table eventually.

"Serious meant that I could imagine our life together, that I believed there was room for you where I lived. I thought and thought. I was going to figure it out and come back to you the next year with everything all planned." He spoke lightly, but his heart felt heavy. "But…while I was trying to figure it out, I was finishing up at Oxford. I had resolved to myself that I'd take a first in classics—it would prove to a great many people that I belonged here. I've always had something of a head for languages. So I thought about you and I studied Greek and Latin the entire summer. Then I threw myself into my final year at Oxford."

"You speak Greek? And Latin?"

He huffed. "Mostly I read them. Speaking is an entirely separate matter."

"So you got a first in classics instead of figuring it out?"

He exhaled. "Well. I thought I had figured it out. And

I knew I had done well on the examinations. Perhaps I did too well. Because when the lists came out, I'd achieved no honors at all. I inquired, of course, but I was told that the faculty had judged it...unlikely that I had performed so well. English, they said, was not my native language. So it was impossible I could have done so well without assistance. I was instructed not to pursue the matter, or my reputation would suffer."

He heard her inhale.

"What was there to do," he said, "but for me to make a joke of the results? It was either that or force a lengthy inquiry into my capability, with the result that many would think me a cheat. I chose not to force an inquiry."

"But...*isn't* English your native tongue?"

"I grew up speaking it and Cantonese. English predominated much of the time though."

"And I still don't understand what that has to do with your proficiency in Greek or Latin."

He shrugged again. "In a sense, maybe they were right. Growing up speaking two languages—my mind knows how to make space for additional tongues without too much work. It's almost as if I were cheating."

"It's not anything like it."

"In any event," he said, struggling back to his own thoughts, "that was...what it was. I had this whole plan involving my aunt and people I was going to prevail upon to make you welcome... And I realized it was all a pack of lies a week before the Trials when the situation with Oxford fell on my head. I couldn't even protect myself. How could I protect you? I should have come that year anyway, but I was...ashamed, I suppose. How could I ask you to join my world when *that* was what I had to offer? I couldn't be serious, not with *that.*"

"Jeremy." There was a hint of reproach in her voice.

He went on as cheerily as he could. "So I tried harder. I went to a political salon, but they never did listen to me." No need to point out any of the things they'd actually said. "Not until I started telling jokes. It turns out, they were happy to laugh. They've always been happy to laugh with me. At Eton. At Oxford. Nobody wants me to be serious, but if I'm willing to have a little fun, well, they're willing to play along."

"Jeremy." She had said his name twice now, each time differently. He didn't know if it was reproach, a request to stop, or her condolences.

"It's been going on so long," he continued. "Ever since I came back here for school. I could always tell a joke. You wanted me to be serious, but I don't even know how. And if I did know it, I don't think they would let me."

She shivered against his back. "Jeremy. You know that's not what I meant. I didn't mean *stop joking.* I wanted you to be serious…" Her voice choked a bit. "About me. About us."

"I know." He exhaled. "And I understood that. But how could I be? I could not be serious without telling you what my life was like, and I did not want you to know." He shrugged. "It's all well and good for *me* to make a joke of everything, but that's not the way your character runs. You would get angry. How could I offer you a life of anger?"

She didn't say anything.

"I almost came the second year. I went to Dover by

train for the Trials, and I walked along this trail, all the way, until I got to the top of the hill, looking down into the village. I could see your house. I tried to imagine how I was going to ask you to join me, knowing what it would mean. And I could not do it. I could not make myself do that to you."

They had come to the top of a hill. From here, they could see the sea over one final rise. Dover was hidden by the final slope. The waters were dark, lit from behind by the last bit of sun coming over the hills. He could smell a hint of salt, and he heard a gull cry.

"So I left," he said. "I turned around and walked away and took a train to London and a steamer to Hong Kong and a junk to Guangzhou because the only person who could tell me how to go forward was my mother."

He thought he heard her sniffle against his back. "What did your mother say?"

Jeremy had told his mother about Wedgeford in his letters before. He'd told her about the people he met and what he thought of them before. He hadn't told her about the other wrinkles—him owning the village, nobody knowing who he was—until his most recent journey.

Jeremy blew out a breath. "She told me that I needed to ruthlessly prune out all the poisonous vines in my path." He swallowed. "And she told me that I should accept no less for myself than I would for you. I didn't understand what she meant. What was I supposed to do, disestablish Oxford? It couldn't be done." He shrugged. "But I came to Wedgeford anyway, because I couldn't stay away. For the first time... I think I finally understand what to do."

"Your list," she finally said when they'd almost reached the bottom of the hill. "The list you were making for your aunt…"

"I'm not sure if that idea was pure genius or horrific idiocy." He put the reins in his teeth to free up his hands and swiveled in the saddle, just a little, so he could see her. "Honestly, I didn't intend to oblige. I made everything up on the spot when I saw you."

Chloe huffed. "Really?"

"I told my aunt when I returned that I was going to marry. She did offer to help me find someone, if I gave her a list. I realized after a day that there was little point in having the discussion. We would never agree on anyone." He held up one hand, fingers touching thumbs to make a circle. "Here is the group of people my aunt would think suitable." He held up the other hand, raising a single finger. "Here is the person I'm willing to marry." He stretched his hands out as far as he could. "As you can see, the number of people in both groups is…zero. I wasn't making her a list to *find* a candidate for me. I made her one so she would know she couldn't."

He could scarcely see Chloe, turned about as he was, but he wanted to see her, at least a little, for this. He turned just a fraction more.

"What list are you going to send her?" Chloe asked in a subdued voice. "The one about…intimidating and determined, et cetera, et cetera?"

Jeremy shrugged and gave her his best, most charming smile through the reins in his teeth. "Chloe. I think you know the content of my list, and *not* just because you made it."

She swallowed and looked at him. There was an incandescent quality to her, her lips slightly open, her eyes so wide. For one long moment, it didn't matter that he was twisted on his saddle. It didn't matter that they'd been apart for three years. None of it mattered.

And then, suddenly, it did. An owl hooted to his right; out of nowhere, a pair of rabbits flashed across the path, one after the other, darting as fast as only rabbits pursued by a predator from above could.

His horse spooked, stepping back. Then it reared. The reins ripped from between his teeth.

It was too late to do much of anything. He lurched out of his seat, flying through the air. He could only hold onto Chloe, twisting in that final split second so that she landed atop him.

His back hit the grass, knocking the wind out of him. His whole body stung with the impact, and for a second, he was too dazed to register anything but the shock of landing.

Slowly, his mind began to notice additional points. The heat of Chloe on top of him. The feel of her breath against his neck. Her body against his. The seep of water into his back.

He sat up quickly to squelching noises.

"Damn it." He looked around in the darkening gloom. His horse hadn't gone far; he could still see her in the gloaming. "Chloe. Are you well? Unhurt?"

She was on top of him. Her hair was spilling over her shoulders. It was the first time he'd seen her with her hair out of place, and the sight stole all words from him. There was something profoundly intimate about seeing her like this, the last remnants of the sun lighting her face, her hair unbound. The weight of her seated on his legs, warm, ready for him to catch up and pull closer.

She blushed scarlet, as if suddenly realizing their respective positions and scampered to her feet. "I'm well!" she enunciated loudly from the position she fled to, almost ten feet away. "I'm very well!"

Her skirt was stained with mud and green streaks of grass.

Anyone who saw them would think… They would think…

Jeremy shut his eyes, because now he was thinking what everyone would be thinking: What if, in one of these little valleys, he had stopped and taken her to the ground and kissed her and pushed up her skirt? He wanted it. He wanted her like that, serious and focused on him. He wanted her to *want* him. To desire him with the same intense, soul-stirring greed that took hold of him. He wanted her to hold on to him and never want him to go.

"Jeremy," she shouted from across the distance. "Are *you* well?"

Well enough, obviously, if this was where his thoughts drifted. Well enough to stand, albeit not without some awkwardness due to the unfortunate stiffening in his trousers. It was going to be even more awkward when he called his horse to him.

"Don't worry about me." He stood and tried to brush mud off his trousers, an act that ended up smearing mud all over his hands and spreading the stains. "I'll be just fine." He frowned; he didn't like the way his mare was just standing there when normally she would be nosing her way back to him, nudging him to see if he had treats in his pocket. "I'll just…call my horse so we can see how she's walking. And we'll be back on our way."

With her touching him again.

"Yes." She nodded. "That would be a good thing to do."

"Here, girl," he called. His mare just looked at him. He had avoided using his horse's actual name this entire journey. He stood in place for another half minute, wondering if there were any possible way around it. "Here, here."

"What's the problem?"

"It's…her training." Jeremy looked up. "She only responds to her name. Even if it's just…me calling her." He had named her when he was sixteen. It was not so much that he *regretted* the name, but… At the moment, it was a bit awkward.

"Well. Call her name then."

There was nothing for it. "Chloe," he called. "Here, Chloe."

From ten feet away, the human Chloe turned to look at him, her eyes widening.

His black mare took a few tentative steps toward him —enough that he could see that one of her legs was dragging a little.

"Ah." Yes. As long as he focused on his mare, he wouldn't have to look at human Chloe.

"You named…your horse. After me."

"Maybe it's a coincidence," he muttered untruthfully and walked briskly over to the mare rather than meet Chloe's eyes.

There was nothing in her hoof; the shoe on her drag-ging leg was solidly in place. But when he urged her to walk, she still favored her right foreleg.

"Ah, Chloe girl. This is why we don't jump at rabbits, don't you know?" he murmured to her. "We don't let ourselves get spooked, because when we do, we do silly things and end up spraining our leg. That's no good."

"Is she injured?"

"Not seriously, I don't think." Jeremy looked around. On the far side of the valley, sheep grazed. He doubted there was any sort of predator here that could do her any actual harm. There was grass to eat and a little water here and the temperature at nights this time of year was warm enough that he could leave her a few hours, if necessary. And his footman was arriving via train… "She'll just need a little rest, won't you, Chloe?"

"Did you *seriously* name your horse after me?"

"Might have done," he replied, and rather than give a clearer answer, he changed the subject. "You must be worried about the time." He bit his lip. "It will work out, I think. We're not so far from Dover that walking will take more than half an hour. And we can hire a cart to take us back."

"You're changing the subject."

"No, no," Jeremy said with a flash of a grin. "I would never do so. I'm just expunging one subject before I get to the one you brought up. The subject remains unchanged, just hidden from notice momentarily." Hopefully it would stay hidden long enough for her to forget. "It will take a little while to find someone willing to take us back to Wedgeford in a cart at this hour, and besides, it will be hours until my…" Footman, he almost said, but he didn't yet want to raise the question of exactly *how* posh he was. "My person," he amended. "It will be a while until my person arrives. That's just as well. We can find rooms in the inn to wash off a little, so we don't return looking like…"

Looking like they'd rolled around together on the solid ground. Which they had, just without real enjoyment.

His mind flashed back to all the things they could have hypothetically been doing in little fields, hidden from view. He thought of the feel of her fingers against his hips, of her body against his, and he swallowed.

Chloe came to stand beside him. He glanced over at her, at the look on her face, so hard to read, the wrinkle in her brow as she contemplated him.

"You have definitely changed the subject."

"We don't have to talk about my horse," he muttered. "It's *obvious* I named her after you. It's also obvious why."

"It is not obvious. Not to me."

He took off his hat and ran his hands through his hair. "Many reasons, actually. Extremely varied. Too multitudinous to enumerate. And you know them all anyway, because you're extremely clever and nothing gets past you."

"Then it should be no hardship to list three." She looked directly in his eyes. "Just three, out of your entire multitude."

He met her gaze. "One."

"Two."

"One." He raised his eyebrows at her. "We're busy, remember? We haven't time to dwell on all my feelings."

She exhaled. "One then. Have at it."

"Chloe is my very favorite name in the world," he told her. "Every time I hear it, my heart lifts and I want to smile. There. Are you satisfied?"

She beamed at him. "I suppose I'll accept that," she said. "See to Chloe the Second and let's start walking then. We haven't any time to spare."

It took him ten minutes to unsaddle his horse, set her on a lead that wouldn't let her hobble after him on a bad leg, and whisper reassurances to her. Then they started the journey again. Chloe the human walked briskly next to him. She didn't ask about his horse or anything else. She just bit her lip and stared ahead of her.

"I've decided," she said, five minutes into their walk.

"What have you decided?"

"I have been thinking," she told him. "All this time ago, you left Wedgeford, and you went out into the world. I had rather imagined you out there, being carefree and wealthy. I don't really know what people like you do regularly." She pressed her lips together. "You don't have to cook or clean or…anything, really. You must have a great deal of leisure time."

"I mostly make jokes."

"Yes." Her voice seemed incrementally softer. "You made jokes. Because people *hear* your jokes."

"That sounds so dismal." Jeremy frowned. "You have neglected to mention that I am also exceptionally entertaining."

She ignored this. "And nobody in England ever saw you, or wanted you for you, or thought of you as anything but a means to acquire some additional family wealth, and it would all work out as long as you, Jeremy, disappeared."

"Ridiculous. Don't say 'nobody ever' in that tone of voice. I've been coming to Wedgeford for years now."

They were picking their way through streets with actual cottages on them now.

"My father told me…"

He waited, listening.

"He told me that he wasn't my father." She got the words out in a rush. "He was my mother's brother. And all this time, he has been taking care of me."

Jeremy could feel his eyes widen. However much a shock this was to him, it had to be more so to Chloe. "How do you feel about that?"

"He thought I would be angry, I think." She looked pensive. "But instead, I just feel so…lucky. How many children are orphaned at such a young age, and brought up with so much love?"

The street they were on ended on something that might rightfully be called a thoroughfare. Wagon tracks were marked in the dust, and houses rose on either side.

"We're almost there," he said. "There's an inn near the station. I'll go telegraph my aunt and see if I have replies from my…um. You know. Can you find transportation?"

She nodded.

Jeremy looked over at her. "I'll get some rooms at the inn so we can clean up a bit while we're waiting."

Up ahead, he could make out the golden glow of streetlamps nearer the center of town.

She turned to him. "What if there's only one room in the inn?"

The question was so absurd that he stopped in place. "What? Why are you asking?"

"Dover may have a great many visitors. You said we'd get rooms at an inn…but what if there is only one room? We must plan ahead."

He blinked at her. "I don't understand. Are we really trying to craft a plan for the unlikely possibility that an inn will be almost full? We'll go to another inn, if it is."

Somehow that seemed to agitate her further. "A great many people may be staying at that inn, with the intent of coming to the Trials early tomorrow. The inn may be crowded and it would take too long to go to another."

"Well, we only have to clean up a little. If there's only one room, we can take turns using it."

For some reason, she looked displeased at this entirely reasonable answer. "Jeremy. You aren't helping."

"I thought I was being very helpful. Doesn't that 'just one room' thing only happen in stories?" He looked over at her, at the stubborn set of her jaw, and suddenly realized what she was implying. "What sort of stories have you been reading anyway? I've been wondering about that 'theoretical experience' you mentioned earlier. Rather than talking about Dover's inn capacity, I think this would be an excellent time for an in-depth discussion of your reading materials."

A faint blush rose on her cheeks. "If you've read the stories, you know what you are supposed to say. If there's only one room, we could *share* the room. Together."

He turned to look at her. She couldn't be saying what he thought she was saying. They couldn't share the room *together*. They were going to undress. Take off their clothing. Have it cleaned, and… Right, he was still stuck on the "take off their clothing" part of his imagination.

"I can't undo all these buttons on my own," she explained.

He was fairly certain she was lying; she had to do all those buttons on her own at home.

She held up her hands. "My hands are muddy, see? I need you to help."

"Chloe." He wasn't thinking properly; he needed to think. "I can't say what you want me to say, and it's all your fault because you made me promise not to seduce you."

"Oh, no." She let out a choked noise. "I *did*. That was horrifically inconvenient of me."

For a moment, she chewed on her lip, thinking. They passed on to a broader thoroughfare, more crowded. It wasn't until the white walls of the Dover Priory station came into view that she stopped and grasped his elbow, pulling him into a dark alley. She was close, so close. Her hand was on his arm, and she tilted her face up to his.

"It was conditional. You're bound only if I don't make a *numbered* plan." She sounded so earnest. "I'm only missing the numbers. So. Here we are. After we finish our business, it will go like this. One, we will go to the inn. Two, we will inquire after rooms. Three, if there is only one room, then…we will be in the same room. Four, we will remove our clothing. Five…" She trailed off, slotting her fingers together in a manner he thought was intended to be suggestive, but just looked slightly nervous. "*You* know."

"No," he said in fascination. "I don't. Go on. I really would like to hear what comes next."

"Five," she said, "you…and I…do…things. You know. *Those* things. Seduction things."

"This theoretical experience." He bit his lip to contain a smile. "What exactly did it consist of?"

"What do you think?" she snapped. "Once when I was in a bookstore, I slipped off to the back and read a medical textbook. It was *extremely* informative. In broad strokes."

He let out a chuckle. "Broad. Strokes. I'm sure it was."

Her hand convulsed on his arm. "It was, perhaps, lacking in non-medical perspectives. Now do you accept my plan or do you not?"

"Is it really a plan if it's a conditional plan?"

"Yes," Chloe said decisively. "It is. I, of course, would never be so brazen as to plan my own seduction. But sometimes, fate makes a certain course of action possible. Maybe even inevitable. You can plan for fate. That's all I'm suggesting we do: let fate decide." Her cheeks flamed and she looked away. "I did not think you would need any convincing on this score, you and your broad strokes."

"Chloe." He wanted it too much to be able to come up with a counterargument.

"*If* there's only one room," Chloe said. He suspected she was blushing still, but he could no longer make out the color of her skin in the dimly lit alley. "If there's only one room, I plan to remove my gown and everything underneath. That satisfies the condition of the promise you made to me… So *you* can plan for whatever you like."

14

CHLOE SHOULD HAVE BEEN EXHAUSTED BY THE TIME she stood outside the inn where they'd arranged to meet. She'd been awake since five in the morning and it was evening now. Her only respite had been a canter across ten miles, at the end of which she'd been thrown from a horse. Yet all she could feel was a sparking anticipation climbing up her spine.

That sense only grew when Jeremy came around a corner, coming into the square before the Priory Inn. It was full dark, and while there was a lamp not far from the inn's door, she was standing in the shadow cast by the building. He scanned the square; his eyes were crinkled with what she thought might be worry until his gaze landed on her.

She lifted a hand in a little wave. She felt assailed by a whole flock of nerves now. What might they be about to... No, she must be honest with herself. She *hoped* they were about to...

So much for honesty. She couldn't even think it.

He came to stand by her. Close to her…so close she could see his features in the dark shadows. Close enough to feel the heat of him, six inches distant.

Not close enough.

"Did you have an answer?" she asked.

He nodded. "My person will be here on the train arriving at ten in the evening."

She had often thought to herself that she could not imagine Jeremy's station, and this brought it home. To have servants in London, available at any hour, who would bring whatever he wanted any distance he demanded when they should be abed? It seemed wasteful and luxurious all at the same time.

"I hope you're offering your person a bonus."

Jeremy made a face. "Of course I am. What do you take me for?"

"We've never really spoken about it."

He wrinkled his nose and changed the subject, as he always did whenever they touched on his wealth. "What of you? Did you manage to find a way to return?"

She nodded. "There's a man with a cart who was intending to take some ale in to Wedgeford early tomorrow. I've…ah…convinced him to make the journey tonight."

"Convinced him?" He gave her a smile.

She didn't smile back. "I had to offer extra for a space in the visitor tents outside Wedgeford this evening," she said. "And a little bit besides. And I don't have the money, so you'll have to pay him."

"Why do you look so embarrassed? I already told you I would."

"He and his son will come and help us in the morning, so... That's it." She nodded.

"The money is meaningless. Think nothing of it."

"I wish I were just thinking of the money." Her face flushed. "We have two hours until your...person arrives. And the inn..." She trailed off.

His gaze seemed to sink into her. Two hours. Two hours, alone at an inn. She wanted it. She shouldn't, she knew, but she did.

"Did you inquire after rooms?" he asked eventually.

It wasn't even strictly necessary, she should have said. They could wait in the common room. They were muddy and grass-stained, but it would be so late upon their return to Wedgeford that the only person who would see was Chloe's father, who would never spread gossip about her. All he might do was add more spice to Jeremy's food in retaliation.

She didn't say that. "No."

He let out a little aggrieved noise. "You're *trying* to let other people take rooms. I'm telling you, a place like this *never* has only one room available. Not even on the verge of the Trials."

"If it has only one room," Chloe said, "then it's fate and the right thing to do."

And if it was just fate, she couldn't blame herself for giving in to what she had wanted for so long.

Jeremy let out a sigh. "I'm trying to be very serious about you, sweetheart."

He hadn't reached out to touch her in all this time, so she did it for him. She set her hand against his cheek.

He let out a noise and tilted his face to fit into her palm. "Chloe."

"You can be serious on the way home." She sounded so severe when she said that. Too severe. She knew what and who she was: cold, efficient, intimidating. That's what everyone thought of her at least.

Inside, she didn't feel like any of those things. How could anyone think her cold when she was boiling like this? When she wanted him? When she'd wanted him forever? On the journey over when he'd calmly recited all the ways that people had pushed him to be nothing but a joke who eventually disappeared and was forgotten by his children, she'd wanted to go out into the world and kick them all in the shins.

In lieu of that, she just wanted him to know that *one* person in the world didn't wish for him to disappear. *One* person wanted him to seek his own happiness.

Jeremy set his hand over hers on his cheek and slowly turned her fingers, so that he could place a kiss in her palm. She felt her entire hand curl, her entire being light up.

He didn't let go of her either. He kept hold of her hand and bundled her close so that his arm fell around her. Then he led her inside.

The innkeeper was a small, thin man who looked them up and down, sizing them up in an instant. There was their clothing, stained with grass and mud. Jeremy's hat was half-mashed in from their earlier accident. Then there was their *race*. Chloe had a moment of clarity. They must look like absolute riffraff.

"We," he bellowed, "have no rooms available. Do you

understand?" He said these words very slowly.

"Ah." Jeremy straightened, pulling his arm from around Chloe's shoulder. "My good man. I think you misunderstand. My wife and I have had a small mishap with our transportation."

The man blinked, as if surprised to hear Jeremy speak the Queen's own English, but then snorted. "And lost your purse too. I know how the story goes."

Jeremy's hand went to his pocket with a frown before he smiled. "No, my purse is right here. How much for two rooms, then? We'll be going on to Wedgeford later tonight, so you may relet the room to any late arrivals, but we're happy to pay the full amount for the evening."

Two rooms. Chloe bit her lip. Her heart had jolted painfully when the innkeeper had said *no rooms available.* Now, all he had to do was say that there was just *one…*

The man blinked as Jeremy removed a handful of coins from his purse.

"We would greatly appreciate water for washing, as much of it as your staff can spare," Jeremy said. "And if there's a way to have our clothing brushed in an hour? I know we can't expect it to be fully clean in that time, just comfortable enough to wear for a few more hours."

The innkeeper focused on the coins Jeremy had laid on the table. "Ah… Yes. Yes, that should all be possible. Very possible."

Chloe couldn't stand the suspense any longer. "How many rooms did you say you have available again?"

"Oh." The man's face tilted up in contemplation. "I… misspoke earlier when I said we had *no* rooms. We have four rooms left still. Two will not be a problem, not at all."

Chloe felt her heart drop. Four was such an unlucky number. Fate was *not* on her side.

"Well then," Jeremy said. "We'll—"

It came to her in a flash then. Fate? Fate *shouldn't* have been kind to her. Her mother had perished, leaving her alone with a young, bereaved, impoverished uncle. He'd been dragged to England, promised a great sum of money, and then abandoned with nothing in a country where he knew nobody. And yet they'd persevered. They'd found a place that was theirs, made a sauce that was theirs. They'd flourished despite everything. Fate was *precisely* what she made of it, and in this moment, she didn't *want* fate to provide four rooms.

Before Jeremy could complete the sentence, she grabbed his purse from his hands and stared down the innkeeper.

"I *thought* you said you had four rooms," she said, "but are you sure—perhaps you meant—surely there is only one?"

The innkeeper stared at her in puzzlement. "I'm positive. It's definitely—"

She pulled a handful of random coins from Jeremy's purse and slapped them on the high table in front of them. She refused to look at Jeremy at her side. He could hardly complain about this; he was wealthy, wasn't he? As long as she didn't see exactly how much she was offering this man, she wouldn't have to let the wastefulness of it bother her.

People said she was cold. Efficient. Intimidating. Well, time to be as intimidating as she possibly could be.

"I *think,*" she said in her most demanding voice, "that

if you recount the number of rooms, you will find that you only have *one* room left."

"I…" He looked at Chloe, then at Jeremy, then at the coins.

"You have *one room,*" Chloe informed him. "Exactly one. Only one. At this time, that is the *only room* you have available to us."

The innkeeper looked at Jeremy. "Sir?"

Beside her, Jeremy sighed. "Yes," he finally said in incredibly flat tones. "You heard the lady correctly. You have only one room. We are exceedingly lucky that we arrived in time to find it."

"I…see?" The innkeeper nodded, extremely puzzled. "We have only one room? But it's the best of the four we have remaining, I suppose. Is that the right thing to say?"

Chloe exhaled in relief. She let her gaze slide over to Jeremy. He was looking at her with an expression she could not quite understand. He seemed almost unable to look away, and that made her feel shy, knowing what was to come.

"Oh, drat it all," she said in an unconvincing monotone. "We shall have to share our quarters."

"Really," the innkeeper cut in, "if you don't wish to, then—"

"We do!" Chloe sang out. "It's perfect! Please stop talking!" She shoved the coins across the table at him.

The man just looked at her, then at the money. "I… see. Very well."

"One room then." Jeremy's voice sounded husky. "Your only room."

15

JEREMY LET THE DOOR CLOSE BEHIND THEM WITH A quiet snick. The room seemed shrouded in silence. It was far enough from the common areas that the faint hubbub had vanished. Thick draperies at the window muted all the outside sounds. There was nothing here but the erratic pounding of Jeremy's pulse in his ear. The room itself was plain but clean: a little dresser, a basin, a sliver of soap laid out next to that. Two steaming buckets of water from the kitchen had been brought up by maids, and a stack of towels laid beside them.

Chloe walked in ahead of him, her back straight and determined.

He'd come back to Wedgeford believing that he would adore her every bit as much as he had before. He hadn't realized that he would come to adore her more with every passing hour, his affection growing until this moment. Even at her most bedraggled, she was unquestionably the most beautiful, the most desirable, woman on earth. And she'd made a numbered plan to seduce him.

It seemed excessive. She shouldn't have needed to count past one.

Matter-of-fact as always, she spooned a dipper of water into the basin and washed her hands, then her face, before discarding the dirty remnants into the empty pail meant for waste.

"Jeremy?"

Jeremy swallowed and turned to her. He didn't want to assume too much.

"If we're going to get our clothing brushed, we need to get out of it swiftly. There's no point waiting." Her eyes met his with something akin to a promise.

"Of course." He swallowed and thought about moving toward her. Thought about what he could do, where he might touch… Somehow just the thought of so much as their fingertips meeting, harbinger of everything that was still to come, froze him in place.

"Jeremy." His name sounded like a song on her lips. "Jeremy, Jeremy, Jeremy. What are you waiting for?"

"Um." He stood three feet from her. What *was* he waiting for?

His face burned; he swiftly turned away from her. His hands shook as he took off his jacket, then his tie. He could probably undo his shirt buttons without too much worry. She'd seen him without a shirt before. He'd made sure of it, once when it was hot and the opportunity had offered itself.

"Jeremy," Chloe said, her voice close as if she had crept up behind him. "Are you *shy?*"

He jumped, heart thumping. "Ha ha. Me? Shy?" His voice sounded uncharacteristically odd to him—pitched high, his words tripping out a little too fast. "That's absurd. Why would I be *shy?* I'm never shy about anything."

There was a longer pause. "Do you not want to?" She sucked in a breath. "Oh, no. I'm so sorry. I hadn't meant to assume—you had said—I, maybe, I misread the situation?"

No. He couldn't have her *uncertain* of him, not when he'd worked so hard to convince her otherwise. He turned and reached for her.

It was a mistake. She'd taken off her gown while he'd been doffing his jacket. Now she stood before him in her chemise and corset. He felt himself stunned all over again, stunned by detail long imagined but never before seen. The curve of her waist. The light brown tops of her breasts, warm and inviting. The shadow of her legs through the fabric of her chemise.

He yanked his hand back to his side before he could touch her.

"Ah." She smiled, but there was a hesitance in her smile. "You *don't* want to. Well, that's entirely understandable." Her gaze tilted downward, and she rubbed at a darker spot on her hem. "My chemise isn't too bad—I can make do from here with a bit of a hand towel."

"No," Jeremy said. "It's just—my hands are dirty, and you look so clean."

She snorted. "*I* look clean? The lighting's not *that* bad. Look." She pointed to her neck, where he could see her pulse beating. "See? Mud." Her upper arm was next. "Dirt." Then her ankles, fine and perfect. "More mud." Her eyes went to his with something of a challenge. "And if you get more dirt on me, you can always wash it off. If you want." She swallowed. "But only if you want. I know I can be a bit much when I make up my mind."

Damn it. "It's not that." He struggled for words to explain. "It's not that I don't want...that I don't want you." He needed a moment to think. "Can we just...put our clothing outside the room for now? The maids are waiting."

He couldn't look as she finished undressing; he counted the towels instead, and determined there were enough to dirty a few before they had a chance to wash. He stripped himself of shirt and shoes and socks and underthings as swiftly as possible, and then wrapped a towel about himself in some semblance of modesty.

He gathered up the pile she'd made of her clothing. That...looked like basically everything? Not that he carried a comprehensive catalogue of a woman's underthings in his mind. Agh. Thinking about making a comprehensive catalogue of Chloe's underthings was not a good idea.

He opened the door a crack and shoved everything through to the maid who waited for them before turning to Chloe.

She'd looped her bulky towel around her shoulders. It mostly covered her hips. Everything else—her ankles, her calves, her knees, the long expanse of her thighs—was visible. Jeremy swallowed and turned right back around.

"It's absolutely not that I don't want you," he said. "It's that I want you so much I can scarcely stay in my own skin."

She let out a startled breath.

"It's easy enough for men," he continued. "Just a little rubbing in the right place and it all works out. But from what I hear…it's not so easy for women."

Her head tilted. "From what you hear? What do you mean, *what you hear?*"

He bulled on, refusing to acknowledge that part. "I suspect the real reason they tell women not to have intercourse before marriage is so that women won't know if their husband is any good at it until they're committed for life."

"Jeremy," Chloe said behind him. "Are you telling me you're *bad* at sex?"

He threw up his hands. "It's definitely a possibility!"

"Have you had complaints?"

"Technically? Never."

"Have you had compliments?"

"Oh, absolutely." Jeremy turned once more to face her. "Every time I've had intercourse, the woman in question has praised everything about me. My style. My technique. My cock."

Turning had been a bad idea. She was close—so close —and her hair was loose, fanning across her shoulders. The line of her collarbone was right *there,* light brown and begging for his lips.

Also, he was talking about his cock and they were wrapped in towels.

He'd said it sarcastically, so she would understand what he was actually saying. Instead, she seemed to take him at his word. "*That* is more like what I expected. So why are you so worried about *me?*"

"Chloe, I've never actually had intercourse."

Her eyes widened and her mouth dropped.

"What?" he demanded. "When was I supposed to have done it? I've really only ever wanted one woman in my life."

"You!" She rubbed her temples. "You could have mentioned this beforehand! Vast, you said! You claimed to have vast experience!"

He lifted the corners of his mouth in a wan smile. "Surprise?"

"Jeremy." She sounded exasperated and pleased and entirely unsure what to make of that. "Damn it. My plan was to let you tell me what we needed to do. You can't just not *know*. I didn't plan for this."

"I'm sorry."

"You should have informed me of this when I was making the plan. I would have..." She trailed off. "I don't know. I would have tried to find a book or something when you were off doing whatever it was with the telegrams from your servants!"

He couldn't help himself. The thought of Chloe wandering around Dover after dark, in a muddy gown, asking for either pornographic bookshops or medical texts, after the day they'd had... It set him off. He started snickering.

"It's not funny!"

"It's hilarious," he told her. "It's *extremely* hilarious. We're hilarious. We're going to have to figure this out on our own. Unless you'd like to go down to the common room and enlist some help."

"Be serious."

"No," he told her. "If I'm serious, I'm scared. I'm

scared because…you're you. You're the brightest light I've ever met. You're sweet and perfect and lovely and…" He moved closer to her, holding onto his towel. "And you have this freckle right here." He reached out one finger to her neck, tapping the little brown spot. "It's been driving me wild since I was fourteen, Chloe, and if I think about how much I've wanted you and how long, and how if I make *one wrong move* I might lose you altogether… I can't be serious, Chloe. It's too much."

She looked up at him with brilliant eyes. "I hate to tell you this," she said in a quiet voice, "but you've made an extremely large number of very wrong moves, and you have yet to lose me. Logically, you should have realized that you are allowed to make mistakes."

"Well… I'm…" He winced slightly. "I'm not *trying* to make mistakes. And I don't want you to think you must tolerate nonsense. Do you know how precious you are?"

She just looked at him. Then she turned away, back to the basin. The towel around her shoulders fluttered, giving him a glimpse that made his mouth go dry. She cast one glance at him over her shoulder, before she let her towel slide to the ground.

Jeremy's mind seemed to go blank. Thighs and shoulders and neck had been enough to almost tie his tongue. Now he could take in the entire naked expanse of her, turned so that he could see that profile of breast and buttock. Every thought in his mind—incoherent as those had been—seemed to shatter and blow away like dust on dry wind.

There was only one thing he could say: "Uhh."

She took a handcloth and wet it in the hot water, then

turned to him. Oh, no. Looking at her straight on didn't help. From here, he could trace the curve of her breasts, the dusky brown of her nipples, the indentation of her navel, the dark hair between her thighs.

"Here." She gestured with the cloth. "If you'll just drop your towel, I can clean you up."

"Look at you," Jeremy said in awe. "With your full sentences and your conjugated verbs. I am in awe of your cognitive capacity."

She was blushing, a dusky rose that spread from her nose all the way down her chest. "*That's* what you're thinking about right now? My conjugations?"

"Don't listen to me," he told her. "Just…look at you." He met her eyes. "Will you come here?"

A nod, and then she came to him in soft strides. He reached out with the hand that wasn't holding on to his towel and took hold of her hand. It seemed the safest place to touch; he'd held her hand before, at least.

But when he took her fingers, he realized that she was trembling. He looked up in her eyes, dark and wide and focused on him.

"Oh, Chloe. Are you scared?"

"Nervous," she admitted. "I'm extremely nervous in the moment." She ducked her head. "Nobody's ever… But I don't want to seem…"

She didn't finish, and Jeremy had a moment of clarity. All the things he worried about—about not being enough, about her coming to her senses—*she* was thinking the same things. *She* was thinking that he might leave her, or change his mind after he saw her naked. *She* was thinking all of that, and so she'd gathered up all her bravery and tossed it in his face, offering up the very things that frightened her. That was his Chloe: brave and sweet and giving.

Jeremy let go of his towel. "Chloe," he said. "Don't worry about how you seem. I want you to be…just you. Nobody but you."

She looked up at him.

"The truth is," he told her, "I'm not like you. I don't make lists. I don't have rational explanations for everything. If you asked me why I wanted you, I wouldn't be able to give a carefully thought-out account. I could only say that you make me feel like the home I want to live in."

He took the cloth from her and turned her to face away from him. It was easier that way, to not have to face her immediately. She'd washed her face and hands and smoothed her hair back into place, but the journey had left a fine layer of dust almost everywhere else. He stroked the cloth down her neck, down her spine. His hands were trembling: Even with the rough, wet fabric between them, this felt terribly intimate. Close, in a way that the anticipation of mere sexual pleasure could not explain.

"It leaves me at a disadvantage," he said. "Between the two of us, you could choose anyone in the entire world who met your standards. I can only choose you."

He could see her press her fingers into her eyes from behind. "Idiot." She sniffled. "You're such an idiot. I can't believe I'm in love with an idiot."

In love. His whole body seemed to vibrate with the force of that. *In love.* He found himself smiling with the joy that welled up inside him.

"Well," he said with his best attempt at cocky confidence. "That's it then, for you. It's a terrible choice, but you've made it and here I am. Turn around, if you'd like me to get your front." As long as he sounded matter-of-fact, he would be able to retain some of his dignity.

She took a deep breath and did so, turning slowly, her eyes seeking his out for reassurance. She should never be allowed to doubt.

"God," he whispered, glad for the wet cloth in his hand, giving him the excuse he needed to reach out. He wasn't sure if he would have dared otherwise. "Chloe. You're…so."

He couldn't quite bring himself to touch her breasts, not yet. Not even with the pretext he'd been so perfectly given. No matter how much he wished to do so. He set the cloth against her collarbone. He could feel the warmth of her body through the damp coarseness of the towel. He stroked down and across, still not quite daring.

The cloth rose and fell with her breath.

"You're so perfect," he whispered.

She let out a surprised laugh. "Oh, is that *really* what you're thinking?"

"Um." He ventured down another few inches, circling one breast with the cloth before coming up to wash the other. "No. Mostly I'm just giving thanks right now for whatever it was that made this happen."

Her eyes shone up at him. "You know," she offered shyly. "You can touch me anywhere you like. I promise I won't mind."

"Anywhere I like is…" He shook his head. "It's too much. I like everywhere, Chloe. I'm not sure you should offer so open-ended an invitation. I'll end up clinging to you like a limpet."

She reached out and took his hand in hers. "This is just like you." She shook her head severely. "All talk of clinging. No actual clinging."

"Here now!"

"Let me provide some assistance. Here." She sat on the bed, feet pulled up underneath her, and gestured him to sit next to her. When he did, she pressed his fingers to one breast, splaying his fingertips wide. "I want you to touch me here."

The texture of her nipple was soft at the edges, pebbled skin rising in a hard, light-brown nub. He'd imagined touching her here far too often. He'd imagined how it would feel, how just the feel of her breast would make him ache to touch more.

He had hoped she might one day allow it. He had never dared to hope that she might ache for it too—ache as much as he did. But her gasp as he circled her nipple was unmistakable. Her whole body shifted toward him, hips pressing forward on a little exhalation.

"Jeremy," she said. "*I'm* the one who is supposed to be shy. You're supposed to laugh at me and take charge."

"Am I?" he breathed. "Or am I supposed to touch you until you're so desperate that you'll climb on top of me and take what you want?"

She exhaled, her mouth opening a little. "Oh. Can we do that?"

"I don't know," he shot back. "Can we? *You're* the one who read a medical text."

She let herself fall back on the mattress with a thump, looking up at the ceiling. "Why are you so *like* this? Is it because you're shy?"

"I'm not being shy." He gingerly lay next to her. "I'm approaching you with the reverence that you deserve. It's hardly the same thing."

"*That* was reverence? What's wrong with medical texts? Please explain."

"Nothing is wrong with medical texts for medical procedures, but I don't think you want me using a scalpel at the moment."

"Jeremy."

He ran his thumb around her nipple, and then brought his other hand to her hip. "Sorry," he said as she shivered under his touch. "I can scarcely help it. My mouth just moves and noises come out. You might have noticed that I have this problem. It's the nerves."

"Hmm." There was laughter in her voice and a smile on her lips. "Nothing to be nervous about. From what I've heard about first times, it's mostly a quick fumble. Which is good. We don't have that much time. Maybe we should get it over with while we still can."

He wanted to ask her precisely why her medical text had touched on this. But he couldn't; he had to defend his honor, such as it was.

"Now, see here," he told her in mock indignation. "I may have never actually *had* intercourse, but I've imagined it. A lot. That's basically as good as actual practice."

She let out a delighted laugh. "Is it? Is *that* your vast experience you boasted about?"

"You have no idea," he told her, "how many times I've thought about you while bringing myself off. I've become a regular expert at holding myself ready until the relevant time. You'll just have to tell me when the relevant time comes."

He leaned in to kiss her. It was different, kissing her when she was lying full out on a bed. Her body was naked, and his skin was bare. Kissing her meant pressing his chest against her breasts. It was different, and so, so good. Her lips tasted so sweet, and he put his hands on her face, pulling her close, kissing again.

"Oh, no." She pushed him away, her eyes alight. "You must tell me. How many times have you thought about me while bringing yourself off?"

"Who can possibly do arithmetic at a time like this?" he muttered into her neck. "Lots. Lots multiplied by many years."

"*I* can do arithmetic. Give me the parameters."

He kissed her neck. "Started when I was...oh, fourteen. Continued on a regular basis." He kissed down her collarbone. "Persisted until last night. Are you satisfied yet?" His tongue dipped against the swell of her breast; he could almost taste a hint of the rose soap the inn had given them. His whole body was responding to her—his breath, cycling in time to hers, his hands, molding themselves to her heat, his cock stiffening, heavy and red with anticipation.

"You think me so easily satisfied? That bodes ill for what is to come. You haven't given me enough information to do a calculation." She sounded entirely unaffected. "*How* regular a basis? Monthly?"

"Monthly!" He found her nipple and took it in his mouth. She made a noise, desperate and wanting, and he swirled his tongue against the tip of her. That taste of rose soap washed over his senses, prominent for a moment, before giving way altogether, vanishing into the softness of her skin. Her back arched against him, pushing up.

"Well." These words came out on a gasp. "I do have to have *some* idea what I'm getting myself into, don't I? Because even if it's monthly, twelve times a month…that's over a hundred times. I'm shocked, Jeremy. If that's basically like intercourse, you're an absolute libertine."

"If I'm to be counted a libertine if I think of having you *monthly,*" he said, shifting down her body, "*imagine* what you will think of me when you hear the truth."

"More often than monthly? Do not say you've thought of this once a fortnight?"

"Maybe if I'd been lucky enough to fall in love with a less inspiring woman." He raised his head to glare at her. "But look at you. You are not a once-a-fortnight woman."

"Am I not?" There was real pleasure in her voice. "Am I a once-*weekly* woman? Because that's well over *four hundred* encounters you've engaged in. You're a hardened rake."

"You'll have to forgive my promiscuity." He sighed into the skin of her hips. "But you have once again severely underestimated my capacity."

"Have I?" She sounded delighted. "How very wicked of you."

"Can it really be so wicked if it's always been you? Every single day?"

He'd come to her pelvis. Her legs slid open for him; he could smell her, salty and enticing, all at the same time.

He'd never felt tentative in his imaginings, and he tried not to be so here. He slid his thumb between her legs, sinking into the slick heat of her. God, the warmth of her body was better, *much* better. Her head tilted back and she let out a sigh.

"Very," she whispered. "Truly wicked. Your heart is blacker than I had contemplated. Saying such things—you cannot imagine what you're doing to me. It's cruel." There was a soft smile on her face.

"However can I make it up to you?"

Her eyes met his. She swallowed. "Show me what you've thought about."

So he slid down her body just a little further, and set his mouth to her sex and licked. She let out a cry, pressing up against him.

He wasn't sure what he was doing—in his imagination, everything he did was always good for her—but she was there to guide him. To turn her hips just so, to press up and say, "Yes, Jeremy, there, right there." To set her hands on his shoulders and push when it wasn't right, and to pull when it was.

"There," she told him, as he licked across the nub, "not so hard—just like that, exactly like that. Please. Please keep doing that."

He had imagined so much about her, so many times. Imagination, it turned out, was poor preparation for the reality of her. In his imagination, he could only want. Here, nestled between her legs, he was learning the truth of her. Learning her taste. Learning the squeeze of her thighs against his ears, the sound of her voice as she grew closer to climax. His own lust rose in response, the heady greed running through his veins a more palpable thing than it had ever been before, and he learned that too. He learned it alongside the temperature of her skin, the clutch of her fingers.

He had known that she was demanding; he had put it on his list. He hadn't understood how this would translate in bed, not until he learned the way she told him what she needed. And he'd never known how lovely it was to give her what she so clearly wanted and to be rewarded with the tension in her shoulders, gathering, gathering, gathering…

"Don't," she said. "Don't stop—right there, like that. Keep doing that. God, Jeremy, I'm going to—"

He learned what she felt like against his tongue, waves of heat pulsing through her, passing into him and stoking his own need. He'd never been so hard. She made a noise in her throat, and his fingers clenched into her hips. Her back bowed, tensing further, and then every muscle seemed to relax around him as she lay panting beneath him.

It was better than anything he'd ever contemplated, and he hadn't even touched himself.

He slid his hands up her sides, soothing her, waiting for her to regain her breath.

"You can't tell me you imagined *that,*" she finally said. "You're still… You haven't…"

"I never imagined you helping me so perfectly," he said. "But I wouldn't want it any other way."

She looked at him, sitting up, and then blinking in confusion. Her hand went to his knee. "You *don't* want it another way? Not at all?" Her fingers slid up his thigh an inch and his cock twitched in response.

"Um." He swallowed. "Maybe one other way? For now?"

"Something-thousand times spent imagining, and *this* is all you were planning?"

"I can wait," he said awkwardly while his cock protested the very idea. "If you'd…prefer."

She reached out and set her hand against his face. "I did not come all this way to be debauched by a libertine, only to forgo the full experience at the last minute."

Sweet. She was so sweet when she said that, and he wanted her so desperately.

Her nose crinkled. "Technically, I suppose it's *after* the last minute, as it were."

Their eyes met. He smiled at her and then leaned in to kiss her. Kissing was good. She was warm, so warm, and she opened up to him, not holding anything back.

The first time he rested his cock against her thigh, she let out a gasp, as if it excited her and not just him. When he pushed against her, he saw stars.

"Yes," she said. "Yes, Jeremy. *Please.*"

It had not occurred to him that she might want his pleasure the way he'd wanted hers. The idea excited him. He pushed against her again, moving their bodies so that his legs were bracketed by her thighs. So that the tip of his cock pressed into her belly and their hips ground together.

"Good," she said, as if she could feel the sparking want inside of him. "It's so good."

Again, and again, until he could feel the heat rise in her. Until she was no longer loose from her own release, but eager once again.

He adjusted himself so that the tip of his member

dipped into the heat of her. She was slick against his head, and she made a little noise as he pushed against her.

There was no give. For a moment, he couldn't figure it out—the heat, the slick—he pressed into flesh that didn't give way. Then she reached down and adjusted him, fingers hot against his member, and so good that he had to bite his lip to keep from spending at her touch. A small motion, and the tip of his cock met wet heat. He slid forward. In. Just an inch, but she was scalding around him, and tight, so tight. So good. He exhaled, exulting in the pleasure.

She bit her lip beneath him.

"Darling." He held his hips steady, freezing. "Did that hurt?"

"No—not really. Give me a moment."

Easy enough to give her a moment when he wanted her to have the rest of his life. God, he loved her. He loved the feel of her around him. He couldn't quite help pulling out a hair, and then pushing back in.

"That." Her hands went to his shoulders. "That's nice —just a little of that."

He hadn't intended to, but every thrust went in a little deeper. Her breath caught; he steadied her, kissing her, until he was fully inside her, balls pressing into her. She felt good, so good, around him.

"Chloe." He leaned his forehead against her. "Sweetheart."

"That's…" Her hips pressed against his. "Move, maybe?"

Maybe. He smiled down at her. He was gentle as he shifted forward, holding his own desires in check as best he could. Still, each hot, wet slide inside her sent his wants sparking. This was her. This was Chloe. She felt so perfect. He felt like fire danced inside him with every stroke, threatening to engulf his heart, his lungs.

He wanted to memorize the feel of this. To remember it forever. To feel her lips on his jaw, her hands on his shoulders, the tightness of her passage gripping him.

She moved under him, repositioning herself. "Move more," she whispered, and so he did. Every thrust seemed to send electricity racing through him, bringing him closer, closer—

"Not quite right," she told him.

He paused, gritting his teeth, and breathed into her shoulder. "What's not right?"

"It feels good," she said, "but—not good enough?" Her eyes opened and she looked at him. "Not in the right way. I need something more, something more like before. When your mouth was on me."

He looked into her eyes.

"I'm sorry," she started to say, "I shouldn't have said—I didn't mean to ruin—"

He cut her off with a kiss. "You *should* have said," he whispered into her mouth. "You *must* say; I can have it no other way. You see, I have been imagining this with you every day of my life, and you must give me the opportunity to make you desire me as much as I want you."

He pulled back. She had a smile on her face, but her eyes glistened.

"Thank you," he said. "Thank you for trusting me to be good to you."

"Jeremy." She sounded almost weepy.

"Here," he said. "What if—like this?" He changed the angle of his thrusts.

She shut her eyes. "Not…quite."

"Like this."

"No." She put her hand between them, between her legs. "Still not. Right here. That's where I need it. Like this."

He set his hand over hers, feeling the way she touched herself. "There," she said. "Like that. Just like that. Oh, God, that's it. Like that. Keep doing that."

He had not thought it could get better. But it did. It was so much hotter this way, so necessary to feel her clenching around him. To hear the little involuntary noises she made, to feel her approaching her climax once again, this time as he was inside her.

He could feel it happen—her whole body tightening around him, heightening the heat that rose in him. He could feel her back arch underneath him as he thrust inside her. He gritted his teeth as she came around him.

He pulled out as she let out her last cry. It took him three shuddering strokes before his body clenched, tightening, pleasure racing through him, and he spilled on her stomach.

His chest heaved; they looked into each other's eyes.

She looked down first. "Next time," she said with a smile, "I want to help with that. Or…" She sounded almost shy. "You could do that inside me."

Next time.

"We're not married. It's risky enough as it is. I don't think we should be doing that at this point."

Her eyes went to his, and there was a hint of hurt in them.

This was it. This was the point where he was supposed to reassure her. *We're not married, but we should be,* he should say. *We could be. We must be. I want nobody but you. Marry me. Marry me as soon as you can.*

But there was a tremendous unfairness in asking her such a thing when she did not yet know what marriage to him entailed. She knew he had some property and a good amount of wealth, but she couldn't possibly imagine the truth. *Marry me. I'm a duke. I'll need to spend my life ruthlessly pruning poison vines that could strangle us both.*

He couldn't ask until he told her everything. And he could tell her now, but...

They had little enough time to clean up; he had to meet his servant at the station, get her father's herbal formula, and send the man to take care of Chloe the horse. There was still their return to Wedgeford. She had a father to take care of, bao to craft, and a sauce to launch on the morrow. Her own *father* had suggested he wait.

She was going to find out how badly he had lied to her. She might despise him—even more now that she'd given herself to him. He was going to hurt her; the only question was whether she could forgive him for doing so.

Jeremy could do a lot of things to her, but he'd told her he would try to lift her burdens. Now was not the time to *add* to them. Not when she had so many other things that demanded her attention.

"Chloe," he said. "Sweetheart. I have something I need to ask you."

She nodded.

"Technically, I have two things I need to ask you," he said, "but one of those things… I think we should have that conversation after the Trials when you'll have time to think it over. And the other…depends on that thing."

"Do you actually think I will need much time to think?" She smiled at him.

Her smile, so sweet and trusting… It hurt.

"I don't know." He ran his hand down her shoulder. "I really don't know. But you told me who I am. I'm a wicked libertine. There are probably some things I should tell you before I ask you any serious questions."

She swallowed and looked away.

"Look. I know right now that I should tell you how I feel and tell you that I want you for the rest of my life. And I do." He leaned down and pressed a kiss to her forehead. "But it wouldn't be fair to say any more. Not now. So I must ask this instead: Will you wait one day?"

She looked up at him. There was a hint of confusion in her expression, but only a hint, and even that gave way after a moment. It felt wrong, that her lips should curve in a gentle smile. It felt wrong to ask her to trust him when he hadn't earned it. When he didn't *deserve* it.

But she was doing it anyway.

"Yes," she whispered. "Yes, Jeremy. I will."

16

THE LAMPS WERE ALL OUT AT HOME, WHICH WAS hardly a surprise given that it was almost one in the morning. Chloe's whole body felt sore. It wasn't just the pleasant soreness remaining from what had happened with Jeremy; it was the hour cantering over the downs to Dover, the fall from the horse, followed by the two and a half hours in the cart that had taken them back to Wedgeford. Her back felt as if the cart had found every loose stone on the road home.

But she'd made it. She stood outside the alcove where her father made his bed.

"Ah Ba?" She spoke in a whisper, not wanting to wake him.

"Ah Lin." His voice came from his room.

She peered in. "Not asleep?"

There wasn't much light, just what filtered through the front windows in the main room. Little enough of it made it all the way back here. At least he was in bed lying down. That smell of sick-room persisted, stronger near his bed.

"I had a little headache." He sighed, and she could hear the covers rustling. "I was a little worried about you too."

She almost opened her mouth to inquire why he was worried about her before she realized that he had a real, honest reason to worry...one that had rather proven true.

No reason to mention that. It was a good thing he couldn't see her expression in the dark.

"I have the formula," she said instead. "Let me boil you some."

There was a pause, as if he were somehow contemplating whether he could refuse. "Mmm," he finally said.

It gave her something to do, and that gave her time to think as her hands went through the motions of adding water to the kettle and putting it on the fire, grinding out the dried root before adding in the other herbs.

She hadn't really been able to think on the way back. Jeremy had been there with her, and her mind had been distracted by the smile he gave her, the way he'd squeezed her knee when the cart driver wasn't looking, the way he'd looked away almost guiltily when he thought she was watching the road.

The water came to a boil and she poured it into the clay dish, covered it, and counted in her head until it had steeped sufficiently. Then she decanted the liquid into a porcelain cup, straining it with the lid. Better to take care of her father before trying to understand...that. She took the cup back to his alcove.

"Here." She sat on the bed next to him, helped him come to a sit, and gave him the cup.

He took a swallow.

"How is your condition?"

"Not so bad," he said, which she suspected was a lie if a headache had kept him awake. "I can still move my hands, and there's only a little bit of pain elsewhere. I'll be fine in the morning."

"You'll be what you are in the morning." She sniffed. "You don't need to be fine."

He sat up a little straighter. "We need to finish the bao in the morning. And the booth…"

"We can do that a great many ways, with or without your immediate assistance."

He huffed. "But *I* need to—"

"Ah Ba taught me to be resourceful. I'm not going to disrespect him by refusing to use the skills he taught me. I'll make do, no matter where you are. You do not need to be useful for me to love you."

"Hm." He sounded upset. "Then why did you go all that way to get the formula?"

"So you could feel better. That's enough for me."

He finished the cup and handed it to her silently.

"Do you think you can sleep now?"

He nodded. "I hope so. We'll see." He lay back down, and she retreated into the other room, just far enough that she could hear his breath. Even. Steady. Slowing. All those were good signs.

Chloe should go to sleep. She knew she should. She had a great deal to do tomorrow—she would have to wake up at five as it was—and it was now deep into the night.

Still, before she made her way to her own bed in the little alcove on the other side of the cottage, she stopped for one last thing.

"Ah Me." She bowed before her ancestors' shrine. She didn't have any food, and she didn't want to light any incense, not at this hour of the night. "And...Baba?" She wasn't sure how to address the man who had sired her and given her the bracelet she always wore when she'd only recently learned of his existence.

The tablet engraved with her mother's name seemed a familiar shadow in the darkness, quiet and unjudging.

"Ah Me," Chloe said at a whisper. "Will it surprise you to learn I had intercourse?"

There was no answer to that, but still she found it comforting.

"I suppose I should not have done it." There were a dozen reasons she shouldn't have, in fact. "But...I did. I'm not sure if it was a mistake. It might have been. Jeremy seemed almost solemn on the way back."

That was what had seemed so odd. Jeremy was almost never serious, but he'd scarcely cracked a joke. He'd looked at her as if he were about to lose her, and she didn't understand that. *She* had always been the one losing *him*.

"It's silly." She put her hands together. "But I love him. And I know that's what all the naive girls who are led astray say, but it's still true. I just do."

Chloe had thought of her name in confusion for so many years, wondering if her mother was disappointed in her. But she'd never felt disappointment in these moments they shared together. Only accepting silence. And now that she knew what her name meant, it felt important to sit here in front of her and confess her fears.

"Ah Ba might tell me I was wrong to trust him. But is it so wrong to think him trustworthy? The worst thing he's ever done is disappear for a few years. And I understand that now."

She could imagine all sorts of gentle reproof. *You know Jeremy Yu is not his real name. You know he's never even talked to you about anything. The two of you haven't spoken of how any of this could work, and there is a massive difference between a woman from a village who wants to sell sauce and...him. What if he wants you to be his mistress? If he hasn't talked about these things, don't you think there's a reason?*

But those were her own doubts, not her mother's. Every time she talked to Ah Me, she felt only one thing: love.

"It's not that I have proof he's trustworthy," she said in the face of those doubts. "It's more that... He hasn't said it, but I don't think *anyone* out there trusts him. His aunt wants to pick a spouse who hates him. The people around him want him to disappear."

Chloe looked up and exhaled.

"This may be selfish. It may be foolish. But *I* want to be the one who trusts him. I want to believe in him, because he deserves it. Ah Me, am I being silly?"

As she had before, she sat, head bowed, waiting. Condemnation never came.

Don't worry, Ah Lin. Everything is going to be just right.

Chloe smiled. "Thank you." She bowed again. "Good night, Ah Me. Baba."

———

Jeremy had arisen at five in the morning, leaving his room in the inn as swiftly as possible. He arrived at the spot where Chloe's booth would be erected and made his plans. They had a scant few hours to get the booth ready before the crowds started gathering. They'd have to be efficient, indeed.

The cart driver's son, who had come with them in the cart from Dover, arrived soon after, yawning and stretching. He had picked up the handcart, packed with the mobile Chinese-style range and the materials for the booth from Chloe's home earlier. They set up the booth, then the range, before starting to hang the colorful bunting.

If Jeremy had known what it would do to him to have Chloe—to know her, to touch her, to kiss her all over… He would never have done it. He could not stop thinking of her, not while he wound the coarse blue fabric up and over in decorative twirls, bringing the cloth overhead before stretching it out across a section of the green to a nearby tree. A few more lines of bunting between the booth and the branches formed a makeshift canopy.

Forty-five minutes later, Chloe arrived, walking alongside the cart. The carter drove; her father sat next to him. Mr. Fong surveyed the wide village green with a judging expression on his face.

Jeremy went to greet him. "Mr. Fong!" He smiled. "Allow me to make you comfortable. Would you like some tea?"

He didn't have any tea. They had only just set up the range, and without coal or pans, it was just an empty slab, black holes cold and empty. Jeremy grimaced. "I can fetch something from the inn. Along with biscuits, or sandwiches or…"

He trailed off at the look Mr. Fong gave him, a sharp glower from beneath his eyebrows.

"Or…not." Jeremy smiled too widely. "Whatever you like."

Mr. Fong turned away and Jeremy watched as he started fussing with the arrangement of the materials they'd brought in the cart. The cart driver and his son laid out big vats of the dough Jeremy had helped knead, alongside more vats of pork filling. Coal, steamers, pots all found their places.

Chloe came up beside Jeremy to rearrange the bunting where it attached to the booth. "You are acting *extremely* oddly," she muttered. "Stop it; he's going to get suspicious. Just act normally."

"What are you talking about?" he replied in hushed tones. "This is how I normally act."

"It really isn't. Stop whispering to me; he'll suspect something."

Jeremy made an anguished noise. "Don't *say* that. Don't even think of suspicions. Repeat after me: 'There's nothing to suspect.'"

"Oh, absolutely. So if we told him, then—"

"Here," Mr. Fong said behind them. They both jumped, turning. But Mr. Fong was just holding a little bun out for Chloe's inspection. His eyebrows rose at their mutual flinch, but he continued on. "This size—a little smaller than usual, so they'll steam faster. I'll test a few for breakfast."

Chloe went over to help him make the bao, rolling out little circles of dough.

"Wait." Mr. Fong stopped her as she spooned a dollop of pork filling into the first circle. "We need to add something to that one." He reached into his pocket and removed a little twist of paper. He ripped it in half, pouring red powder on top. "This one's for Jeremy."

"Ah Ba." Chloe sighed. "Really? How long are you going to be doing this for?"

"Apparently at least one more day," he said, his eyes flickering to Jeremy, "especially after last night."

Jeremy's reaction was entirely involuntary; he and Chloe looked at each other, matching spots of guilty red on their cheeks.

"Last night?" Chloe said in a high voice. "What about last night? Nothing happened last night!"

It wasn't very effective as denials went, but it could have been worse. Jeremy knew this, because what he said was: "Please don't kill me."

Mr. Fong turned what felt like a predator's gaze on Jeremy. Jeremy could feel anguished, pained heat rising from the back of his neck.

Oh, God. The absolute worst thing he could have said and there it was, already out of his mouth. Mr. Fong stared at him a moment longer, then tapped a finger against his chin, turning to his daughter.

She stared mutely back.

He finally shook his head. "You're both ridiculous," he muttered. "Nobody wants to know about any of *that.*"

"Know about…what?" Jeremy said.

"There's nothing to know!" Chloe chirped. "Nothing at all!"

"I'm reasonably aware of my surroundings," Mr. Fong told them. "You're both acting extremely strangely, and I would appreciate it if I could imagine a great deal less based on your clearly guilty faces. Do I ever make it obvious what *I'm* doing?"

"Ha. That's ridiculous. You don't…" Chloe trailed off, her eyes widening.

Mr. Fong rolled his eyes. "Exactly. You have no idea. Give me the same courtesy."

So saying, he turned back to put the massive pot over the range, holding his hand a few inches from the liquid to check the temperature of the water. He acted as if the discussion had never happened.

Jeremy looked at the man. For all that he was Chloe's father, he wasn't actually *old*. He looked like he was maybe thirty, and while he *had* to be at least a decade older than that, he was scarcely even middle-aged. So of course it wouldn't be surprising that he…that he…

No. He couldn't bring himself to contemplate it.

"That's…" Chloe looked into the vat of dough. "I am going to pretend that…he never said that. It didn't happen."

"It didn't happen," Jeremy agreed. "And there are bao to be made. Here, let me help." And luckily, after that, there was too much to do to waste time with embarrassment.

17

By the time ten in the morning rolled around, Jeremy was already exhausted. Chloe had badgered Mr. Fong until he agreed to take a rest. He had retired to sit under the tree twenty paces distant. But the day had really only just started. Jeremy's thoughts disappeared into an endless routine of rolling yeasty dough into circles and handing these to Chloe to fill, over and over, until his fingers felt imaginary dough even when he took a break to stretch. They sold a tray or so during the morning. By midmorning, the rush began to start with a man who came up to the booth, looking with interest at the batch of bao that was coming out of the steamer.

"What's inside?" one man asked, and Jeremy stepped forward.

"It's a pork bun," he said. "A little like a meat pasty."

"Meat pasty." The man looked at it. "Why's it white, then?"

"It's been steamed rather than baked. That's all."

"Hmm. Give me two then." He laid a coin on the table.

Jeremy had never acted as a servant at table. It was a lot of fun to do so—to take the money, to hold his back stiffly, as if he were a footman with a tray, and to hand over two buns, glistening in the paper wrappers they'd been steamed in.

"Here you are, my good sir."

The man gave him an odd look, but he took one bun out of its paper and bit into it. He paused, chewing, before his eyes widened.

"What's inside?" His voice was muffled with his mouth still full. "It's good."

Jeremy just smiled at him. "It's pork cooked in Wedgeford Brown, with a handful of other flavorings."

"Wedgeford Brown." The man shook his head. "Never heard of it." He took another bite. "Never tasted anything like it either. Is it like curry?"

"It's not really anything like curry." Jeremy frowned, and then tried to imagine how a baker might speak of his wares. "It's only the most delicious sauce in all of England—available now for the low price of a shilling a jar. Think of what this sauce could do to soups and stews and pasties."

"You can buy it?" The man leaned forward. "Just a shil—" He caught himself. "Ah. I mean." He cleared his throat. "I suppose I could manage a jar at that price."

"You seem like a fellow who knows a good price when he sees one," Jeremy said, leaning in conspiratorially. "This is an introductory offer, just for the Trials. After that…" He trailed off suggestively.

The man's eyes widened. "In that case, I'd better get two."

The man left, juggling his jars and his other bun.

"What have you there?" he heard someone say.

"Ah, those meat buns over there—best I've ever tasted," came the reply, indistinct in the noise of the growing crowd. "Try some while you still can."

"I didn't know you were so good at selling buns," Chloe said behind him.

Jeremy just smiled at her. "You didn't know I was good at saying words and getting people to do things? Really? And you claim to have *known* me?"

Chloe blinked. "Oh. Excellent point. Carry on."

The crowd grew thicker and hungrier; the bao disappeared as soon as Chloe opened each steamer basket. For two straight hours, Jeremy didn't have time to do anything except smile and take money and hand over buns. Finally, the jar of coins at his feet was almost full and the crowd had thinned out, going back to the Trials.

Beside him, Chloe handed him a pair of bao and a mug of tea. "Sit down," she said. "Take a break. They'll be back in a crush for dinner."

He sat down with her. He didn't know how she managed to look the way she did—fresh, with her hair still in its perfect bun. She'd been working the steamer baskets all day, and she had not one hair out of place. She sighed and rolled her shoulders back, stretching, while she ate her own bao.

There were a lot of things he could say. *Look, aren't I useful?* That was one of them. *By the way, I'm the duke.* That was another.

What he actually said was this: "Please never hate me."

She paused, mid-bite, to look at him, her head tilted in confusion. "It seems rather unlikely at this point."

"Oh." He took a bite of his own bun and washed it down with a swallow of water. "Good. I think."

"Have you ever lied to my father and stolen his method for making sauce?"

Jeremy grimaced. Technically, he'd been lying to everyone in Wedgeford for ages. So… At least fifty percent yes.

"Trust me," she said, unaware of the direction of his thoughts. "I have only enough hate in my heart for White and Whistler...and certainly no emotion like that for you. There's no need to fret so."

Jeremy finished his bun. That was the hell of it. He *had* stolen. There *was* need to fret. He'd stolen from everyone in Wedgeford. They knew he was rich, but they imagined that he was...maybe some kind of simple country gentleman or a trader's son or something. Not the actual duke who owned all their land. They'd treated him as a compatriot, taken him into their confidence, and made him feel like this place could be home. And he'd been lying to them all this time.

He had stolen their friendship, their good-will. And why? *I don't want them to know I own everything. They'll act differently.*

The reason seemed so pale, now that he was on the verge of explaining everything. He'd robbed them of the chance to make their own choice as to how they would treat him.

Stay, Chloe had told him. *Grow,* Mr. Fong had

suggested. But had he poisoned the ground before he had the chance to do either?

He'd been afraid. He'd questioned himself. He'd doubted. But if he had been so afraid that they would act differently, fearing that he would hold his property ownership over their heads…

There was a very simple solution to that problem. He could have just given them the property outright. He'd already changed his will for Wedgeford's sake. He hadn't *had* to attend the festival in silence, saying absolutely nothing about his ownership while he continued to own the homes of the entirety of the village. The land of Wedgeford had come from a long-ago female dowry; it wasn't even entailed. He could have just…given it away.

It had never occurred to him until this moment. *Root out every poisonous vine,* his mother had told him, and this was the first time it occurred to him that the thing that had poisoned every second of his time in Wedgeford was something he could change.

He *was* a thief. And a coward. Who lacked imagination.

He put his head in his hands.

"Jeremy?" Chloe looked at him. "Whatever is wrong?"

"I'll tell you." He had to; he had put it off too long. "I'll tell you when we're finished here tonight."

She nodded and appeared almost concerned; he felt he had one last thing to add.

"You mustn't feel as if you are obligated to stand by anything you've said over the last few days."

"What have I said?"

"You can hate me if you want. When you know. If you think I deserve it."

She just looked at him, one eyebrow raised. "You are acting very, very oddly. I suppose it's because you're tired."

He'd stolen enough from her. He wouldn't steal her momentum at the instant she stood poised for victory. He stood. "Come on. Time to get the bao ready for the next wave."

———

By the time evening came, Jeremy felt about as capable as a wet dishrag. Mr. Fong had retired to rest, but the crowds were thick, and it was clear that despite their best estimates, they were going to run out of buns. They had already sold all their jars of sauce.

Just as he was selling the first buns from the last tray, someone came up behind him.

"Posh Jim!"

Jeremy turned, trying to find a smile through his exhaustion.

It was Mr. Wilderhampsher. He had dirt on his face, mud on his shoes, filth ground into his trousers, and grime smeared all over his jacket. There wasn't a spot on him that remained uncontaminated with some disgusting substance. He was grinning.

Jeremy found himself brightening.

"Mr. Wilderhampsher!" He managed to make himself heard over the clamor of people in line, hoping to get the last of the buns. "How was your day?"

"It was utterly splendescent!" Mr. Wilderhampsher's

beaming face indicated that this was intended as the highest of compliments. "I was with Lee when we found the Minders' Wedgelot!"

"Amazing! Good job!" Jeremy cheered him, taking another couple of pennies and passing over two more buns.

"Of course, *he* carried the Wedgelot." Mr. Wilderhampsher demonstrated the Wedgelot carrying technique, hands high over his head. "And I did the little thing to keep others away." He mimicked the protective stance—arms at right angles, moving in a circular pattern.

"Good job!"

"We got all the way over the Wedge before we lost the Wedgelot to the Uppers."

Jeremy nodded. "That happens."

"But! We got it back! We ran up a tree and snatched it from their hands as they passed under."

"Truly amazing," Jeremy gushed. "I told you it would work out."

"And they've given me a name. A true Wedgeford Trials nickname. I'm now Mr. Whajusay." The last was said so quickly the words blended together.

"What?"

"Mr. What-Did-You-Say." Mr. Wilderhampsher looked so absurdly pleased by this development that Jeremy could only nod thoughtfully.

"Congratulations. Look at you. You've made friends!"

"I can't wait to come back here next year."

Jeremy gave another pair of buns to a customer. Beside him, Chloe handed over more still. They were down to their last basket.

He stopped and knelt next to Mr. Wilderhampsher.

"A little advice," he said, low enough so as not to be heard by Chloe.

"Yes?"

"If you meet a girl," Jeremy said, "and you fall in love with her…"

Mr. Wilderhampsher's nose wrinkled. "Ugh. I'm not here for *girls.*"

"Or anyone else," Jeremy amended. "Or even if you just make a friend or three. Speaking from experience, I should tell you…"

Mr. Wilderhampsher leaned closer, and Jeremy bent to his level.

"Don't wait a decade to tell them who you really are."

Mr. Wilderhampsher pulled back, making a face. "That… That sounds like…oddly specific advice. Are you trying to tell me something?"

Jeremy straightened, laughing, and cast a glance over at Chloe. "Yes." He ran his hand through his hair. "It's definitely…oddly specific. And yet very good advice."

As weary as Jeremy was, he was not looking forward to the end of the day. The last of the buns had been sold; the bunting had been taken down, the cart driver and his son had loaded everything up. Jeremy had gone through and scrupulously cleaned up excess paper left on the green by the crowds, and by the time he'd returned to the spot where the booth had been—now disassembled and packed in the cart alongside the range and the steamer baskets—he had no more excuses.

They were finished, and it was time to tell Chloe. He swallowed.

She turned to him, happiness shining from her face. "Jeremy!" She greeted him so warmly, as if he deserved her brightest smiles. "Look at you. You look so tired. After all your hard work, we'll scarcely be able to call you Posh Jim at all."

"No." Soon, she'd know his real name and title. He gave her a wink even though he felt sick to the pit of his stomach. "It may not come naturally to me, but I *am* capable." Finishing the joke came easily, despite the uneasy swirl in his belly. "Capable-ish."

"Well, I'm not even capable-ish any longer." She came to stand by him. "I'm so tired I could just collapse right here and sleep for five days."

"Don't. I'm too tired to guard you from inclement weather."

Her head tilted, perhaps catching for the first time that his smile was a fraud. She looked up at him. "Jeremy? Is everything well? What's wrong?"

"Nothing is wrong," he told her, and then caught himself. "Nothing except the things that have always been wrong."

He caught hold of his bravery, examined it, and…

And once again, found himself not up to the task. "You're tired. We should talk in the morning." What was the difference in twelve hours when it had already been twelve *years?*

For a long moment, she didn't say anything. Twilight was falling; she looked up at him, her eyes searching.

"You regret last night." Her voice was low.

"No." He reached out for her hand, before realizing how very public they were in the moment. And then he realized that unfortunately, she was right. "Not as such. I regret how I handled it. I'm afraid I owe you something of an apology. And a confession." He sighed. "Two confessions. But we're both exhausted, and it'll be better in the morning. Maybe?"

She looked down at his hand, where he'd reached for her. "Now *I* won't be able to sleep, worrying. Come, Jeremy. I'll send the cart ahead and have them unload it all into the barn. Walk with me."

"You're tired."

"I am," she said. "But you look so sad, and you're never sad. Today was remarkable for my father and me. We sold all the jars we made and all the buns. I can't bear seeing you sad today. You know that, right?"

If she was brave enough to say such a thing to him—outright, in public, with others perhaps listening in—he could be brave enough to tell her the truth. To beg for her forgiveness. To tell her that he'd give her all the time in the world to consider, and to hope that maybe—after a month, after two, perhaps—she would get over the shock of it all and understand. All he could do was hope.

She checked the cart one last time, gave the cart driver one final payment and a bonus, and the directions to take everything back to the barn, then came back to Jeremy. Slowly they left the green. They passed the rock where she'd talked about kissing, and the path that led up the hill, where they'd actually kissed. The road was still populated at first; they stopped every five steps to talk to someone. Over a bridge, down a smaller track, and eventually, they left the throngs behind.

"How bad is it?" she finally asked. "By your face, I'd say that whatever you need to say is horrible."

He exhaled. "It is." He wasn't sure where to start; that was the problem. He'd had all these years to think of how to do it, and he still couldn't decide on the proper order. Tell her he was the Duke of Lansing? Or ask her to marry him? If he asked about marriage before telling her the truth, she wouldn't know what she needed to make a decision. And if he told her first, she would likely be so distressed she might not stay to listen to the question that followed.

That made the proper course clear. If what he'd done was so unforgivable that she couldn't bear to hear him, he needed to start with the unforgivable item first.

"Chloe. There's no easy way to say this."

She was staring at him in something like horror. "You're already married."

He tilted his head in confusion. *"What?"*

"I was just trying to think what could possibly be so bad that you'd look like that. You look like you're about to pronounce a death sentence on me. It was the worst thing I could think of."

"I—no, that doesn't even make sense." He almost wanted to laugh. He wasn't sure if the actual truth was worse or better. "How does anything I've said and done square with that?"

Chloe shrugged. "It sounds like you've done something *extremely* bad. *That* doesn't make sense either, because you're you. I'm just extrapolating."

"Stop extrapolating!"

"Did you kill someone? Are you here to hide from the authorities?"

"That is also extrapolating!" He made a fist. "This is hard enough as it is without your inventing sins for me. Will you *please—?*"

Oh yes. Reproaching her was probably an *excellent* way to start this conversation. He cleared his throat and wiped a hand across his face.

"Please. Please allow me to say what I have to say. I've put this off so long, and it's so terrible. I don't want to say it, but it cannot wait any longer. Not one second. Chloe, I love you. I want you in my life forever." He paused, throat closing on what he had to say.

She frowned at him. "That's it? That's the bad thing that has you looking at me like that? I already knew that."

"You did?" He frowned. "How did you know that?"

"You've told me twenty times since you arrived."

"That's—that's just—never mind. Look. How am I supposed to confess? I wasn't supposed to say that yet. I'm getting it all mixed up. Chloe, *I'm* the duke."

There. He'd said it. Badly, but he'd said it. His breath seemed stuck in his lungs, as he waited for her horrified reaction.

Instead, she looked up at him with a befuddled stare. "What?"

Right; the truth had to come as a shock. She probably hadn't even rightly heard what he'd said.

"The Duke of Lansing," he explained to her. "The

fucking duke. His Grace Good Riddance. The Duke Who Didn't. That's me."

Still she did not say anything.

"My full name is Jeremy Alan Yu Ging Lung Wentworth, Duke of Lansing, Earl of Marbury, Viscount Wilde, Baron of—"

Her eyes lit. "Ging Lung! What character do you use for Lung?"

"Um." He blinked. "Dragon. But Chloe—"

"You know, my father—SiuLiung—he uses the same character, just pronounced the Hakka way. I had no idea. What an extraordinary coincidence!" She frowned. "Or maybe it's not that extraordinary. He's twenty-four years older than you."

"Chloe." He felt as if he were moving through thick mud. The going was painstakingly slow, and the ground threatened to suck him under. "How is that the thing you are focusing on at the moment? Are you listening to me? I'm the Duke of Lansing. I own your home. You owe me fifty-three years of rents."

That did stop her. She folded her arms and frowned. "Surely not. We've only lived here the past eighteen years."

"Are you not surprised?" he demanded. "Or angry? Or dismayed?"

She put a hand on his elbow. "Jeremy."

He shut his eyes. "Yes?"

"I am not dismayed. Just a little confused."

"That explains it." He sighed. "It must come as an immense surprise to you; of course you may take time to consider."

"No," she said. "Not that. I am...having a moment of difficulty comprehending...one other little thing."

One *little* thing.

"No," he said bitterly. "You comprehend it perfectly well. I am the horrific fiend who owns all your land. You *all* owe fifty-three years of back rents to me. I took advantage of your friendship, your goodwill, your—"

"Jeremy," she said, "will you please wait just one moment before you go on a tirade?"

"I know how it looks, asking you to marry me." He put his hands in his pockets and looked away. "It's no good either way. If I *didn't* tell you, you wouldn't know what you were getting into, and that wouldn't be fair. If I *did* tell you... I don't want you to feel as if you must do anything, simply because of the stupid situation with the land and the rents and all of that. If you wish, before you answer, I'll have my solicitor draw up a deed of conveyance."

"Jeremy," she said. "Will you *please* listen to me? I have a question, and I think you must answer it."

"It's true." He looked down at her, afraid of losing her once she truly understood it. "It's all true."

"Listen!" She made an exasperated noise and took hold of his shoulders. "Jeremy, were you under the impression that nobody knew who you were?"

He blinked. His entire mind went blank. "Ah?" There was a roaring in his ears; his entire body felt like he might blow away on a strong exhale. "*What* was that you said?"

"I think you heard me. Do you think nobody knows you're the duke?"

"What." He wanted to finish the sentence; he really did. The problem was that he didn't know how. *"What."*

"What?"

"What," he repeated stupidly.

"There is no what." She shrugged. "Everyone knows you're the Duke of Lansing."

He was struggling to fit his mind around this. "Did your father tell you recently? He told me he wouldn't mention it."

She was beginning to smile. "Oh, you giant oaf. Are you under the impression that you're anonymous?"

"Um." He looked up at the night sky. Stars were beginning to come out, bright and beautiful. It had not exactly occurred to him that he *wouldn't* be. "Yes?"

"Let me see if I have this straight. When I was in Dover, and you were off at the station, someone mentioned their cousin Tom in Shanghai to me. I've never even been to China. Did it matter? No. They think all Chinese people know each other. There is precisely one half-Chinese duke in all of Britain...and you somehow think that the village of Wedgeford wouldn't be continually informed of his existence?"

"I..." He hadn't thought of that. He hadn't thought at all.

"You cut a ribbon in the May Day parade in London last year. There were tens of thousands of people in the crowd! Did you think, in that massive assembly, that there was absolutely nobody from Wedgeford?"

"But." Jeremy swallowed. "But nobody ever said anything? How—that—I don't understand."

"Well, first of all." She rolled her eyes. "It's Wedgeford

rules. We don't go around asking people where they're from. It's awkward and unmannerly."

He'd realized that. He'd understood it. He just hadn't...comprehended precisely how it might apply to him.

"Secondly," she said, "you always seemed a little embarrassed by it. If you'd *wanted* us to call you something besides Posh Jim, you'd have said so."

"That's true, but..." He still could not complete a thought.

"And finally," she said, "do you mean to tell me you *haven't noticed* how much people tease you?"

"Tease me." He bit his lip. "People tease me?"

"You know. Going up to you and saying things like, 'Ha ha, do you think the duke will like what I've done to his field?' and such. Do you think we spend all our time talking about the Duke of Lansing when you're not here?"

He felt as if he'd been struck by lightning. He felt... He didn't know how he felt. It was impossible to comprehend. They...knew? How did they all know? How could it be possible? And what did it mean?

That they'd known, and they'd still treated him the way they had... He wanted to laugh with the relief that rushed through him. And he thought that he'd loved Wedgeford *before* this moment. Ha.

"It was fairly obvious that you were embarrassed by your station," Chloe said. "Everyone liked you, and it would have been horrific to have to bow and scrape and 'Your Grace' you the entire time. Nobody wanted it, least of all you. Ignoring it seemed like the best option for everyone."

"Except for the teasing," he muttered. They'd been teasing. They'd been *teasing?* His entire world seemed to shift on its axis.

"Yes," she said with a laugh. "Except for that."

What in all the *hells*. That had been *teasing*. He hadn't even realized. If that had all been teasing…good God, the entirety of Wedgeford was *hilarious,* and he'd never given them credit for it.

"I feel," Jeremy said, his head still ringing, "that I am getting away with something really awful here. Everyone is supposed to be furious."

"There's nothing terrible about being loved," she told him. "People liked you. That's all that happened. You are allowed to have that."

He still could not quite grapple with the concept. "It's late," he finally said, rather than answering this. "We… obviously have a great deal to discuss. There's still a lot we have to go over. But before I let you go for the night, before we both collapse of exhaustion… I love you. I want you. I need you rather desperately. Please tell me you'll marry me."

She smiled up into his eyes. "Jeremy." She reached out and touched his face. "Yes."

18

CHLOE STILL WASN'T QUITE SURE WHAT HAD happened today. It felt like six days of repetitive, unrelenting labor, all crammed into one. The way she'd held her breath when the crowd first started trying the buns… The press of business, without a second to spare, during the onslaught of meal-times.

That, and the heavy, uncounted jar of coins, would have been enough to leave her somewhat dazed.

Now there was this. Jeremy's hand was in hers. He'd asked her to marry him. He'd accompanied her home. None of it seemed quite real; she was so exhausted that she thought it might all be a dream, that it would surely end when her eyes opened.

But here they were, fingers twined together, nearly to the end of the road, down which she lived with her father. Just one more bridge over a little stream, through the copse of trees, then past the ancient yew that marked the edge of their property. She could see the windows of her home lit up beyond those branches. Her father was waiting.

Jeremy had asked her to marry him. It *still* didn't seem real.

He squeezed her fingers. "You really will marry me?"

Maybe he felt as unmoored as she did. "I really will," she answered.

If this was not a dream—and she wasn't certain—she had no idea how it would work. There was too much to consider. She couldn't leave her father; she hoped Jeremy wouldn't expect such a thing. And the thought of abandoning her father's sauce company, just started…

People would say that there was no need for her to pursue such a thing, if she were a duchess. Money would be no object, after all.

Except Wedgeford Brown had never fully been about money, not really. It had been about reclaiming what should have belonged to her father by right and had been stolen by avarice. It had been about revenge.

Were duchesses allowed to make sauce? Jeremy wanted her; she knew that. He loved her, even; she also knew that. But she wasn't sure there was a place for her ambitions in his life.

"I will treat you so well," Jeremy said, stopping in the copse of trees just before they got to her house.

She was afraid if she asked any of these questions, the moment would burst like a bubble of soap. "Oh, don't start with that." She smiled at him. "You've always teased me. I've always liked it. There's no need to do differently now."

He leaned into her. His breath was warm against her

ear. "Chloe. I've been thinking about Wedgeford. And Wedgeford Brown."

Five days a year; that was what he had given to Wedgeford thus far. Would it become the same for her?

She didn't want to choose between this place and the man that she loved. Chloe shut her eyes. She was going to choose him; she was fairly certain she would. It would not make sense to explain to him that their engagement had left her feeling a bit at a loss.

She looked up at him. "Don't talk of it now, I beg you. I'm so tired. We can work out the details later."

For now she could pretend. She could pretend that their life together would always be like it had been these past few days—with him supporting her, helping her find herbal formula, hiring help for her business.

She was better for his presence; he'd proven it these last days. She could not have a sauce empire if she did everything herself. Without him there yesterday, she would have tried to do everything and managed…far less. She would have been grumpy and frustrated the entire day. She needed someone to remind her to be human, to leave space on her lists. She needed someone to make her laugh.

But…did duchesses even have lists? Did they get to carry board clips and taste sauces?

She took both his hands and pulled him in, until his body pressed against hers. She could feel every inch of him, the muscle of his legs pressing against her skirts, his hips against her pelvis. Their foreheads touched so that she could breathe his air.

"Chloe." He didn't pull away. "This is…not the best

idea. I love you." He swallowed. "I also…want you so much."

Maybe it was because she was exhausted. Maybe it was because she was just a little scared. Maybe it was because this felt like a dream that could end at any moment, and she wanted to hold on to whatever memories she might make.

Chloe pressed herself against him. He let out a little groan.

"Chloe…"

"Maybe you're not alone." She looked up at him. "Maybe I want you just as much."

"We shouldn't." He swallowed. "Last night… I know we're getting married, but it's still a risk. And that's not why I asked, I want you to know—not because I think you might be pregnant. The only reason I took you to bed yesterday, knowing the risks… It was because I already knew I wanted to marry you."

He was sweet, so sweet. She almost wanted to protect him from himself. She smiled up at him instead.

"Jeremy," she said.

He cupped her cheek in his hand, leaned down, and pressed his lips to hers. He could have opened her mouth, dipped his tongue in—any of the things he had already done. But he didn't. The kiss should have felt chaste, in comparison, and yet there was such yearning in it, such desire in that short press of their lips that it left her wanting so much more.

"Beautiful girl." He kissed her again, this time a little longer. "Tired girl." Another kiss, this one the longest of all. Their lips clung together; she didn't want to give him up. "I should let you sleep." But he didn't let go of her.

Maybe she was being selfish, trying to hoard every possible experience while she still had the chance. Maybe some part of her still believed that this wouldn't work out...that despite his protestations, he would leave and she would have only her memories once again. She wanted —she needed—more to recall.

"Jeremy." She looked up at him in the darkness. "I'll sleep better if I'm not still needing you."

He let out another groan. "*You* need *me?*"

She did. She thought of what had happened in the inn last night—the way he'd touched her, his hands on her hips. The way his body had joined with hers, twining together. The way he'd thanked her for trusting him.

She'd not had time to ponder it since; they'd been so busy. But her body had been contemplating all day, and now that it was night, it remembered. It remembered the way he set off electricity in her veins. Her flesh remembered the pleasure of his touch, and she wanted him.

She let out a shaky breath and gave him her deepest vulnerability. "I'm scared. I'm scared that you'll leave again."

"Chloe." His hand came to her face, touching her gently. "Chloe."

"You'll come to your senses," she said. "You'll realize how hard it will be, you'll decide—"

"Chloe." His lips brushed her nose. "I know you're scared. I can't blame you. I don't know how to solve the problem of the entire world, and I wish I did for you. But life will not be harder with you; it will be wonderful."

"But—"

He caught her in another kiss, hot and openmouthed. She felt as if he were swallowing her fear and giving it back to her, transmuted into pure desire.

"Chloe," he murmured when he pulled back, "what part of 'I want my wife to have exactly your qualities' made you think I could ever want someone who was not you?"

Chloe knew a bit about fear. Fear stemmed from hurt, and he'd hurt her before. Fear was not easy to banish; telling herself she should not feel it was an exercise in futility. It knocked at her door because it knew it could have easy entry. She'd never been able to bar it fully from her life, only to cordon it off with lists and plans.

But pushing that fear away, tamping it down in the bottom of her soul and pretending it did not exist? Acting as if it were some spectral creature that would devour her if she looked it in the eye? That would never answer.

And so Chloe took the remnants of her fear, the last portions of the hurt she had felt, and for a moment, she let herself feel every last inch of it in its full glory. Maybe this was the last time they'd ever kiss, the last time he'd ever explore her with this sense of worship. Maybe on the morrow, she'd wake up and discover there was no way through, that this was a dream that could never be.

He kissed her again, his hands running down her sides. Alongside her wistfulness, lust rose. Not just lust for his body, but lust for him. For *them*. For a future without hurt, without any of this fear.

And with that desire came determination.

Maybe this was the beginning. Maybe she was holding

on to fear because if she let herself feel how much she wanted him—how desperately she wanted him to stay in her life and talk to her about sauces and fold her bao and take her to his bed—she'd make herself vulnerable to disappointment.

She imagined her fears of frailty and abandonment as a heavy, spiked ball deep inside her. But she'd dealt with fears before. She thanked them for keeping her safe, acknowledged them for the work they had done in bringing her to this moment. And then she imagined taking that spiked ball out of her, holding it out as if it were a dandelion puff...and blowing all that fear away, to scatter in the wind.

She took his hand and pulled him through the small copse of trees, up against the aging yew. The branches spread around them, casting shadows in which they could hide.

"Jeremy," she said, looking up at him. "I love you."

"I love you." His hands came to her skirts; he pushed her back a step, then two, until her spine rested against the yew. The branches spread, low and twisting, forming a little platform that seemed to embrace her. "I love you." His hips ground into hers.

Were there difficulties? Yes. But Chloe had encountered difficulties before, and they'd all proved susceptible to her. Did she not have lists? She had lists. She and Jeremy could make a truly excellent list together.

His hands fumbled in the fabric of her skirts, and so she helped him—lifting all the layers, guiding him to where he could take down her drawers.

"God." His fingers slipped between her thighs. "I love you. I love you so much."

What was she truly afraid of? She thought back to the moment they'd entered the inn in Dover last night. She had wanted there to be only one room… and so she'd made it happen. She'd cheated, yes, but cheating was a form of winning.

It had not been fate. It had not been magic. She was Chloe YiLin Fong. Her father's bracelet sat on her arm; her mother's earrings brushed against her neck. She had been named to rise on wings that made no sound, and so she would do so now.

She undid the buttons of his trousers, taking the hot length of him in her hands.

"Chloe," he gasped. "Chloe, we don't have to—"

"Do you *want* to?"

"Yes." He leaned in close. "So much. So much. But I want to be so good to you. I don't want to annoy you with my wants."

"You're not annoying me." She tilted her face up to him. "I want you too, and I am not going to let my fears dictate what I have. Let me want you as much as you want me."

Her legs were bare to the cool night air; his hands were between her thighs, feeling her slickness. Her fingers were on his hard cock.

"God." He put his forehead against hers. "I want you. I always want you."

She had no idea what she was doing. Instinct made her curl her leg around him, opening herself up. Instinct made them press together, the hard bar of his erection pressing against her opening. He thrust against her, shallowly, once, then twice, before rearranging himself and sliding in an inch.

For a moment it seemed as if there were no room for him. She exhaled slowly, feeling the hard tip of him, then inhaled and felt her body soften. He pushed in another inch, carving out space inside her.

"Jeremy." Her hands went to his shoulders; his arms came around her, holding her in place.

"Chloe." His head rested against her shoulder. "Chloe. So good."

He thrust again, a little less shallowly, slipping deeper inside. Every nerve she owned seemed to catch fire as he did. She wanted him, more of him. She opened wider, wrapping her other leg about his hips. He took her weight, adjusting without a second thought and thrusting even deeper into her.

"God," she whispered into his shoulder. "You belong here. You belong with me."

It didn't matter how difficult it seemed. Chloe was named for the sound of feathers, and she could almost hear them now.

He sank into her fully, his hips pressed against hers. At this angle against the tree, every thrust of his pressed something vital between them, sending little sparks out.

She gave herself over to him, to the feel of him taking her, to the clench of her hands on his shoulders. She gave herself over to the sensation, winding higher and higher.

She could not help the moan that escaped her lips, high and keening, when she finally came.

He pulled out a moment after, thrusting against her hard before coming into his hand.

For a moment there was only sensation, the heat of their bodies where they pressed together. The trickle of sweat down her face. The cold air of the night. The gentle press of his lips against hers. The press of the bark against her dress.

She came back into herself breath by careful breath.

"Chloe." His lips brushed against hers. "I love you."

"I love you too." She could feel the determination swelling in her heart. True, she could not see how it was possible for them to be together. Even if they were, she might have to give up so much—so many pieces of herself that she wasn't sure how she could stay who she was.

And yet she also knew she would make it so. She refused to let it be any other way.

"I love you," she said. It was a promise.

He found a handkerchief in his pocket and gently cleaned them off. He let her down on her own two feet. She rearranged her skirts, brushing them back into place, and then he kissed her again.

"We must talk in the morning, sweetheart."

"Talk," she said, giving him a smile. "Just talk?"

"*Just* talk. Among other things, I need to talk to your father."

"Then I'll meet you back here tomorrow at seven."

"Seven?" He let out an exhale. "Nine, please."

She couldn't help but laugh. "At nine."

He walked her to the door of her father's house. And there, he pressed against her, kissing her one last time.

Their tongues touched; he tasted hot and sweet. It

should have been a carnal kiss, the way it seemed he wanted to devour her. And yet, despite the heat of it, it was so much more. *This,* the kiss seemed to promise, *this is going to last forever.*

He pulled back and looked her in the eyes.

This was where the dream ended, she suspected. This was where reality started. On the morrow, they'd talk over all the details they might not be able to see past. On the morrow, she would insist on what she wanted.

Her list was simple.

Everything. Chloe wanted everything.

19

"CHLOE IS OUT IN THE BARN," MR. FONG SAID, JUST before nine the next morning. He looked at Jeremy the way he always looked at Jeremy—as if he were a thing to be tolerated, and then, just barely.

"Oh." For a moment, Jeremy thought about avoiding this next conversation. But that wild impulse lasted only for a moment.

"She'll be back shortly," Mr. Fong said. "Breakfast is nearly ready. Do you wish to join us?"

Jeremy swallowed. "Might I help?"

This was how he found himself in the kitchen a few minutes later, in his socks, with a mortar and pestle, a pile of fragrant, lightly cooked herbs, peanuts, and some fried tea leaves.

"Just grind them," Mr. Fong said casually while he threw chopped leeks and tofu in a wok, searing them.

Luckily, enthusiasm worked wonders on a mortar and pestle. "So," Jeremy said as he put his shoulder into the task. "I asked Chloe if she would marry me."

He glanced over at Mr. Fong. He picked up the wok in one hand, mixing the vegetables without looking over.

"She said yes," Jeremy said. "She and I…still have a great deal to talk about, but I wanted to say that no matter what, I would never separate you from her. You'll always be welcome in our home."

Mr. Fong flicked him a level look. "When you say you have a great deal to talk about…"

Jeremy sighed. "We did talk about my being the Duke of Lansing, yes. Briefly. She may still run screaming when she hears particulars, in which case you may be rid of me yet."

"She has liked you all these years," Mr. Fong said. "If that were going to happen, it would already have happened."

The door opened, and Chloe came in. "Ah Ba, I have the— Oh. Jeremy, you're here." She looked back and forth between them. "I'll let you two talk then, and just go and pai to—"

"One moment," Mr. Fong said. "What I have to say next is for you both. Jeremy says you're engaged."

Chloe ducked her head. "He came here to talk to you."

Mr. Fong shrugged. "What should I say? You've already made up your mind. I wouldn't hold you back from anything you wanted to do."

Jeremy blinked at him. He had thought there would be more resistance.

Mr. Fong tapped his shoulder and gestured to where Chloe stood near the ancestral tablets. "Go join her," he said. "She should make that introduction, I think."

Jeremy went over to Chloe, and then, following her, knelt in front of the rosewood tablets. She'd shown him them before, years ago. She waited for him, then laced their fingers together.

"Ah Me," she said. "Baba. This is Jeremy."

"I'm Yu Ging Lung," he offered.

"He matters to me," Chloe said. For a moment she didn't say anything else.

Jeremy wished that Chloe's mother was here in the flesh. Between Jeremy's mother, Chloe's father... They had learned so much. He wondered what they would have learned from the woman who had died when Chloe was a baby. It was an incalculable loss.

But Chloe just smiled. "Ah Me," she said. "I think you'd love him as much as I do. He's very funny, and he makes my load lighter."

He looked at the smile on her face, the way her eyes shone. He looked at the little tassels at her ears and the tablet before her, with the character that was a part of Chloe's name, the way that her Ah Me had been a part of Chloe's life even after she'd gone. It was an incalculable loss, but it was not a complete one. Chloe's Ah Me had never been entirely absent.

Jeremy hoped that he would always be a part of her life, and her children's life, and their grandchildren's life... Present in the flesh or not, he hoped that what he did would matter to them.

"Breakfast is almost ready," Mr. Fong called out. "For the lui cha fan—Jeremy, tell me how spicy do you like your food?"

Jeremy smiled. "I like a little heat."

AN HOUR LATER, JEREMY AND CHLOE WENT OUT TO
talk. People were beginning to straggle from their homes
in various states of weariness after the Trials yesterday. But
it was a beautiful day, perfect for a walk together.

Jeremy made a point of holding Chloe's hand. In
public. It was as good as a declaration; he wanted everyone
to know she was his.

"Was Ah Ba very surprised about the engagement?"
Chloe asked.

Jeremy shook his head. "No. He and I had a little talk
the first day I was here where I basically admitted to being
in love with you, and he said something like, 'So why
haven't you talked about the fact that you're the Duke of
Lansing?'"

Chloe put a hand over her mouth, covering a smile, as
they walked over a bridge.

"I stared at him like a carp pulled from the lake. And
he said something about how I was hardly good enough
for you and I was terribly obvious when I stared at you. I
begged him not to tell you who I was and to give me the
chance to expose my secrets on my own." Jeremy frowned.
"In retrospect, he must have found that particular point
absolutely comical. He knew of my misery and chose to
let me wallow in it. Suffice to say, your father was not at all
surprised about this development. He just wanted me to
have a serious discussion with you about it."

"And here we are," Chloe said. "We should have a
serious discussion." She let go of his hand. "Here we are,
being very serious."

"Here I am," Jeremy said. "Being very serious."

They had come to the edge of the green. The green was practically crowded. People were up and about, moving unsteadily in the too-hot morning sunshine. They'd all been celebrating the past night, and if the average villager's celebrations had run more to alcohol and less to the heated kisses that Jeremy had exchanged with Chloe... Well, there was no need to let anyone know of it.

Other people or no, he could not look away from Chloe. The sun was halfway up the sky. Little glints of light caught the dark color of her hair beneath Chloe's straw hat. She was wearing the gold tassel earrings again today, and they swung a little in the breeze. All rationality fled Jeremy's head, and he said the first thing that came to mind.

Unfortunately, that was: "This is impossible."

She had been smiling at him as they walked together —a shy, sweet, welcoming smile—but at his words, she froze, that hint of tender happiness disappearing.

It *was* impossible. Objectively, she looked the same way she always did—prim and proper, her hair in a tidy bun, wearing a gown of some kind of striped dark navy. Her board clip was nestled firmly under one arm. A broad, cream-colored sash hugged her waist in a way that made Jeremy want to wrap his arms around her and keep her close.

She put one hand to the bridge of her nose. "Ah." She exhaled. "You've realized."

"Realized what?"

"How very difficult it will be—you and me..."

It took Jeremy a moment of blinking in confusion to

understand what she had meant. He looked around. It felt as if the entirety of Wedgeford was out picking up bits of trash, removing bunting, and taking down booths.

They were also all potentially eavesdropping on their conversation.

"Chloe, sweetheart." Jeremy looked over at her. "Have you considered inquiring about my antecedents before coming to an unwarranted conclusion?"

Her eyes met his.

"'This is impossible!'" Jeremy repeated himself, enunciating each word. "I could have meant anything by 'this.' I might have been referring to a new steamship record crossing of the Atlantic, or a funny story I'd heard about a rabbit, or—"

"But you did not mean any of those things," she interrupted gravely.

"No. I was referring to the fact that you are more beautiful every time I see you. It's positively outrageous. It should not be possible. And yet! Here you are."

That grave expression on her face cracked. Chloe turned pink. "Do you honestly just…think things like that? Really?"

"All the time," Jeremy confessed. "It's embarrassing how much I adore you. It's a good thing I have absolutely no shame, because *someone* has to tell you over and over how lovely you are so that you will know it hasn't changed. And apparently this entire village is filled with louts who lack either courage or good sense."

"Good sense!" She laughed. "You? No. I don't understand. You know all my worst qualities. Any day, you may come to your senses."

"I like all your worst qualities." Jeremy shrugged. "It seems entirely unlikely that my tastes will change, given how persistent they've been. But what would I know? I'll leave the odious business of finding some semblance of logic in this all to you. I just get the fun job of adoring you."

She blushed and fell in beside him. She was a foot away from him, which was twelve inches too many. God, there were too many people about.

He turned to her. "Well. It's time to do as you requested so long ago. It's time for me to be serious. Pay attention; it won't last long."

"Jeremy." There was a hint of reproach in her voice. "You know I meant…"

"I know how you meant it," he said. "That doesn't mean that we haven't been avoiding some of the more unpleasant parts of reality. I've spent a handful of days a year in Wedgeford; we've never talked about how I spent the other three hundred and sixty. And if you're to spend them with me, we must."

She exhaled, then looked away. "Of course."

"You're uneasy."

"It's just…" She turned to him. "I'm not suited to be a duchess. No, don't argue. You know that; I know that. All of England knows that."

"Chloe."

"I'm not suited to be a duchess." Her jaw firmed. "I have no idea how it's done." She removed her spectacles from a pocket in her gown and placed them on her nose. Then she pulled the board clip out from beneath her arm, took out the pencil, and in one determined motion, started writing. "But I will figure it out. I plan to make a list. If it can be done, I will do it. I shall need a bit of guidance, but…"

"You see?" Jeremy interjected. "How is this possible? Every single time I think you have reached the pinnacle of beauty, you do something like this and level all my expectations. It's uncanny."

"Hush," she muttered. "I'm making a list."

And she was. He watched in fascination as she wrote *What Duchesses Do* atop a creamy sheet of paper. She really would do it, he realized. She would observe and listen and absorb. She'd figure out what she was supposed to do and try to make herself into that person, stiff and proper, all for him.

Stay. Grow. He thought of that advice, straining inside him like a seed ready to take root. And there was his mother's advice, so near to it: *Root out every poisonous vine.* That, he thought, had been a gift for Chloe as much as for himself.

He could never let her try to transform herself into someone she wasn't.

"Chloe," he said, stepping in and putting a hand over her paper. "Everyone who is anyone is going to cut us. You know that, right?"

She looked up at him. For a second, he saw a fierceness in her eyes—the determination that he most loved about her. Her shoulders went back. "No." It was almost a growl. "They won't. I will not allow—"

But whatever it was she would not allow, Jeremy did not find out. At that moment, there was a clatter of horses' hooves. He saw them coming up the road, four perfectly matched bays, trotting in absolute synchrony, pulling behind them a polished white carriage. A *familiar* polished white carriage. Jeremy knew that crest.

His eyes shut. "Oh, for God's sake, Aunt. Really? I sent you the list less than forty-eight hours ago. It's a fourteen-hour journey by carriage. How did you find the time?"

The carriage came to a stop before the inn. The entirety of Wedgeford, Jeremy felt, must have turned in interest. A footman jumped down from the back of this immense conveyance; he placed a wooden step on the ground and opened the door.

His aunt stepped down, touching the footman's outstretched arm briefly.

She was dressed as if for a day at court, in heavy blue skirts embroidered with gold thread, with a jewel-trimmed hairpiece nestled between perfectly arranged white curls. She was dressed to intimidate, and at his side, he heard Chloe inhale.

"Jeremy." She sounded almost frightened. "Jeremy, is that—"

His aunt looked around the green, her eyes narrowing as her gaze came to rest on him. Her chin went up; she marched toward him, determination in every step.

Jeremy reached out and set Chloe's hand on his arm.

His aunt came to stand before him, every inch of her bristling with indignation. She was incredibly short—shorter even than Chloe—so there were not too many inches to bristle. Years of practice, though, had honed her bristle to a fine art.

"Your Grace," she said curtly. She gave him a curtsy that was cutting in its propriety.

It was a good thing he knew her so well.

"Aunt Grace!" He beamed. "You're here! I'm delighted. Allow me to make introductions—Miss Chloe Fong, this is my aunt Grace, the Countess of Clarington. She took charge of me in Britain when I attended school here. I was an incredible trial, but as you can see, if I aged her prematurely, it was only into greater beauty."

"Your *Grace.*" His aunt sighed. "Behave yourself."

"She calls me 'Your Grace,'" Jeremy said in a mock whisper, "but actually, she is the one who is Grace. I always found that confusing."

Chloe looked at him and shook her head. "You're like this all the time with everyone, aren't you?"

Jeremy just gave his aunt a wide smile. "Aunt," Jeremy said. "This is Miss Chloe Fong; she is my fiancée."

His aunt let out a sigh, and he saw her shoulders droop. "Oh, Jeremy," she said in a soft voice, pitched so that only he and Chloe could hear. "How many times must I counsel you? You must *think* before you speak. Saying such things in front of an entire crowd? The breach of promise suit will be *immense.*"

"Oh, dear. That sounds awful." For a moment, Jeremy let himself look chastened before he brightened. "Wait. I know how to avoid a breach of promise suit. What if I simply don't breach my promise?"

His aunt let out another enormous sigh. To his side, Chloe did as well. And then, as if they'd planned it...

"Your Grace," his aunt said, "be serious."

But she spoke atop Chloe. "Jeremy, be *serious.*"

For a moment, both women stopped. His aunt eyed his fiancée with a casual wariness. Then she shook her head.

"You seem like a perfectly lovely village girl," his aunt finally said, "and I understand why he might... Never mind. You must understand that he cannot marry you. It simply won't work. He just hasn't thought about it because he is so terribly thoughtless."

The villagers who had been cleaning up the green had all somehow crept closer. A full quarter of them pretended to search out minute scraps of paper in the grass in the immediate vicinity. The rest weren't even trying to pretend.

It was a good thing, Jeremy realized, that they all knew he was the Duke of Lansing, or all this Your-Grace-ing would have come as something of a shock. He could make out familiar faces close by—Naomi Kwan, who gave Chloe a surprised but happy smile; Kam Ming, who didn't bother to disguise his eavesdropping as anything other than naked interest.

"It's actually the opposite," Jeremy said. "I'm not thoughtless. I just have so many thoughts all at once that they all jumble together all higgledy-piggledy into a gigantic, untoward ball of thoughts."

"It comes to the same thing. You know the two of you will never be accepted, not by any branch of society. You *know* it. So tell me, how do you plan to overcome this?" She waited expectantly, as if hoping she'd stumped him.

Jeremy had never been one for plans. To tell the truth, he hadn't had one at all, and he knew he ought to have done. But in that moment, he realized what he needed to do. *Stay,* obviously. And *grow,* also obviously. But that was only possible if he, like Wedgeford, started in a place that allowed for both. That could only happen if he took his mother's advice and rooted out the poison.

"Your premise is false," Jeremy said. "We are *already* accepted. Look around you."

She looked. And then, she really looked. He could see her gaze landing first on the Uchidas, then on the Kams, then up to the Chens and the Changs and the Watanabes…

"This." She lifted her chin. "This is not society."

"How can that be?" Jeremy frowned. "Wedgeford is so very social."

She pressed her fingertips to her temples. "Stop willfully misunderstanding me."

"Very well," Jeremy said. "Then I will say it outright. You want me to spend my entire life miserable so that I can be around people who will always think I'm never enough. You're the one who hasn't thought. I don't want to do that. I want to stay where I can grow."

At his side, Chloe's fingers dug into his arm.

His aunt looked shocked. "No, of course not. Of course I want your happiness. Of course…" She trailed off, looking around. "But *London* society…"

Jeremy sighed. "To hell with London society. My mother hated it. I hate it. Chloe would hate it. The feeling is returned. Why would I want my children to grow up spending all their time with people who hate them?"

"But… Our family's good name—"

"Ah." Jeremy looked around, as if it were the first time that he'd noticed the tight fist of villagers that had come to stand around them. "Aunt, this is a family affair. Let's take this into the common room in the inn."

She turned her head, frowning at the crowd. "Yes." Her knuckles clenched whitely. "Yes. That is a very good idea. Into the inn for some privacy." She turned and started marching smartly toward that destination.

"As it's a family affair," Jeremy said, with a wink to the crowd, "and as Wedgeford is one big family... Please, I'd love to see you all come along. As many as can fit."

"Ah, Posh Jim!" Kam Ming came up and nudged him with an elbow. "Congratulations on your engagement!"

"Naomi," he called over the crowd. "Any more of the Wedgeford Brown?"

"A single jar. But I'd reserved it for my personal use."

"May I beg a sacrifice in a good cause?"

Naomi looked at Jeremy, then looked at Chloe, then finally nodded. "But only because I know Chloe will get me a replacement."

It took a half hour to arrange the common areas. His aunt had entered, looked around, and demanded a private room. She'd been told there was none to be had—which was true. It *was* the day after the Trials, after all.

By the time Jeremy had greeted everyone, arranged seating, told a joke or two, settled Chloe at the table across from his aunt, and made his own way to sit at his fiancée's side, fifteen minutes had elapsed. His aunt sat on her own bench, her back ramrod straight. She would never do something so uncouth as let her impatience show—at least not to people who didn't know her well. But he could detect a hint of restlessness in the slight narrowing of her eyes.

Chloe glanced at her board clip, laid on the bench beside her.

"Your Grace," his aunt said. "Enough of this unseemly delay. We must talk."

Jeremy glanced over his shoulder. "Ah, I beg your pardon, aunt. The delay may have been unseemly, but it was for a good reason. I have something to show to you."

He gestured, and Naomi came from the kitchens, bearing a bowl. She set this in front of his aunt. It was a simple dish: steamed rice, glistening and white, topped with pork in Wedgeford Brown, with peas and strips of pickled red pepper. Naomi added a napkin at her side, and then chopsticks, and then—as his aunt stared at those instruments in dismay—a knife and a fork.

Aunt Grace looked up. "It's not time to eat."

"No," Jeremy said. "It's necessary. Please. Do take a bite. We will wait."

Aunt Grace gave him a look that promised certain death. The problem was, he'd known her for too long; he'd become immune. He just smiled and gestured to the dish.

After a moment, she gave in. She tucked the napkin into the lace of her collar. She picked up the knife and fork and cut off the tiniest possible end of pork. She put this into her mouth, chewed daintily, swallowed, and set the fork down once again.

"Let me explain," Jeremy said. "This sauce has been the life's work of my fiancée and her father. It is, as you well know, utterly delicious."

His aunt's head tilted in the tiniest involuntary nod, before she caught herself.

"Be that as it may. It is a commercial enterprise." She

emphasized those last words. "Jeremy, I needn't tell you... You must distance yourself from such things as best as you possibly can."

"Nonsense. I've decided that I'm marrying into Chloe's family; she's not marrying into mine."

Chloe started at his side.

"Commercial," his aunt repeated, as if she were uttering the filthiest of all possible curses. "And...I apologize for the indelicacy, but it must be said. It's foreign in origin. You of all people cannot—"

Jeremy met her eyes. "It's not foreign. That sauce was fermented here, with yeasts found in Wedgeford. The idea came from here. It was made here. If tea is British, this sauce is British. If this sauce is British, I am British, and my wife is British, and my children will be British. I need not change myself to belong. I *already* belong; it is the rest of England that is out of step."

"You cannot change reality by spouting lofty words."

"No." Jeremy leaned forward. "But I *can* change what part of reality I choose to raise my family in. I am going to do what my father should have done."

"He *should* have married a different—"

"Aunt," Jeremy said.

His aunt loved him; Jeremy knew she believed that. But she also thought he was a mistake. She would *always* look at him and see an error in the shape of his eyes, the curve of his nose. She might have loved him, yet she had no idea how he needed to be loved.

"If you say one word against my mother, I will never speak to you again."

Root out every poisonous vine. He saw it now, in startling clarity. Some of those vines cared for him, but that didn't make their poison less toxic. He'd made excuse after excuse for his aunt. She loved him. She meant well. She wanted the best for him. None of that mattered.

"I will not hear you speak of my mother that way. I will not hear you speak of my wife that way. And you will never tell my children that they are a mistake. Ever."

"Your mother." Aunt Grace sighed. "What would she think of you allying yourself with…"

"I have already asked my mother's permission to marry Chloe; she has already granted it."

"Wait." Chloe spoke at his side. "You did? *She* did? When did this happen?"

"I *told* you I visited her in Guangzhou." Jeremy shrugged. "She had our fortunes read. We're a very auspicious match. Don't worry."

"Jeremy," his aunt Grace said. "You can't just…do this."

"Ask anyone here, and they'll tell you my titles. I'm His Grace Good Riddance—and good riddance to any who think I don't belong. I am the Duke of Lansing, but I am also the duke who owns most of Wedgeford. I'm the Duke Who Didn't—and I aim to do even less. My first act as the Duke Who Didn't? I'm renting out my ducal estate."

Aunt Grace started to stand in horror. "Jeremy. You *can't*. Your reputation. Your *duties.*"

"Ah, yes. My duties. My second act of not doing those will be to give away all the land in Wedgeford to the people here. There's no reason it should be mine—just an accident of birth. Everyone here is clearly using it better than I would; why should I own it?"

"Your Grace, if everyone simply gave away their property—"

"Then the world would be a much, much better place for everyone except the dukes."

She looked over at him angrily. "It—that's—but—" She shifted tacks instead. "But what of the possibility of building your influence in Parliament?"

"What about it?" Jeremy shrugged. "I've tried scraping and bowing to get other people to acknowledge me. It doesn't make them take me more seriously. I have a vote; they can't take it away. Anyone who wishes to influence me can come here and scrape for *my* vote instead."

"But—"

Jeremy smiled. "Tell them the best way to curry my favor is to buy my wife's sauce."

Chloe turned to him. "Jeremy," she said urgently, "you can't do that. That's nepotism."

Jeremy tilted his head toward her and raised an eyebrow. "So? The entire House of Lords is literally nepotism-as-government. It's not my fault. I didn't make the rules."

"Be that as it may," Chloe said sternly, "using your position that you obtained through nepotism to do more nepotism is unacceptable."

"Think about it from my point of view." Jeremy gave her his best smile. "If I can't employ a little nepotism to favor my friends and family, who *can* I favor with nepotism?"

"Agh." Chloe put her head in her hands. "That's what

makes it nepotism. It's not nepotism if it's for strangers!"

God. How had he managed to get the most perfect woman in the world to agree to marry him? Jeremy grinned at her fondly. "The only strangers I can think of who make sauce are White and Whistler. Do you want me to promote *their* sauce?"

"Of course not," Chloe said, "but—"

"There." Jeremy dry-washed his hands. "It's decided. Nepotism it is then." He looked across the table. "I'm sorry, Aunt. Did we interrupt you?"

His aunt stared at him for a moment before giving out a beleaguered sigh. "Yes," she said. "You've done so continually throughout your entire life, and this conversation has proven no exception. I just want the best for you, Jeremy."

Jeremy inhaled. That was it, really—the entire problem in a nutshell.

He reached over and set his palm over her hand. "Aunt Grace," he said. "I love you. You took me under your wing. You wanted me to understand British society, and I do. You had no idea what to do with me, but you tried. It was difficult, and you did what you thought was best. I will never doubt that about you."

She gave him a tiny, minute nod.

"But it *wasn't* best." Jeremy met her eyes. "It wasn't best for me; and the things you want are not the best for anyone here. I am not going to repeat mistakes simply because they are tradition. Either you will learn to value my family for what they are, or you will not see them. There is no middle place."

"Jeremy." She bowed her head. "I… You know I wanted only…"

Only the best, she would normally say.

"And now you know." He smiled at her. "You've wanted only the best for me, but I have come to a decision. *This* is what's best for me. I'm staying here."

He turned and looked Chloe in the eyes.

"*She* is what's best for me. *Wedgeford* is what's best for me."

Chloe's eyes were shining.

He reached out and gently took the board clip from where it rested beneath her arm. He undid the clip and removed the little pencil, and set the board on the table in front of them.

The first page was the list she'd just started this morning.

What Duchesses Do, it said.

He wrote beneath it in large, square capitals: *WHATEVER DUCHESSES WANT.*

"There." He turned to her. "You said when I came here that I don't get to make your list. Let's keep it that way, shall we?"

She nodded, her eyes bright. "Jeremy. You're... You're so much, you know that?"

"I know." He grinned at her. "I love you too."

And then he looked around at the people gathering around them. "Right, everyone." He smiled. "Chloe and I are getting married. The next two rounds are on me!"

———

THE LITTLE CHURCH WAS DECKED OUT IN SUMMER flowers. Red peonies lined the backs of every pew. The entryway leading to the nave had been decorated with ivy and more peonies in pink. Chloe stood with her father, her heart pounding.

Tradition dictated that the Dukes of Lansing were always married at the cathedral ten miles from the Lansing estate. Chloe and Jeremy had considered it; truly they had. But it had taken one meeting with the bishop—one tiny meeting to discuss what would and wouldn't have to occur —for him to dismiss their every suggestion and instead dictate what a *proper* wedding would look like for the duke.

It had seemed only right that they come to Wedgeford. The little church here hadn't had a vicar in decades; they'd been able to make their own choices. That had allowed them to include what they wished.

Chloe's father leaned in and adjusted her headpiece. She'd seen herself in a mirror. She could scarcely believe that it was her underneath that finery—especially the headpiece of wrought vines and red lacquered flowers nestled among tiny golden leaves.

At her wrist, her Baba's bracelet was warm and comforting. Her mother's good silver earrings were heavy at her lobes, a reminder of where she was from to match the brilliant red wedding gown that proclaimed where she was going.

"There." He looked at her. "You look fit to be a duchess."

She looked down. Four layers of cloth, red silk and red net, embroidered with a phoenix flying amidst peonies, with a few buttercups at the cuffs, just for Wedgeford— she'd never imagined owning anything so fine. It had taken all the months that had elapsed since their engagement in order for the gown to be finished by the Chinese seamstresses they'd commissioned from London.

It had been worth it, to wait for this. If she was going to be a duchess, this was the duchess she wanted to be—a duchess from Wedgeford.

Her father looked at her. "If you're having second thoughts, it's not too late to run away." His lip twitched. "I'll trip him if he comes after you."

He was joking, and yet she somehow knew that he also wasn't. "Ah Ba."

He simply looked at her. "I know you love him," he said. "I think he is a good man. But if I'm wrong, if we're wrong…" He swallowed, cutting himself off, then looked her directly in the eyes. "I will do anything to see you happy. Just know that."

"I know." She smiled at him. "I know."

She could hear the music swelling in the church.

"I am happy," she told him. "I am the happiest."

"Then so am I."

Chloe crossed "get ready to be married" off her list, handed her father her board clip for safekeeping, and took his arm. They stepped into the church.

In the pews to her left, she saw her friends—Naomi and Andrew, Ming, the Chans and the Singers and the Medfords. To her right, she passed Jeremy's aunt Grace, then at the very front, his mother and his grandmother. They had come to Wedgeford a fortnight in advance of the wedding; indeed, the entire ceremony had been planned around their arrival.

Chloe had served them tea and had been welcomed

into their family. They'd been thick as thieves after. Jeremy's Ah Ma spoke excellent English, but Chloe still spoke to her as best as she could in halting Cantonese, listening to her stories of Jeremy's childhood. She talked about how much better Wedgeford was than the ducal estate and about whether she and Ah Poh would stay with them now that Ah Gung had passed away. It had been like getting another mother, one who had taken her in immediately.

And there, at the very front, waiting for her…

It was her first time laying eyes on him that day; she'd not known how he was going to dress. She'd almost expected a Western suit, and indeed, he was wearing grey Western trousers, crisply pressed. But he wore a black mandarin jacket over that, frogged buttons marching up his chest to a banded collar. He smiled when he saw her, and everything but thoughts of him vanished.

She couldn't think of anything as she came up to him, step by step. Her heart seemed full, so full. And the way he looked at her—at her, only her, as if he wanted nothing else…

Chloe wasn't good in front of crowds, and this moment was no different. But she'd made a list for herself, and when she reached the altar and turned to face him… For a moment, she found all her words gone. He met her eyes, gestured with his chin, and she remembered.

"Chloe," he whispered as she came to stand across from him.

"Mine," she responded. "Mine." He reached out to take her hands. "My Jeremy."

That smile of his grew until it seemed impossibly large. "Yours," he said. "Always yours."

EPILOGUE THE FIRST

Six months later

IT HAD BEEN SOMETHING OF A FEAT OF ENGINEERING to finish the house where Jeremy expected to live out the rest of his life in a little more than eight months' time. He'd started construction before their wedding, and it had been the focus of much of his time since. Had he expected to build anything on the scale of the usual ducal mansion, it would have taken years. But this wasn't a place for dukes to impose; it was a place for him to stay and his family to grow.

As it was, the Duke of Lansing's abode in Wedgeford was relatively modest—not quite as large as the inn on the other side of the village, which made it less than one-tenth of the size of the actual ducal mansion, which Jeremy had leased out at an exorbitant rate. He had tried to involve Chloe in the construction at first, but she'd balked—freezing at every penny he'd suggested spending. Finally the two of them had agreed that the house was a thing that Jeremy needed and that Chloe tolerated.

"Surprise me," Chloe had told him. "Also, never mention costs in my hearing again."

So while Chloe had watched the building go up—she could hardly miss it, with the construction a stone's throw from her father's home and the barn where they fermented their sauce—she'd never been inside.

Jeremy was about to lead her in for the first time.

He stood with her just before the stone guardian lions outside the vermilion gate at the road. Snow had fallen last night, covering the backs of the lions and the curlicues of their manes in little cotton drifts of white. Chloe stepped close; she smelled like sunshine and warmth at the end of winter.

"Are you ready?" he asked.

She smiled at him. "I could not be more ready."

He'd brought a length of blue silk; she obligingly shut her eyes, and he wrapped it about her head, blindfolding her.

"Don't let me trip," she said.

"As if you'll have the opportunity. I'm carrying you in, aren't I?"

Her hand squeezed his, and she turned to him, leaning against him trustingly. It should not be a surprise, such a little thing—not at this late date, six months into their marriage. But that she gave herself to him so easily, that she knew all of him and trusted him anyway… It still staggered him.

He pulled her to him and picked her up; she adjusted her arm around his shoulder. There he realized his lack of planning had failed him: he had hired servants; of course he had. But he'd hired a sous chef and a few maids, and not live-in ones at that. None of them were present.

He'd wanted to have time with Chloe alone to explore the place. But there was nobody to open the door and his arms were filled with his wife. Now he either had to put her down or…

Or manage. It took a little fumbling to undo the latch with the free fingers of his left hand.

"What are you doing?" She laughed in his arms.

"Nothing," he muttered, pushing the door open with his hip. "Just…bollixing everything up. Don't worry. You can't see it, so it isn't happening."

He set her on her feet in the middle of the entry, took off his shoes, and knelt to do the same for her, changing them both into house slippers. A staircase rose in front of them. This stair was not as grand as the one in the manor he'd inherited, but it was constructed of a warm, golden wood that seemed to invite the eye up.

He shut the door behind him, turned her to face the stair, and removed her blindfold.

The last months of seeing to the entire construction project on his own had been worth it for the disbelieving gasp she let out.

"Jeremy." She reached for his hand. "This is… It's massive. It's too big."

"That's what they all say about me," Jeremy said with a waggle of an eyebrow, "but really, I'd think you were accustomed to a larger size by now. Don't worry. It *will* fit."

She cast a look at him and didn't comment on that.

"This is ridiculous." She turned to him, but she was smiling. "And it's beautiful."

She had toured his ducal estate before they rented it out. She had not called it *ridiculous;* in fact, she had not used any adjectives at all to describe it. Her feelings had been summed up in one word, spoken after they'd left the premises: "No."

He would take ridiculous and beautiful.

He took her through the downstairs—a receiving room ("A receiving room!" she exclaimed. "But what will we even receive there?" "Visitors," he explained. "This way, if I don't want to see them, I can let them molder and pretend I'm being polite.") and a dining room and a parlor ("Isn't that duplicative?" she asked with a sniff. "We have separate places to receive and to speak?"). He showed her the room for her father in the back, the suite for his mother and his grandmother, who had decided to stay, the servants' areas belowstairs, before taking her up the grand staircase, where there was an upper parlor ("Now you're just teasing me!" she said. "How can there be an upper parlor and a lower parlor?"), several rooms for visitors, a nursery, and additional rooms for any children that might come.

He ended in their bedroom.

"You see what you miss by not living in the ducal estate?" He flashed a grin at her. "Separate bedrooms. In fact, separate suites. An entire separate dowager house, because more than two generations in one household is apparently unthinkable? Don't ask me to explain. I've never understood."

She hummed. "Imagine having all that space, just so you could be more lonely."

"Mmm." He wrapped his arms around her, pulling her close. "Imagine. The only thing here from the ducal estate is the bed."

"Oh?" She turned to look at the bed with interest. It was a light wood with high posters and golden velvet curtains embroidered in red. "Is that the *actual* ducal bed?"

"No. *That* was too large and ungainly, and quite frankly, it's ugly. Good riddance. This came out of the dower house."

"Well. It fits here. I like it." She smiled up at him. "It's strange to think. You must have carted all this past my father's house right in front of my nose, and I've been so busy that I didn't even notice a thing."

It was true; she had been busy. After their success with Wedgeford Brown at the Trials, they'd been inundated with orders. They'd sold out their entire available stock within the first week; by the end of that first month, they'd had orders laying claim to every jar that they could produce for the next nine months. Chloe and her father had spent long hours securing a source for good quality broad beans and teaching others enough of the process that they could assist in the production of more sauce.

After the first month, Jeremy had called on his man-of-business to sit down with her and to talk to her about how to not do everything herself by the simple expedient of hiring people and then—this had proven to be the trickiest part—letting them do their jobs.

"My brilliant wife." He placed a kiss on her cheek. "At this rate—what with me giving so much away, and you getting so much business, you'll soon be wealthier than me."

She huffed. "Unlikely."

"Extremely likely," he responded. "We just need to extrapolate out a sufficient length of time in the future. Maybe by the year 1920."

"Maybe by the year 1990," she responded. "And we'll both be dead by then, so it won't matter."

"Maybe we won't be." He smiled at her again. "Maybe I'll have a full century with you, and then some. Maybe it won't be enough."

She turned to him, perhaps recognizing the warmth in his voice, and hooked her index finger in the waistband of his trousers, pulling him closer.

"No." Jeremy smiled at her. "A century definitely wouldn't be enough."

The edge of her thumb found the bare skin of his abdomen, and he sucked in a breath of anticipation.

"This bed…" Jeremy waggled an eyebrow. "You know, it's in desperate need of a trial."

"Is it?" She smiled at him. "But Jeremy, we have a whole upper parlor for that." She wound her fingers in the button fastening his trousers.

"And a lower parlor." He pulled her in close, leaning over her until their lips were a finger's breadth apart. "And a receiving room. And—at the moment—absolutely nobody is around to hear you receive. Nobody at all."

"Well then." She undid the first button of his trousers. "We had better get started."

EPILOGUE THE SECOND

Eight years later

IT WAS NOT THE NICEST INN IN BRISTOL, BUT THEN, Chloe, her husband, her father, and their two children were not there for anything other than tea. Tea, and a little bit of revenge.

The tea, so far, had been middling—boring little cucumber sandwiches and brown water steeped too long in leaves sadly lacking in aroma. Ah Ba seemed unimpressed. As he should; he'd never have countenanced anything so bland to be served to his progeny.

May had taken her sandwich apart rather than eat it, a vexed look on her face as she waved the soggy bread around before attempting to beat it into the wooden table with unsteady fists.

"No," she said to her brother when he also reached for a sandwich. "It's nasty!"

Chloe hid a smile. "Ah Yit, don't smash your sandwich if you don't want it."

"But Mama." Chloe was faced with the most adorable pout. "No flavor. I don't like it." She raised a toddler fist again to wreak more vengeance on the bread.

Ah Ba glanced at her with a hint of a smile, as if proud of his grandchild's excellent taste.

"Ah Yit." Jeremy moved to sit beside her. "I know. Life is difficult. Sometimes bad things need to be smashed."

May nodded.

"So if you absolutely *must* smash your sandwich," Jeremy said, "do it on your plate with a fork. See? *This* is how you smash a sandwich. *Politely.*"

Chloe gave her husband an extremely unamused look. He winked back at her.

But May didn't care. Having unfortunately been given permission, she picked up a spoon and proceeded to use it to dig holes in the bread.

"Mama," she said. "Look! I smashed. Politely."

"Semi-politely," Chloe corrected, and then sighed, looking upward. "I'll take it."

Behind her, she could hear another patron talking. "That," he said, "is the Duke of Lansing, if you can believe it. Here, in this inn. He does as he pleases."

Chloe couldn't wait to get back to Wedgeford, away from these stupid whispers.

"You can smash the other half of your sandwich," Jeremy was saying, "but first, you must eat at *least* one food. Can you do that for me?"

"I heard he visits China. That he's been there almost as much as he's lived here in England."

Untrue. They'd been to China once. She'd wanted to look for evidence of her father. She'd found a record of marriage, and that had given her a name, a history, a family—all gone now, so many decades after the end of the Taiping Uprising. But at least she'd been able to get an ancestral tablet for him.

It had been a good trip. Almost as good as what she anticipated now.

Ah. There. Chloe sat straighter in her seat as two people came into the inn. One of them was dressed in a dark-brown coat that had seen better days. He had a lengthy handlebar mustache that was desperately in need of trimming. The other man, with thick sideburns that could have housed three magpies and their nests, was dressed in a dark-blue coat with patched elbows. They came in and flopped down in two seats near the fire.

Chloe looked at her father.

"Sirs." The innkeeper came over, his face arranged in an uneasy almost smile. "Mr. White. Mr. Whistler. I... I want you to know, you have been, over the years...excellent customers. But...at this moment...it is most unfortunate that I should have to mention it..." He sighed.

Mr. White—the man in blue—blinked at the innkeeper. "Sir. You cannot possibly mean to refuse our custom. We've had some minor setbacks, of course, but they will be dealt with in short order."

"No, no," Jeremy was saying to their daughter. "Smash with a little less force. You only want to break the sandwich, not the plate."

Chloe exchanged a look across the table with her father. He was smiling—a small smile, to be sure, but it radiated delighted anticipation.

"To be sure, to be sure. But, sirs." The innkeeper

ducked his head. "Your account has been in arrears for some months. Perhaps you might consider some payment to bring it more current?"

"Some months." Mr. Whistler looked at the man. "But we've been coming here for *years*. Is there no loyalty to be had?" He frowned, looking at the board where the day's dishes were written in chalk. "And it's your fault we're in arrears anyway, you and everyone like you. You've got Wedgeford Brown on the menu tonight!"

The innkeeper made a placating gesture. "You've been in arrears for twenty-two months, to be exact. And the Wedgeford Brown was by particular request. Just for tonight."

"Who would request *that?*" spat Mr. Whistler.

Jeremy turned around, still wielding a spoon. He was spattered with little bits of broken cucumber and sandwich. Still, he gave a brilliant smile.

"Gentlemen!" He waved the spoon. "Mr. White, Mr. Whistler, I presume? Good sirs, there's no need to worry about being impolite—we shall, of course, cover the cost of this meal. And whatever beverages may be required to get through it."

Mr. Whistler frowned at Jeremy suspiciously. "Who are you?"

"Ah. I forgot to introduce myself; my apologies. I was too busy smashing this sandwich to recall my manners. I'm Jeremy Wentworth, the Duke of Lansing."

Mr. White flinched back. "You!"

"That's enough introduction for me," Jeremy said merrily. "Here's my wife, the Duchess of Lansing. You already know my father-in-law, of course; you must remember Mr. Fong from the time when he made you a sauce and you robbed him of what you owed him and pushed him out on the street without a penny."

Ah Ba raised a hand. Over the years, his hands had gnarled with age, the knuckles swelling. But Chloe had made sure that he had the best of care, and while he'd had to give up some activities, he still oversaw the mixing and production of sauces on a regular basis. The two men stared at him for a moment, eyes wide, then looked at Jeremy, then back at him.

"Oh, no!" Mr. Whistler gave a hearty—and fake— laugh. "Whatever do you mean by that? We're all friends here."

"Are we?" Ah Ba looked around. "I see my son, my daughter, and my grandchildren, all of whom I would call my friends. What are you?"

"Friends, of course, of course!" Mr. Whistler said. "Bygones and all that. What happened back then—well, it was only the mistakes that friendship must allow, really. Cultural differences and all that. What a dreadful misunderstanding we have all had."

"Oh." Ah Ba tilted his head and looked at Chloe. "It was all, apparently, a cultural misunderstanding. That was a normal occurrence in Britain. Hmm."

"Papa," said Archie, "are *these* the bad men?"

"Ah Ciu," Jeremy said in Cantonese, "remember what I told you? Don't insult people in English. It's not nice."

There was a long silence as Mr. White and Mr. Whistler tried to smile in a mildly friendly fashion at Mr. Fong.

"That's so nice to hear," Chloe put in. "We're all

friends. Doing the things friends do. Sharing a meal. That sort of thing."

The two men exchanged glances.

"Excellent," Mr. White said in puzzlement.

"Very excellent." Mr. Whistler beamed. "Ha ha. Why would you hold a grudge? That would be silly, I'm sure."

"We have always been friends," Ah Ba said, with that long slow smile. "How nice to know that. Chloe, what is it that British friends do? I am apparently not good at cultural nuance."

"Ah Ba," Chloe said, "they *just* told us. Friends ruin each other's businesses. At least in Britain, they do."

Her father tapped a knuckle against his chin. "Of course. I would hate to omit such an important token of friendship."

This awkward moment was interrupted by the return of the innkeeper. He had brought more cucumber sandwiches and a pot of tea, which he placed on the table before the two men.

Mr. White picked up one of the sandwiches and examined it morosely. "So." He looked up. "It was on purpose. All of this was on purpose."

Her father just smiled. "It was a beneficial side effect."

Mr. Whistler exhaled slowly. "See here. I'm sure we can come to terms. Mr. Fong, I want you to think of the opportunity we gave to you."

Her father's eyebrows rose.

"Without us," Mr. Whistler said, gesturing at the two of them, "your daughter would never have married so well. Surely you must harbor *some* sort of thanks in your heart on that account."

"Oh, certainly," Ah Ba said. "Are we not buying your dinner? Too bad about your sauce. And your income."

"We're friends," Mr. Whistler said after a long, uncomfortable moment. "Surely we can come to an agreement."

Ah Ba looked at Chloe. She looked back at him. "No," they said in unison. "We can't."

Mr. Whistler stood. "This is unaccountable. We are gentlemen! You cannot deny us!"

Mr. White just stared at them. "But what will I do?"

Ah Ba just shrugged. "What was it you told me back then? Ah, yes. You can labor with your own hands. You should be capable."

"But—"

"But you just said," Chloe cut him off. "You just *said* what a huge favor it was for Papa when you sent him off with nothing. You just said it was friendship to toss someone off without a penny. You couldn't have been *lying,* could you? It seems only right that you be given the same opportunity we had."

There was a long pause. Mr. White looked at Mr. Whistler. After a moment, they stood from the table together.

"You'll regret this," Mr. White said.

Mr. Whistler nodded. "You'll regret this forever."

"We've already forgotten," Jeremy said, reaching out with a clean cloth. "Ah Yit, let me clean your hands. Smashing is dirty work."

"I want another sandwich," May said.

"To eat?" Chloe intervened. "Or to smash?"

The spark that lit May's eyes was not as cunning as she imagined. "To...eat."

Her daughter was a terrible liar. Ah, well. Unfortunately, she'd get better at it. Jeremy was an excellent teacher who adored his children. Chloe stood. "I think we've all had enough smashing for today."

"I hope you feel good about yourself," Mr. White was saying. "I hope you feel good about everything you've done here!"

Chloe picked up her board clip. "Thank you," she said absently. "I do."

"I didn't mean it! I was being ironical."

"Mmm." Chloe's list of daily tasks today had been very manageable. She'd seen to a few shipments, overlooked their new warehouse... That left only one item that needed to be checked off.

Ah. There. *Revenge.*

She put a line through the word. It felt good. It felt *extremely* good.

"Look." She turned to Jeremy, holding up her board clip. "A perfect day! I finished everything on my list."

He took her arm and gave her cheek a kiss—a little too long, a little too lingering, promising that more was to come.

"Are you even *listening* to me?" she thought she heard someone say.

"I'm so proud of you, dear," Jeremy said, stepping to stand between her and the men across the way. "Shall we go?"

Chloe nodded. "Let's."

About the Wedgeford Trials

I got the idea for a book set in a tiny village that had a yearly festival, run since antiquity, which attracted people from all stations in life all over Britain all the way back in 2013 or so when I watched a documentary called *Wild in the Streets,* about a tiny village that has a yearly festival, run since antiquity, which attracted people from all stations in life all over Britain.

The town of Ashbourne in Derbyshire has been holding a "Royal Shrovetide Football Match" since medieval times. (It's not football as we know it for whatever you might mean by football.) Teams are decided based on where you are born; visitors come from all over to take part. It's been called "royal" ever since the Prince of Wales (later King Edward VIII) showed up to a game in 1928 and got a bloody nose.

The Wedgeford Trials are decidedly different from Royal Shrovetide Football, of course, but I've loved the idea of a small town made temporarily large ever since I heard of it.

About Unnamed Sauce/Wedgeford Brown

When I first started writing this book, I thought that I would have Chloe and her father just introduce soy sauce to Britain. Then I started doing research and discovered that soy sauce was introduced in Britain in 1679 and it went through periods of such widespread popularity that in the mid-1700s, people would bring along soy sauce cruets when they traveled. Now I'm just mad that I haven't been putting soy sauce in my books before now.

White and Whistler are obviously not based on real people, but there are two historical facts (or maybe historical apocrypha) that underlie the story of Unnamed Sauce in the book. (1) Worcestershire sauce was supposedly named after a British noble returning from India who wanted to recreate the taste of a dish in Bengal. So it's not actually a British-British sauce. (2) The first time Lea and Perrins put together the ingredients for Worcestershire sauce, they thought it was disgusting. They gave up and left it in a barrel. Months later, it was delicious.

About Chloe's Father

Chloe's father has what is called in the book "wet wind inflamed joint disease," which is what we would call, in the West, rheumatoid arthritis. Traditional Chinese medicine understands physical ailments very differently than Western medicine. In the early 1900s, TCM's treatment—

some thousands of years deep with research and work at that time—would almost certainly have been ahead of the West.

About the Rest of the Book

I could fit the things I knew about my maternal grandmother before I started this book in maybe fifteen minutes of conversation. She went by the English name of Nora and was born on Maui in 1904 to Chinese parents—my great-grandfather, who had come to Hawaii as a laborer in the late 1800s, and my great-grandmother, whom he had purchased as a wife. Nora was (according to the immigration documents we have) her mother's sixth child. Her ethnic background was Hakka (although they used Cantonese pronunciations for names).

At the age of three, she returned to China with her mother. There, she lived in extreme poverty. She was homeless for a while and hungry often. At a very young age, she joined a girl gang to survive, and dreamed of a different life. At the age of fourteen, she returned to Hawaii. She had two years of schooling at that point, and she'd heard that education was free in the US. In the 1920s, she graduated from high school and then went on to get a college degree from the University of Hawaii. She met and married my grandfather and had six children. Child number six was my mother. My grandmother died when my mother was very young, and my mother has no direct memories of her.

That is almost everything I knew about my grand-mother before starting this book. She was a strong, smart, ambitious woman, an anomaly in relation to everything else I heard about China. And, I thought, well, that's the way it is. Anomalies happen everywhere.

Then I wrote this book.

The Hakka People

The word "Hakka" in Chinese means "guest people." Whether the Hakka are an ethnic or a cultural minority is up for some debate. What is not up for debate is that they came into southern China from the north sometime in the tenth century. They tended to be very poor and brought their own traditions with them. Since most of the easily cultivated land was already inhabited, the Hakka farmed hillsides and other less arable lands.

Hakka men and women, as a general rule—and this might have been in part because of poverty—took on substantially more equal roles. Hakka families didn't prac-tice foot binding and rarely practiced plural marriages. They also didn't adhere to strict divisions of labor. Hakka women did many things that were considered men's jobs.

Taiping Tianguo

"Taiping Tianguo" refers to the name given to a rebel government that seized a significant portion of southern China between 1851 and 1864. The name, translated into English, is "Heavenly Kingdom of Great Peace," and—spoiler alert—this was a misnomer.

The "Heavenly" part of the name came from the fact that its founder, Hong Xiuquan, claimed to be the younger brother of Jesus Christ. The rampant inequality prevalent in China at the time, exacerbated by the First Opium War, created a perfect storm for an uprising. In many ways, Hong was a visionary (whether you agree with his vision is another story entirely). He was also Hakka, and that cultural influence is evident in the kingdom he so briefly formed. Taiping Tianguo—at least on paper—believed in the equality of women and men. Hong redistributed land and money to those in need, and women and men were equally eligible; women, even married women, were able to own their land outright.

In 1853, he opened the imperial examinations to women for the first time. Some two hundred women took the examinations, and Fu Shanxiang (a woman) took first place. Women in Taiping Tianguo served as chiefs of staff, chancellors, secretaries, commanders, generals, commandants, and soldiers. The precise title I gave Chloe's mother —"Deputy Chancelloress of the Winter Department"— was held by a woman. Details of the achievements of women during the brief period when there was a Taiping state can be found in Vincent Y. C. Shih's *The Taiping Ideology* (1967).

Discovering this was something of a revelation for me. I had always seen my grandmother as an anomaly. And maybe she was, but I had not realized how wide and deep that anomaly went. That she came from a cultural background that had opened the imperial examinations to women explained so many things to me. My grandmother was not a departure from her culture; she was an exemplar of it.

But this was set against the backdrop of a civil war on a scale that is almost unimaginable. In the US Civil War, around 600,000 people died. In the Taiping Rebellion (and/or Uprising, depending on how you view it), estimates put the death toll between 10 and 30 million. Entire cities were devastated; hunger was widespread in its wake. Parts of China still struggled, not yet recovered, decades later.

This in part fueled some of the early waves of the Chinese diaspora.

My family left southern China in the 1870s and 1880s ("left" is not quite the right word; initially, some members were taking work elsewhere while the majority of the family remained in China. It was only after a generation or so that the families started permanently living elsewhere). There is no longer anyone living who remembers precisely why they left; I have asked. The family oral history that has remained is mostly about poverty and bandits, and while I do not have direct confirmation that these dots connect in my family's case, in many ways, this story, for me, felt like I was writing a subsection of my own family's diaspora.

A Question Mark on Chinese Cultural History

Some people might find it surprising that Jeremy's mother would insist on staying with her parents, given that many Chinese people believed that upon marriage, a woman ceased to belong to her parents' household.

In response, I have only these two anecdotes from my family history. Anecdote the first: In 1883, one of my great-grandfathers first came to Maui as a laborer. At the time, he had a wife and two children. He returned to China and his wife and told her he loved Hawaii and wanted to live there for the rest of his life. She told him that she was her parents' only surviving child and she wasn't going to leave them, so he could get lost. Now you know why my great-grandfather purchased his second wife, who ended up being my great-grandmother.

Anecdote the second: After my grandmother got married and started having children, she wrote to her sister, who was still in China. "Please come help," she said. "I am drowning in babies, and if you come, I will teach you English." (This is obviously not a direct quote.) My great-aunt was married at the time, but her husband was terrible. She left immediately.

General cultural trends are never absolutes.

A note on language

In general, I tried to rely on my mother's style of speech in choosing when to use a non-English word. Thus, for instance, when my mom talks about the practice of ancestor worship, she uses the verb bai instead of pray (I used the Hakka word pai in this book, rather than the Cantonese) and the word hoeng (again, my mom uses the Cantonese word rather than the Hakka one) to refer to incense sticks. (I asked my mom if I could include this in my author's note, and she wants me to tell you that she considers ancestor worship to be a violation of the first of the Bible's ten commandments against idolatry, and she hasn't practiced it since she was a child. I told her that none of you would judge her for this, and I'm fairly certain I'm correct.)

I also (generally) tried to use Hakka where the speaker would use primarily Hakka and Cantonese where the speaker would use primarily Cantonese. The exceptions (that I know of): I used the Cantonese word "bao" to refer to meat buns because the word came up far too often from too many people to use both the Hakka "pao" and the Cantonese "bao" to refer to the same things without confusion; I ended up using the Cantonese word because it's more recognizable in Western society. I likewise used the Western "tofu" instead of the Hakka "tau foo." I also referred to the Heavenly Kingdom of Great Peace as "Taiping Tianguo" (Mandarin) as the Mandarin transliteration is standardized in history books at this point.

Finally, I used the Mandarin word qu to refer to yeast microorganisms. While I didn't go into Chloe's father's history, he spent time in Nanjing where he apprenticed to a maker of sauces and studied ancient Chinese texts, and so I imagined that most of his early discussions (and therefore acquired vocabulary on the subject) were in Mandarin, rather than Cantonese. I also just like the way qu sounds.

About the food

When I started writing this book, I got a copy of

Linda Lau Anusasananan's *The Hakka Cookbook: Chinese Soul Food from around the World,* which is a delightful book that details Hakka recipes collected by the author from Hakka communities around the globe—from China to diaspora near and far. I made over half the recipes in this cookbook while I was working on this book.

Many of the foods that Chloe's dad serves are my interpretation of recipes from Anusasananan's cookbook—altered,of course, with my thoughts on how those recipes were adapted to the diaspora community that Anusasananan described compared to the diaspora community in which Chloe's family lived.

I could probably write an author's note on the food in this book alone, but this is already the longest author's note I've ever written, and it's probably not the place to spam you with thousands of words alongside photographs. Instead, I've set up a food glossary on my website with pictures, descriptions of my thoughts, and recipes. You can find the food glossary at http://cmil.co/foodglossary.

A note on naming, transliteration, and language drift

Hakka, Cantonese, and Mandarin (among other languages) all use Chinese characters, with the result that while the meaning of a character remains constant, those characters are not always pronounced the same.

Trying to transliterate Hakka in a historically accurate fashion is something I struggled with for...basically the length of this book, until I gave up and came up with a semi-consistent scheme. Hakka is not a single language (sidenote: what is and isn't a language is wildly up for

debate, and is, especially when it comes to the question of
the Chinese family of languages, a deeply political question in the modern world because of China's One China
policy, so let's pretend that I'm saying "language" or
"dialect" as you prefer); it is a family of languages, one that
in the mid to late 1800s was already split into language
families that had drifted far enough apart that they were
not mutually intelligible.

The Hakka (mostly because of the poverty) were a
substantial part of the first waves of labor emigration from
China; those who remained in China have been subjected
to Chinese pressure to reduce the usage of languages other
than Mandarin. Many Chinese people who emigrated in
the early days either had their names transliterated with
little care by officials who wrote down whatever they
thought they heard (my grandfather's extended family, for
instance, encompasses two separate spellings of their
family name), or, after standard transliterations were
accepted, had the characters for their name looked up, and
were assigned a transliteration that was either Cantonese
or Mandarin, irrespective of whether they would have
pronounced their name that way. So looking up immigration records and guessing what names would have
sounded like is also not a great start.

For the transliteration of Hakka in this book, I have
mostly used *A Hakka Index to the Chinese-English Dictio-
nary of Herbert A. Giles,* by D. MacIver, published in
1904. This is not a perfect choice; transliteration attempts
by Western folk, especially in 1904, have significant issues.
But it is at least a semi-consistent choice, or at least it
would be, if MacIver's index were comprehensive. It is not.

Where MacIver's index is lacking, I've used the modern transliteration on wiktionary.org. The exception to this is "nyong tofu," which MacIver transliterates as "yong" and everyone else in the entire world pronounces as "nyong."

There's also the question of how to render generational names. In 1890, there was no standard, agreed-upon way to transliterate or treat generational names to non-Chinese culture. My grandfather (who was Yue Cantonese) seems to have referred to himself as "Choy" (his personal name) and used his generational name (Tsok) as a middle name in English. (He also used a separate business name: Choy Kee—which did not include his generational name at all.) (There was a point in drafts in this book where I mentioned Chloe's father having a separate business name, used on the labels for the sauce, but I decided that it required too much explanation for what was essentially a not-super-relevant point.) My grandmother (who was Hakka) signed her Chinese name as "YukIn," capitalization on every transliterated character, on official English documents.

I thought about choosing one convention for everyone for the sake of consistency, but decided that inconsistency was actually more historically accurate. Thus, Jeremy's Chinese name is transliterated as Yu Ging Lung, with the generational name treated as a separate name, while Chloe writes hers as Fong YiLin.

The characters for these names do not properly render on all e-readers, but you can find them on my website.

Working from there, Chloe's mother was Fong Nyuk-Min. In Chinese, the family name (Fong, meaning fragrant) comes first. There follows the generational name

—a name given to all children of a specific generation (this is fairly old-fashioned, and many modern Chinese no longer follow this convention). For men, that generational name often comes from a family poem, where each generation gets a successive character in that poem. For Hakka women, according to Jessieca Leo's *Global Hakka: Hakka Identity in the Remaking*, the generational name was usually chosen by the grandmother.

My grandmother and Chloe's mother share the generational name character meaning jade or treasure. At the point when my grandmother was named, this was transliterated as "Yuk" from Cantonese and "Nyuk" in Hakka.

Chloe's Chinese name is Fong YiLin. The second character in her name, the generational name, is the character which sometimes means wings and sometimes means feathers. (Some of you will recognize the real-life person whose family name shares this character...who definitely exemplifies wings.) The final character, her personal name Lin, is composed of two radicals. The leftmost one is jade again. In the epilogue, Chloe's daughter's name is HiYit—Yit meaning bright or daybreak—and again, the second character is composed of two separate characters, the topmost one being Chloe's generational name of feathers.

All this would be vastly easier to see if I could put Chinese characters in e-readers with the certainty that they would transliterate properly!

Where possible, I've used the modern accepted transliteration of Chinese place names. This does pose some issues in terms of place names that are now commonly accepted in Mandarin versus Cantonese. I spent hours giving myself a headache trying to figure out whether I should use the names that would have been used in England at the time, versus modern ones, versus modern transliterations of the historical Cantonese... Ultimately, I decided that a lot of people spent a lot of time getting headaches before deciding on the current naming scheme. I wasn't going to come up with a better solution just because I was also giving myself headaches, but I might certainly hit on a worse one.

The one instance where I don't follow this is the name of the village where Chloe's father comes from—Look King village. "Look King" is the transliteration used in my great-grandfather's immigration interview for the place where he comes from. I believe the village where my great-grandfather came from has now been subsumed into a much larger city, and if there's an administrative subdivision that still bears a name that resembles "Look King," I don't know what it is called well enough to find it. I wanted to include this reference to my family history more than I wanted consistent transliteration of names, and so here we are.

GLOSSARY

This glossary is available on my website at http://cmil. co/tdwd-glossary/ with audio pronunciations. The glossary there includes the names used in the book, as well as the Chinese characters (which are not included here because they do not render properly on all e-readers).

Ah - *used in both Hakka and Cantonese* - affectionate prefix added to names / relationships

Ah Ba - *used in both Hakka and Cantonese* - father (affectionate)

Ah Gung - *Cantonese* - maternal grandfather

Ah Me - *Hakka* - mother (affectionate)

Ah Ma - *Cantonese* - mother (affectionate)

Ah Poh - *Cantonese* - maternal grandmother

Baba - (widely used in Chinese dialects, but the tones differ) father

bao - *Cantonese* - a bun filled with something, usually steamed. See the pork bao entry in my food glossary.

Hakka - translates literally as "guest people," refers to an ethnic/cultural subgroup that migrated to Southern China somewhere between the 2nd and the 10th century.

hiong - *Hakka* - joss stick / incense

jook - *Cantonese* - a porridge/gruel made from cooking a grain in a lot of water for a long time

kuk - *Cantonese* - a class of yeast inoculants used to ferment (among other things) soy sauce, vinegar, and several kinds of wine. See **qu**.

lau tai - *Hakka* - little brother

lui cha fan - *Hakka* - translates literally as "thunder tea rice," a dish made by frying herbs and tea leaves, pounding these in a mortar and pestle (hence the "thunder" in the name), and pouring the resulting green soup/tea over cooked vegetables and rice. See the lui cha fan entry in my food glossary.

pai - *Hakka* - pay respect or worship

qu - *Mandarin*- a class of yeast inoculants used to ferment (among other things) soy sauce, vinegar, and several kinds of wine. See **kuk**.

Taiping Tianguo - literally, "Heavenly Kingdom of Great Peace." Refers to the rebel kingdom formed by Hong Xiuquan in Southern China between 1851-1864.

nyong tofu - literally, stuffed tofu. Tofu triangles with a bit removed from the center, filled, stuffed and then braised. See my nyong tofu entry in my food glossary.

ACKNOWLEDGMENTS

This is a book that has taken somewhere between years and months to write, and so first of all, I want to thank you, the person who is reading this now. So many of you have showed me patience, kindness, and generosity. Your emails and messages have helped me remember why I write. Thank you all.

I spoke with my mother multiple times while writing this book, and in turn, she searched old letters from family and spoke to cousins in China. My mother is seventy-seven, and I'm grateful to have been able to spend this time with her.

The last handful of years have not been the easiest, but so many people have made them bearable—such a vast number that I must mention many people at this point by group instead of individually by name: The 'Rona Writing group, who helped keep me motivated to write with regular updates, and encouraged me once I started writing again after my own bout with (probably, but there were no tests) COVID19; my multiple WhatsApp groups, who cheered me on and told me (when my ideas weren't stupid) that I should stop being so hard on myself (and who told me when my ideas *were* stupid, and to move on); the amazing group of Fanyu friends whom I met between September 2019 and February 2020, who have brought joy, delightful fan art, and amazingly decorated cookies into my life; my therapists; *Keep your Hands off Eizouken,* an anime, for reminding me to write for myself without fear of failure; Sydette Harry, for reminding me what the work looks like, and what it doesn't.

Mr. Milan, Pele, and Silver, provided a lot of general love and breaks from the writing. Silver has been getting up there for a while now. While I wrote this book, he curled up on the carpet in my office, waiting to catch my attention. He needed help reaching his food, so every hour or so, he'd meow for me to lift him up, and I'd pet him and give him a boost and drink some water. He was a truly excellent cat. He passed away the day after I wrote the initial draft of these acknowledgments.

For specific help on this book, my thanks to everyone who read it and provided comments and editorial feedback: Rose Lerner, Lindsey Faber, Michelle Li, Rawles Lumumba, Robin Bond, Martha Trachtenberg, Savannah Frierson, Lillie, and Anne Victory.

My thanks to Stephy Lee and Michelle Huang for their help with the Hakka language, and to Dr. Xiaorong Ding at the Denver TrueMind center, who graciously took time out of her day to advise me on the use of Traditional Chinese Medicine in treating rheumatoid arthritis.

Last, but never least, a word about the assistance I received from one person. When I knew I would be writing a character who was managing chronic pain, I contacted Corey Alexander. Their advice—succinct but to the point—made this book a better book.

I have also been thinking about why romance is structured the way it is for many years, and what the alternative would look like. In 2017, I had a conversation with Corey that sent me off down a research rabbit hole, and had me diagramming alternate plot structures, trying to figure out how to make them work in romance and what that would mean. The first fruits of that conversation are reflected in some of the choices I made in this book—specifically, how to handle the reveal about Jeremy as a duke.

Corey was one of the kindest, most thoughtful, people I have ever known. They passed away shortly before this book came out. I am devastated that they are no longer in this world, and hope they know how much they were loved and appreciated.

2020 has been one hell of a year. If you have read this far, I am glad you are still here with us.

CPSIA information can be obtained
at www.ICGtesting.com
Printed in the USA
LVHW091653121220
674025LV00041B/1004

9 798685 689276